As I was putting on my coat, the doorbell rang. I looked out the window.

What the hell?

Daniel Kazan stood on my doorstep.

I went cold. *How dare he?* I flung open the door. "What are you doing here?" I exploded.

Confronting him,  inches taller than me and exu— my hackles. He raised hi— —ing expression on his face. As if he were trying to calm me down or reassure me.

"I just want to talk to Hannah. I came early to catch her, before she leaves for school."

I squared my shoulders. "Get out of here! You've been told to stay away from us!"

His face was in shadow. "I think it's fair to want to see Hannah. I've waited a long time."

The guy is nuts. "She's not Hannah—she's my daughter. Maddy."

"You're keeping her from me." He was leaning toward me, and I had to keep from falling back. I couldn't let myself seem weak. If he thought he'd intimidated me, what would be his next move?

My heart pounded. My hands were curled tight, my nails biting into my palms. "Damn right I'm keeping her from you. Now get off my porch before I call the police!"

What if he wouldn't leave? I should call for help—but my phone was inside, and I didn't want to leave him on the porch unattended.

Praise for Not Your Child

"*Not Your Child* will please suspense story readers. …It's a hard-hitting thriller that will keep readers engrossed to the end, adding unexpected twists and turns to provide delightfully intricate inspections of motive and reality."

~*D. Donovan, Senior Reviewer, Midwest Book Reviews*

~*~

Finalist and second-place winner, 2021 Daphne du Maurier contest for Excellence in Mystery/Suspense.

"Wow! Just Wow! You had me from the start!"

~ *Candis Kennard,*
Judge, 2021 Daphne du Maurier awards

~*~

"Lis Angus' *Not Your Child* is a tautly written thriller that begins with every parent's worst nightmare—a missing child—and ratchets up the tension with unexpected plot twists. Lis explores the complex relationships between parents and children and what can happen when a child's yearning for independence leads them to a dark place. A gripping debut that will keep readers engaged until the very end."

~*Michelle Hillen Klump, author of A Dash of Death*

~*~

"When a man makes a mistake regarding a young girl's identification, his obsession turns to insanity, and her mother will do anything to keep her daughter safe. Inside the heads of all three characters, *Not Your Child* is a tense tale proving maternal instinct can go beyond blood."

~*Jaime Lynn Hendricks, author of Finding Tessa*

Not Your Child

by

Lis Angus

Not Your Child

Cover Art by *Jennifer Greeff*

The Wild Rose Press, Inc.
PO Box 708
Adams Basin, NY 14410-0708
Visit us at www.thewildrosepress.com

Publishing History
First Edition, 2022
Trade Paperback ISBN 978-1-5092-4118-7
Digital ISBN 978-1-5092-4119-4

Published in the United States of America

Dedication

To my two daughters, Jess and Amanda, and the heart-stopping times I thought I'd lost them.

Prologue

RCMP Constable Kenneth MacCormick parked his SUV at the edge of the road, stopping short of the accident.

The snowstorm had definitely ended. The Alberta sky was a brilliant blue, and the sun reflecting off the snow-covered fields was blinding, though it brought no warmth. The temperature was minus 21 Celsius.

Snow was piled high on either side of the road. He walked ahead to the scene marked off with flares, his boots crunching on the snow. Jerry Kowalczyk from the Ponoka detachment was waiting for him. "Mac, you're not gonna like this."

Mac nodded to Jerry. "You were first on the scene?"

"Yeah, first police. George Sanders called it in—he saw it when he came by with the snowplow this morning."

They stood side by side, gazing into the deep ditch and the pickup truck half-buried in snow at the bottom. The truck lay tipped on its passenger side, nose against the far bank.

"Are those your footprints?" asked Mac.

"Yeah, mine and George's. He went down to see if anyone needed help, saw there were two people but they were dead. I went down too to make sure."

Mac considered the scene. "So what happened

here?"

"It's a mess. Looks like they were hit head-on; the whole left-hand side of the cab is smashed in. The driver's airbag inflated, but that wasn't enough to protect him. The woman was in the passenger seat and didn't have her seat belt on. She went through the front windshield."

Mac whistled. "Whatever hit them had to be travelling at quite a clip."

Jerry cleared his throat and spat. "Yeah, for sure. But that's not all. There are a lot of other footprints down there, partly full of snow. Somebody else was there before us, a while after the accident but before the snow stopped. They did quite a bit of walking around the vehicle. I have no idea what they were doing."

Mac frowned. "Anything else?"

"Well, there's a baby's car seat in the back seat. But it's empty."

Chapter One

Daniel almost didn't notice the two girls that morning. He was busy reattaching Tucker's leash to keep him close. In dog years, Tucker was older than Daniel's sixty-three, but he still tried to run like a pup. Daniel relaxed against the park bench, the October sunshine warming his shoulders, idly listening to bird calls and the nearby Ottawa traffic.

But something about the girls caught his eye. At first just that they were there, walking on the other side of the narrow downtown park. Not quite teenagers, as far as he could tell, still at that coltish age. One girl with dark hair, one blonde. They chattered to each other as they approached.

Then one of them laughed, the blonde with the bouncy ponytail. He froze, spellbound. That face, that hair, that dancing figure. It was like seeing Kelly again. That's how she moved as a young teen, all loose arms and legs, partway between gawky and graceful. And the laugh—Kelly laughed like that.

Just like that.

The girl smiled like Kelly, too, with a slight twist at the side of her mouth.

For a moment he was back there, with Kelly on the farm. She was reaching to catch the softball he'd thrown to her, practicing for the team tryout at school the next day. Patricia stood on the front porch, about to call them in for supper.

He blinked and shook his head, returning to the present. There'd been too many of these times lately, when he found himself lost in memory.

Refocusing, he saw that the two girls were leaving the park.

Another thought struck him. No, it was a crazy notion. But the idea refused to budge.

Could she be...Hannah?

No. Just a trick of his brain. How could she be here?

But he couldn't tear his eyes away. Now he couldn't let it go. Almost without volition, he rose to follow the girls. The girl.

"Here, boy." He didn't need to pull the leash—Tucker trotted beside him.

Daniel strode along steadily, dodging pedestrians, staying half a block behind the girls. They crossed the street ahead of him, but he made it across before the light changed.

Uneasy questions batted at him. How could Hannah turn up here, after all these years? It was too good to be true. It must be his imagination. He'd been wrong before.

But he kept moving, making sure not to let the girl get too far ahead of him.

She does look like Kelly, Patricia's voice whispered in his head. *That's not imagination.*

He took a deep breath, trying to clear his mind. He'd been hearing Patricia's voice more often lately. Sometimes it was a comfort, like she was still with him. Other times, it gave him shivers.

It doesn't matter how she got here. Just don't lose

her now!

****

The girls went through a gate into a schoolyard. Kids were milling around, some tossing balls or running, others standing in groups or pushing each other. About a dozen clustered near the door, starting to crowd into the building.

Daniel only hesitated for a minute. He'd be kicked out if anybody in charge noticed him, but he needed to know more about her. He tied Tucker to the fence and entered the schoolyard.

The two girls stopped to chat with a boy, then headed into the school.

Daniel moved forward and tapped the boy on the shoulder, a short redhead with glasses. "That girl you just talked to…"

The boy turned to him, squinting. "Which one?"

"The blonde girl."

"You mean Maddy?"

Daniel nodded. *Ah, that's what they call her.* "Is she in your grade?"

"Nah." The boy shook his head

"What's her last name?"

But the boy had already turned away. Daniel tried not to show his frustration.

Patricia was in his head again. *Don't lose her. You need to find out where she lives.*

He'd have to follow her home.

****

That afternoon, he went back to the school. He and Tucker walked up and down the street, keeping the schoolyard gate in sight, waiting for school to let out. He couldn't watch all the exits, but if he missed her

5

today, he'd try again tomorrow.

Just after 3:15, she appeared. Blonde ponytail swinging, backpack on her shoulders, in a group of kids. The group split up at the corner. She crossed the street beside the same dark-haired girl she'd been with that morning.

Daniel followed, again staying a half block behind them. There was more mid-afternoon traffic than he'd expected. Taxis honking, buses rumbling by. Could be tourists, coming back from the Parliament buildings.

Several times he had to pull Tucker into a storefront doorway to avoid bumping into clumps of pedestrians on the sidewalk.

The girls turned and entered the park; they seemed to be retracing their route from the morning. He hurried to cross the busy street, holding Tucker's leash tight.

A musky damp-leaf odor filled the air, mingling with a faint scent of wood smoke. Daniel stayed well back, matching the girls' pace. Then they stopped, turning to face in his direction. He stopped too, trying to act casual, bending to pet Tucker. When he looked up, they had vanished.

Where did they go? Hurrying ahead, he saw a set of steps rising from the park to a residential street. He mounted the steps with Tucker close beside him. At the top, he peered around a leafy shrub. The two girls were entering a small red brick house on the left.

Chapter Two

I rushed in the door after a long day at the clinic. Maddy was upstairs in her room; I hardly ever saw her before dinner anymore.

Chicken breasts were thawing on the counter, and I was rinsing vegetables at the sink when the phone rang. It was Nicole Obata. "Susan, did Maddy mention anything about a man following her and Emma today?"

"What? No I haven't talked to her yet."

"Emma said there was an older man, with a dog. He was outside the school this afternoon, and when they got to the park, he crossed the street behind them and followed them along the pathway."

That didn't sound worrying. "It's a public pathway. He probably was just taking his dog for a walk."

"Maybe. But she said he was behind them all the way to your house."

"What do you mean, to our house?"

"That's what she said. The girls went inside and watched out your window. He came up the steps from the park, stood on your street, and stared at your house."

A prickle of unease washed over me. "Are you serious?"

"Yes. She's sure he was following them."

My unease grew. "Did she say anything else?"

"Not really, but Matthew and I don't like it."

So she'd already discussed it with him. "What are you suggesting?"

"Matthew thinks we should report it to the police."

"Doesn't sound like there's a lot to report. Some guy came and stared at the house." I couldn't imagine the police doing much with that story.

She sighed. "Well, why don't you talk to Maddy, find out if she noticed anything more? And call me back after."

"Sure." I hung up and stared, unseeing, at the vegetables draining beside the sink. Emma's parents and I tried to coordinate our rules for the girls, since they were best friends and did everything together. This fall we agreed to let them walk to school on their own, now that they were twelve. Their route, through our small park and along a few busy streets, seemed safe enough. Maybe we were wrong.

Dinner could wait. I called upstairs to Maddy. After a long minute, she opened her door and came to the top of the steps. "Am I in trouble?"

Why was that the first thing out of her mouth? It wasn't like I was always on her case, though sometimes she acted like it. "No, but I want to ask you something."

She slouched down the stairs and sat on the bottom step, staring at her hands. Her hair, released from its ponytail, fell forward over her face in a blonde curtain.

I wanted to brush her hair aside but restrained myself. "Sweetie—" I started.

She frowned at me, glowering. She'd told me not to call her that anymore.

I began again. "Nicole says a man followed you and Emma today?"

She wrapped her arms around her knees. "Yeah

8

there was a guy. But it was no big deal."

"Was he really following you?"

"Maybe." She shrugged. "He was behind us for a while. And then he came up and stood out front."

"Emma said he was at your school too."

"She saw him there. I didn't notice him till the park."

"Did he…say anything to you? Or approach you?"

"No." She tucked her hair behind one ear. "But he did stay in front of our house for a while. It was kind of weird."

Hmmm. "What did he look like?"

She shrugged again. "He was just some old guy. He had a dog with him. A big yellow one."

I sighed. "Why didn't you phone me? Or at least tell me about it when I came home?"

She rolled her eyes. "Why? We handled it. Emma came into our house until he went away." She bit her lip. "Maybe he was just lost."

Well, I didn't want to make more of it than it deserved, or project my unease onto her. "Come into the kitchen so I can make dinner while we talk."

Maddy followed me, stooping to pick up Oscar, our aging tabby. She stood by the window with him gathered in her arms, her face buried in his fur.

I began chopping the vegetables and chicken I'd assembled for a stir-fry. "Did the guy seem threatening at all?" I asked.

She slid into a chair at the kitchen table. "Just forget it. He didn't really do anything."

Scraping a pile of red pepper cubes to the side, I started on the mushrooms. Time to change the subject, before this escalated into a full-blown argument. "Can you set the table, please?"

The stir-fry came together quickly, and we talked about other things as we ate—Halloween, school, TV shows. But thoughts of the guy watching our house hung on in my mind.

****

I phoned Nicole after dinner. "Maddy didn't really have anything new to add, but it sounds like he was definitely following them."

"I told you Matthew thinks we should report it."

"All right." I still didn't think the police would do much about it, but I could see that Emma's parents wouldn't let it rest. "I can phone them." That way I'd know what was said.

A civilian clerk answered my call; she took my information and said an officer would call me back. I sighed. "How long will that take?"

"I'm not sure. Someone'll get back to you as soon as possible."

I half-expected a long delay, but I had hardly finished filling the dishwasher when my phone rang. "Good evening, Ms. Koss." A woman's voice, gravelly.

Actually, it's *Dr.* Koss, but I never insist on the title. Some psychologists do, but I've always thought it seems pretentious.

She continued, "I'm Constable Marie Boucher. You called a few minutes ago." She sounded mature, authoritative, with a light French accent. I repeated my story. She asked a few questions about the man's appearance and actions. "Do you have any other details?"

"All we know is what I've told you."

"All right. Thank you. I'd like to come by and

speak to both girls, if that's convenient."

****

Waiting for the police to arrive, I had a few minutes to call Jenny. She's been my closest friend since university—my mainstay for support and reassurance. Skipping preliminaries, I told her about the guy following Maddy and Emma.

"You sound worried." I could hear concern in her voice.

"I wasn't, really, until the police officer said she wanted to interview the girls."

She paused. "What did she—?"

"I'm not sure why she wants to interview them. But it made me wonder if this is more serious than I thought."

"Well, wait and see what she says." A second later she added, "Would you like me to come over later?"

I smiled at her impulse. Trust Jenny to offer support. "No, that's not necessary. I know you get up early for work."

"Okay. Let me know what happens."

****

Nicole joined me in the kitchen as I made tea. She and Matthew had both come over with Emma. "I'm glad you called the police," she said, her forehead creased in worry. "We don't like the idea of some guy following the girls."

I swallowed. "Let's just see what the officer has to say." I still wasn't sure what the interview could achieve. Adding a plate of Oreos to the tray, I nudged the mugs and teapot over to make space. We headed back to the living room.

Matthew sat at one end of the couch, tapping his

fingers on his knee. Emma and Maddy had crowded close together at the other end. Nicole perched on one of the easy chairs, leaving the second one for me. I'd turned on lamps earlier—a floor lamp and two smaller table lamps. They gave a warm light to the room but cast dark shadows in the corners.

Maddy's face was flushed. "I've never talked to a policeman. This'll be interesting." She elbowed Emma, who raised her eyebrows and returned the nudge.

"It's a police *woman*," I said.

Maddy's eyes widened. "Cool." She leaned forward and grabbed two cookies, handing one to Emma.

Nicole started to say something but stopped when Matthew gave her a sharp glance. He reached over and squeezed her hand. "It's all right," he said. "The girls will answer the officer's questions, and then we'll learn what happens next." He and Nicole were both around my age—early forties—but sometimes his manner made him seem older, more serious.

The doorbell rang, and I opened the door to a dark-haired police officer in uniform. I guessed she was a little younger than me. "I'm Constable Boucher," she said, "but you can call me Marie." She had a capable, no-nonsense air that gave me confidence. She shook hands with each of us, then sat in one of the easy chairs. She turned down tea but accepted a glass of water, which Maddy jumped up to fetch, handing it to her with an eager smile.

"Thank you," Marie said. "Now, if you and your friend sit here with me, you can tell me exactly what happened." Maddy and Emma seated themselves on an ottoman in front of her, mesmerized.

She led the girls through their story, probing for details as they spoke. What was the man wearing? How tall? They couldn't remember his clothing, other than it was "regular clothes." No, not a suit. Yes, a jacket—a dark one, they thought. Like a windbreaker. And he had gray hair, no hat.

An old guy, Maddy insisted. Emma agreed. "Maybe like your grandpa was," she said to Maddy.

Maddy stared at her. "Grandpa didn't look like that." But her cheeks were flushed.

My dad had died of heart complications the previous January, just after turning seventy-four. Losing him was hard on Maddy. They'd been close, and she spent a lot of time with him, often with Emma in tow.

Listening to the girls' descriptions, I realized this didn't give the police much to go on.

Marie thanked the girls, then turned to me. "We'll have officers watch for him when patrolling in your neighborhood and around the school. We'll contact the school principal to make sure everyone is keeping an eye out there. But unless the man shows up again, there's not much more we can do."

This was about what I'd expected. But I knew Nicole and Matthew had hoped for more.

Marie closed her notebook. "Here's my advice for now. Keep your doors locked, and let me know if anything more happens."

Mathew leaned forward. "Should we be worried?"

"I'd just say, stay alert. Keep supervising your girls."

He glanced at Nicole. "We could drive them to school and back for a few days," he said. "Instead of letting them walk."

Before I said anything—I wondered if he was overreacting—Marie nodded. "That couldn't hurt."

When she got up to leave, I followed her out onto the porch, closing the door behind me.

"You seem to be taking this more seriously than I expected."

She squinted at me, her face in shadow. "We try to follow up any instances of children being followed."

"Have there been any other reports?"

"Nothing recent, but we've had problems in the past. We've been told to stay on top of anything like this."

Back in the house, I took a deep breath and returned to the living room. "I guess we should stay vigilant. Matthew, you thought we should be driving the girls to school?"

He tilted his head. "I think it makes sense. Just to be safe."

"I can drive them in the morning. Can either of you pick them up after school? My afternoon is packed."

Maddy looked mutinous. "C'mon, Mom. Really? We don't need to be driven."

Matthew frowned at her. "We want to make sure you're both okay. What if he shows up again?"

"So what? There are two of us. And he's old…" She usually saved this argumentative tone for me— staying polite with other adults—but I knew she regarded walking to school as a hard-won privilege.

I interjected. "What does his age matter?"

"We can run faster than him if we need to."

Time to nip this in the bud. "We're driving you tomorrow. End of discussion."

Emma said nothing, sitting quietly with her head bent. Maddy muttered something inaudible.

Nicole and Matthew exchanged glances. Nicole spoke. "If you drive them to school, Susan, I can pick them up in the afternoon."

They got ready to leave with Emma. As I closed the front door behind them, I turned to speak to Maddy, but she'd already headed upstairs to her room.

I pressed my hands against my temples, unsure of what might lie ahead.

Chapter Three

Maddy was half-hoping the man would be back.

She lay in bed, unable to sleep, the events of the afternoon swirling through her mind. It had been pretty exciting.

She hadn't told her mom everything.

After they noticed the guy in the park—and decided he'd been following them—Emma was the one who wanted to escape. "Quick, let's go to your house."

But Maddy hadn't wanted to leave, not yet. The guy had a dog with him. She'd always liked dogs.

Emma was pulling at her elbow. "C'mon. Let's go."

The guy had stopped and was bent over, maybe tying a shoelace.

Maddy gave in to Emma's urging. They scurried out of the park and raced across the road. Maddy fumbled in her backpack, digging underneath her books for her house key. She wasn't used to having her own keys yet.

Emma bumped up behind her as Maddy retrieved the key, and they both crowded against the door. Maddy shoved the key into the keyhole. Emma whispered, "Oh my God, there he is! He's coming up the steps from the park!"

Maddy opened the door, and Emma pushed into the hallway behind her. "Hurry!"

Maddy locked the door and dropped her backpack on the floor.

The girls ran to the front window. They peeked carefully around the curtains, making sure he couldn't see them. Maddy could feel Emma trembling beside her, and her own knees wobbled. The guy was standing out on the street, staring in their direction. Emma's arm pressed hard against hers as they watched.

The man seemed old but not ancient. Thin but strong-looking. White hair, lined face. The dog—a big dog with yellowish light-brown fur—sat quietly beside its owner.

Watching the man, Maddy couldn't help thinking he reminded her of Grandpa. It was a dumb idea, but that didn't stop her from having it.

Finally he turned and went back into the park, the dog following.

Maddy sank to the floor. "Whoa," she said. "That was weird."

"He might not be gone," Emma said. "He could just be waiting in the park."

Maddy glanced at her friend. Now that the guy had left, she was sorry it had ended so soon. Nothing this interesting had ever happened to them.

And he did remind her of Grandpa.

They were still wearing their jackets. She turned to Emma. "Let's go back out and see if he's still there."

"No way! Are you crazy?"

This was the part Maddy hadn't told her mom about.

"Come on. There's two of us. What's he going to do?"

Emma shook her head, arms folded.

Maddy gave up. If Emma was scared, she'd go on her own. "Okay, stay here. Leave the door unlocked so I can get back in fast if I need to."

She ran to the park steps and edged her way down, peering carefully around the bushes to the path below. Her stomach quivered as she crept down the steps, half-expecting the man to be waiting there, but he'd left— she could make him out in the distance, striding with his dog beside him. Heading toward Bank Street.

She'd watched him, wondering if he'd turn and see her, but he didn't.

Now, as she lay in bed, Maddy wondered again about the man. He had definitely been following them. And having him come up the steps and stare at their house…it made her stomach feel like it did when they were waiting for the roller coaster at Wonderland last year. Partly thrilled, partly scared.

Was he dangerous, like her mom and Emma's parents thought? But he had that dog. Aren't people with dogs usually nice people?

Maybe he was just lonely.

She couldn't help thinking about him.

Chapter Four

The girl's smiling face and dancing figure had filled Daniel's mind since he first spotted her. Amazing to find Hannah at last—and to find her here, so far from home.

It's why we never gave up.

He heaved another box of old magazines to the curb. They smelled musty; Aunt Ruby must have been saving them since the sixties. Saturday Evening Post, Life, National Geographic.

When Aunt Ruby's will left the house to him, along with his cousins Gord and Pete—Uncle Jack's boys—they'd decided to sell it. They all lived in other provinces, and none of them wanted to be absentee landlords.

The house would be worth a fair bit. Ruby and George bought it in 1956, and in the meantime this central Ottawa neighborhood had become trendy, with prices to match.

Daniel had volunteered to get it ready for sale. He had the time; he'd already harvested this year's crops. Since Patricia's death three years ago, after a long drawn-out fight with cancer, he had rented out most of the land on his Alberta farm. Without her, he'd lost interest in farming...or pretty much his interest in anything, for that matter.

Except for finding Hannah. That had to be his top

priority, as Patricia had insisted from the beginning.

As the years went by, they'd kept prodding the cops to keep the investigation alive, and they never stopped hoping to find her. She had to be somewhere.

And recently Patricia's voice was more demanding than ever. *It was all your fault, so you have to fix it.*

He knew that was right. He needed to find Hannah, take her back to the farm where she belonged.

And now that goal was in sight. He'd finally found her—in Ottawa of all places. Unbelievable! But this time he was certain. It must be fate that had brought him here.

And Aunt Ruby's house gave him a base to work from while he decided how to proceed.

****

In the afternoon, he returned to the street where Hannah—"Maddy"—had disappeared into the brick house. A lot of the houses were substantial, surrounded by tall overhanging trees. They were brick or stucco, with front porches and second or even third floors. Housing styles from the 1930s or earlier.

He shivered. It had been sunny and warm when he left the house, so he'd only worn a thin jacket. But now a chill breeze had sprung up. With every wind gust, leaves were dropping from the trees and sweeping along the sidewalk.

He needed the girl's last name. The family name. Hopefully he could get that from one of the neighbors.

Somebody with computer smarts could probably find the name online, using the address, but he had no idea how to do that.

He rang the doorbells at a couple of houses. No answer. Well, people were at work. Maybe he'd made a mistake coming here in the daytime.

On his third try, at the house next to the one he thought of as Hannah's, a middle-aged woman came to the door. She frowned at Tucker, who was sitting quietly at Daniel's feet with the leash clipped to his collar. Seeing her nervous glance, Daniel stepped back and wrapped the leash around one of the porch pillars. He smiled at her, hoping to put her at ease. "Ma'am? I'm trying to get in touch with your neighbors next door." He pointed.

She looked over at the brick house. "Susan? Yes."

"What's their last name?" He'd give it a shot. She might not want to tell him.

She squinted at him. "You want to get in touch, and you don't know their last name?"

Daniel didn't have an excuse ready. He swallowed. Thinking fast, he said, "I see their eavestroughs need clearing. That's my line of work."

"Oh?" She gazed at him, her expression uncertain.

"I'd like to leave a note, but I thought it would go better if I knew their name."

She pursed her lips. "Maybe so. Anyway, it's Susan Koss. You could leave a note in her mailbox."

"Is there a Mr. Koss?"

"No, not as far as I know. There's just Susan and Madison. Maddy."

"Is that the little blonde girl?"

"Yes, a lovely child."

"Thank you, ma'am. I appreciate your help." Daniel bent to unwind the leash from the porch pillar and headed back to the sidewalk. He didn't glance back, so he couldn't tell if the woman was still watching him or not.

Chapter Five

I went in to wake Maddy on Thursday morning, opening her curtains to let sunshine stream in. I used to wake her with a little ditty my mother sang to me as a child, but Maddy'd told me several months ago that it was for babies.

When the sun hit her pillow, Maddy sat straight up in bed, glaring at me. "Mom! What are you doing in here?"

"It's time to get up. It's a perfect fall day outside."

She made a sour face, her eyes blazing. "Don't come in without asking. Don't I get any privacy?"

Wow. I could have anticipated that snippy tone, but I wasn't braced for it so early in the morning. I tried to respond calmly. "I just came in to wake you. Time to get up for school."

She frowned at her bedside table, where her phone was sitting. "You didn't need to wake me—I set my alarm. And it's not time yet, anyway; I still have another ten minutes."

"Given how long you take to get ready these days—"

"Oh my God!" She flopped back on her bed and pulled the covers over her head.

At that I left the room, a dull pounding starting behind my eyes. Maddy and I had been having these run-ins more often in the last few months. I knew I shouldn't let them get to me—they were just a sign of the teenage years arriving, I was sure—but my insides roiled every time we argued. And I hated that indignant tone she had started using.

By breakfast, her bad temper seemed to have evaporated. She hummed as she poured orange juice and added milk to her Cheerios, watching something on her phone as she ate.

I sighed. If the atmosphere wasn't exactly companionable, at least it was peaceful. But these quiet moments were few and far between these days.

****

After dropping Maddy and Emma off at school, I realized I'd left some notes at home that I needed for work. This was my second day of driving the girls, which Nicole and I had agreed to do for a while, but the extra time crunch was messing with my organizational skills.

None of us had seen any sign that the man was still around. He was probably long gone.

As I pulled into our driveway, hoping to make this a quick stop, my next-door neighbor Joyce waved and approached my car. I did my best to stifle my impatience. Joyce liked to chat, and I didn't have time for her this morning.

I'd barely opened my car door before she started talking. "Hi, Susan. You aren't usually home this time of day."

I collected my purse and got out of the car without making eye contact. "I'm just here for a few minutes to pick up something." Hopefully she'd take the hint and let me get on with it.

She sidled along beside me as I headed toward the

house. "I wanted to ask you—did that eavestrough guy leave you a note?"

I paused. "What eavestrough guy?"

"He was here yesterday just after lunch. He wanted to know your last name. Said he'd leave you a note about cleaning your eavestroughs."

I stared at my roof. I wasn't in a mood to think about cleaning the gutters, though I supposed they could use it.

"*Did* he leave a note?" she asked.

I shook my head as I started up the steps. "No. I didn't see one. Why?"

Joyce had stopped on the walkway. "There was something odd." When I didn't say anything, she added, "He mentioned Maddy."

I swiveled, staring down at her. "What do you mean?"

"He asked about her, asked if she was the blonde girl."

An uneasy chill crept over me. "She wasn't around yesterday—she was at school. When would he have seen her?"

"He also asked if there was a Mr. Koss."

I came back down the steps to give Joyce my full attention. "What did this guy look like?"

"Do you think you know him?"

"I'm not sure. Can you describe him?"

"I didn't pay much attention. He was an older guy, I'd guess sixty-five or seventy, but he seemed fairly fit. White hair."

My stomach clenched. "Anything else?"

She took a step back, her eyes widening. "Well, he had a good-sized dog with him. Yellow or light brown

I don't know what kind it was. I'm not a dog person."

Heat flushed through my body. *Oh my God.* He was still around—and clearly his interest in Maddy was more than incidental.

Trying not to show my sudden fear, I turned to unlock the front door. "I have to go now. Thanks."

But before going in, I realized I should put her on alert. "Wait a minute, Joyce," I called. She had gone back to her yard but turned at my voice. "I don't have time to tell you the whole story, but that guy has been following Maddy and her friend. Please keep an eye out for him and let me know if you see him again."

She nodded, with a shocked expression that said she wanted to know more. But I had to get going. I gave her a wave as I returned to our porch. "I'll fill you in later."

Closing the front door behind me, I slammed my purse down on the hall table, my temples throbbing. *Not a migraine now, please.* This was not the time to retreat to a dark room, my treatment of last resort for a full-blown headache. I pulled a bottle of Tylenol from a cupboard in the kitchen and popped four, hoping to halt an incipient attack.

I headed to my desk to get the papers I needed, then went back outside, locking the door behind me. A cold gust of wind blew into my face. The air was heavy with moisture, and dark clouds filled the sky. I shivered; fall had arrived. Glancing at my watch, I realized I'd have to hurry if I wanted to get to the clinic in time for my first appointment.

Apart from the wind, everything was still. Joyce had vanished. Bare trees swayed overhead, and dead leaves lay in drifts beside the sidewalks.

The street wasn't entirely empty, though. At the far end I saw two figures, a tall one and a short one. I squinted. A man with a dog.

A man with white hair and a big yellow dog.

No.

My vision clouded, and blood pounded at my temples. *Could that really be him?* "Hey!" I yelled. "Get away from here!"

He showed no sign that he heard me.

I leapt toward my car. I needed to confront him. The door unlocked as I approached—but, fumbling with my purse, I dropped my keys.

Groaning, I threw my belongings onto the front seat and scrabbled for the keys. They had fallen under the car, and I got down on all fours to reach them. Grit pressed into my knees as my pantyhose ripped. *Damn it.* I scooped up the keys and flung myself behind the wheel, tearing out into the street.

But when I neared the corner, the guy and his dog had vanished. I pounded my steering wheel. Blood pulsed painfully in my forehead as I pulled the car to the side of the road to collect myself.

I gritted my teeth. Gradually my breathing settled, and I tried to gather my thoughts. If that was him, what was he doing here in the morning, when we normally aren't home? Was he scoping out our street, our house?

And where was he now? He'd only had time to duck into someone's backyard or move to a nearby street. He could easily return.

But I was late. I had turned on the alarm system before I left, so our house was protected. I put the car in gear and headed for work.

****

I called the police number and asked for Marie. When she returned my call, I was just pulling into the parking lot at the clinic.

"Marie, that guy is still hanging around. He was at our neighbor's house yesterday, asking about Maddy. And I think I saw him on our street about ten minutes ago."

"Slow down. Tell me the details." She led me through the story and said she and her partner would drive around the area to see if they could locate him. They'd also speak to Joyce to see if she had any information to add.

I suspected they'd find nothing, and Marie called me later to say they hadn't caught sight of him. They'd keep up the patrols, though, and she encouraged us to stay vigilant.

My heart still hadn't stopped pounding. The previous incident wasn't just a one-time event. Now it seemed clear that his focus on us was more than fleeting, and I had no idea what he might do.

Chapter Six

Friday morning. Daniel sat at Aunt Ruby's kitchen table, flipping through his tattered black address book. He hoped Mac was at his desk at RCMP headquarters. It was nine o'clock in Edmonton. Should be an okay time to call.

"Mac? Good morning, it's Daniel Kazan. It's a while since we talked."

A moment's silence on the line. "Yeah, it's been a while." Mac sounded distracted. "I don't have anything to tell you. There haven't been any new developments."

Daniel broke in. "It's my turn. I have something to report."

"Oh?"

"I'm in Ottawa."

Mac's voice sounded hollow; he must have put the call on speakerphone. "Ottawa must be nice this time of year. Is that what you called to tell me?"

"No. I'm not here sightseeing. I'm getting my aunt's house ready for sale."

"Ah. So what's up?"

"It's good news—great news in fact. I've found Hannah!"

"What?"

Daniel drew a breath. "I was in the park a couple of days ago with my dog, and two girls walked by. One of them looked exactly like Kelly. I know it's her. It was like seeing a young Kelly again."

Mac sounded skeptical. "What makes you think Hannah would be in Ottawa?"

Daniel stood and pushed back his chair, impatient. Mac wasn't getting it. "I don't know, but here she is. I didn't come here expecting to find her—it just happened."

Mac groaned. "This sounds like a repeat of last time."

Daniel gritted his teeth. "No, it's not. That was a mistake. This time is different. This girl could be a carbon copy of Kelly—she has to be Hannah. I'm positive."

"Hey. I know you wish we could find her, but this is the second time—"

Don't let him talk you down. Patricia's voice was insistent. *You know what you know.*

"I'm telling you, this time I'm sure it's her. And I've found out where she lives."

"Have you been following this girl? That's a bad idea."

"I've been careful. I haven't bothered her. But I know her school now and where she lives." He gave Mac the address. "And I know her name too. They call her Maddy; the family's name is Koss."

Mac's voice got louder, as if he'd moved closer to the phone. "How did you find that out?"

"One of the kids at her school...and a neighbor."

Mac sighed. "So you've been going around asking questions. You have to stop—you'll get yourself in trouble again."

"No, I'll be careful. That's why I'm calling. You have to investigate. I'm positive it's her."

Mac sounded impatient. "If you swear you'll stay away from this girl...I'll tell you what. I have a buddy in Ottawa, in the police there. I'll get him to do a discreet check. At least we'll find out if there's a girl of the right age living there, and get some information. In the meantime, I want you to keep to yourself."

"Sure, okay. I'll be spending the weekend clearing things out of my aunt's house anyway. But you'll follow up, right?"

"Yes, but don't get your hopes up. I doubt it's her."

Chapter Seven

Monday morning arrived, crisp and bright. I was glad Nicole was driving the girls today, so I could get to the clinic early.

I was putting my laptop into my briefcase, ready to head to work, when the doorbell rang. A uniformed police officer was standing on the porch. I hadn't expected anyone, but I was glad to see him—I hoped the cops had finally found the guy.

I opened the door with a smile. "Good morning, Officer." I had to tip my head back to see his face—he was tall, over six feet at least, with a short reddish beard.

He raised an eyebrow, as if surprised at my cheery greeting. "Good morning. Ms. Koss?"

"Yes."

"I'm Bob Russo, with the Ottawa Police Service." He held up his police badge and ID card so I could confirm his identity. "May I come in?"

"Of course."

As he entered, he took off his hat and wiped his feet. I led him into the living room at the front of the house. The room was cheery and welcoming that morning, with the sun slanting through the windows.

"Can I get you something?" I asked. "Coffee?"

"Coffee'd be great, thanks." Now that he'd taken off his hat, I noted his short-cropped hair was almost fully gray. I guessed he was in his late forties, with a face that showed some wear, along with intelligence.

In the kitchen, I touched my hand to the half-full carafe of coffee left from breakfast. It was still warm; I filled two mugs and stuck them in the microwave for a minute. "What do you take in your coffee?" I called.

"A little milk is fine."

When I returned to the living room, he was standing by the bookcase with his back to the room, inspecting the framed photos on display.

"That's Maddy, with the fish," I said, handing him a mug and pointing to a 5x7 photo, one I took at the lake last year. Maddy was beaming, holding up a small fresh-caught walleye. In my mind I could see that glorious morning again. Maddy and her grandpa—my dad—had gone fishing after breakfast and came back excited about Maddy's catch. With Dad gone now, there wouldn't be any more such mornings.

Russo picked up the photo. "Ah. Maddy's your daughter?"

"Yeah. She's the one the guy's been following."

He looked at me with something like confusion. Carrying his coffee, he moved toward one of the easy chairs. "May I sit down?"

"Of course." I sat at the end of the couch across from him and took a sip of coffee. "So I assume you're here to report some progress?"

He shook his head. "I'm actually...we may have a misunderstanding. I'm not here to report on anything."

"What?" I sat up. "You're not here about my complaint?"

"No. I didn't even know you'd made a complaint. What was it about?"

"I spoke to a Constable Marie Boucher. Do you work with her?"

He nodded. "We're both in Central Division. But we haven't spoken about you. What was your complaint?"

I took a breath. "Marie knows all about it. A man followed Maddy and her friend to and from school last week, and he's been hanging around."

Russo put his coffee down and leaned forward, watching me intently. "Well, that may have something to do with why I'm here today."

"I thought...you said it didn't."

"For a different reason," he said. "I'm here unofficially, as a favor for a fellow cop. He's an RCMP officer in Alberta, in their Missing Persons Unit."

I frowned, puzzled. "So what's the favor?"

He sighed. "One of his long-time cases is a girl who disappeared about eleven years ago. Her name was Hannah Byers. She apparently was abducted as a baby, taken from the vehicle where her parents died in a hit-and-run accident."

I shuddered. "How awful. But what does that have to do with me?"

"My buddy has stayed in touch with the girl's grandfather. She's never been found; she'd be twelve years old by now."

I stared at him, suddenly uneasy.

"The grandfather is in Ottawa now, and he phoned my friend, Mac, on Friday, to say he believes he's found her. He's...well, he's convinced that your daughter is Hannah."

Chapter Eight

I stared at Russo, stunned. "Are you joking?" Then I sat upright. "Wait, that's him! That's the guy who's been following her, isn't he?"

He raised his eyebrows. "That could be the case, yes."

"So you know who he is?"

"Yeah. His name's Daniel Kazan."

I sighed with relief. "Well, that's a step forward. Now you should be able to do something about him, make him stay away from us, right?"

Russo leaned back in his chair. "I guess there's more to this story than I knew about. Mac—my RCMP buddy—just asked me to check that a girl of the right age lives here." He cocked an eye at me. "Your Maddy is twelve?"

A chill went through me. "She's twelve, all right, but she's my daughter. No question." I shifted in my chair, unable to sit still. "What makes this guy think she's his granddaughter?"

"Apparently he says Maddy strongly resembles his daughter when she was the same age. She was the one who died in the crash. Hannah was her baby."

"That's crazy. He thinks Maddy was his daughter's baby?"

Russo nodded. "That's it."

"And now he's been lurking in our neighborhood.

34

The girls are terrified!" This wasn't strictly true, I knew; the girls seemed to be taking it in stride. I was the one scared stiff by all this. But still.

"I'm sorry to hear that. You said you've been dealing with Marie Boucher on this?"

"Yes, but there wasn't a lot she could do unless they could identify him."

"I'll fill her in about Kazan. And Mac said he told Kazan to stay away from Maddy."

"But that doesn't mean he will."

He frowned. "No. And Mac said this happened once before."

"What? With another girl?"

"Yeah, a girl in Red Deer. There was some trouble. He was following her and saying she was his granddaughter. Though he changed his mind there, said he'd made a mistake."

"So this time it's a mistake too!"

"Probably. But Hannah's disappearance is still an open case, so Mac can't just ignore Kazan."

I stared at him. "What does this Kazan guy think? That I kidnapped his granddaughter?"

"He may not have a theory. He's just insisting that Maddy is Hannah."

My mouth was dry. "This is ridiculous." I scowled, my stomach churning. "So now what?"

"Well, I'll fill Mac in on our discussion. And I'll brief Marie. We can try to get Kazan to back off, at least to stop following Maddy."

I tried to ignore the dull pain blossoming behind my eyes. "What if he won't?" The guy sounded unhinged.

"Probably the best thing would be to convince him

he's made another mistake. That Maddy is actually your daughter."

"How do we do that?"

"I'm sure you have documents, records, proof of her birth, and so on. I'd suggest you pull those together." He got to his feet and put his hat on, adjusting it with a practiced motion.

I stood too. "And then what?"

"Just have them ready. I'll fill in Mac and Marie, and they'll take it from there." He took out a card, wrote a phone number on the back, and handed it to me. "That's my cellphone if you want to reach me."

After he left, I sagged against the front door, listening to his retreating footsteps.

This was unreal. My head was suddenly pounding, and I could hardly hold myself upright; all my energy had drained away. A sudden nausea overtook me; I clapped my hand to my mouth and hurtled down the hallway, making it to the downstairs washroom just in time to vomit into the toilet.

Wiping my face, I stared into the mirror. *I look like shit.*

My ten o'clock session at the clinic was in half an hour. I had to pull myself together. I dashed upstairs to brush my teeth, did a quick repair job to my makeup, and headed for my car.

Meanwhile, Russo's statements circled through my brain. Having Kazan's name was a step forward. But what kind of lunatic would make this preposterous claim?

If he was really convinced Maddy was his granddaughter, I had no idea what he might do.

****

In the clinic waiting room, I watched as the anxious six-year-old I'd just finished assessing put on the jacket his mother was holding for him. "I'll see you again soon, James." The mother smiled nervously, but James ignored me.

The clock on the wall read 12:01. Lunchtime. I'd made it through the morning.

Any appetite I might have had for lunch vanished as the memory of Russo's revelations filled my mind. I hurried back to my office and closed the door.

Before anything else, I wanted to google Daniel Kazan's story.

Entering various combinations of words based on the few details Russo had told me, I pieced together the basics. They added a few bits to the account Russo had provided.

Kazan's daughter and son-in-law, Kelly and Jacob Byers, died eleven years ago in a severe snowstorm in rural Alberta, apparent victims of a hit-and-run collision that drove their vehicle off the road. When discovered the next morning, they were both dead, and their eighteen-month-old daughter, Hannah, had disappeared from the child seat in the back. She was assumed to have been abducted. No sign of her had been found since, despite vigorous investigation.

Kelly was Daniel and Patricia Kazan's only daughter, Hannah their only grandchild. It was a terrible story. I could imagine their grief, and how frantic Hannah's disappearance must have made them.

A later article mentioned that Patricia Kazan died of cancer three years ago. So Daniel Kazan was alone now, his whole family gone.

I could pity him—but that didn't make him any

less dangerous. In fact, those losses could lead to a kind of derangement, and his deluded focus on Maddy could become an obsession. If it hadn't already.

Pacing from my desk to the window, I struggled to tamp down my rising anxiety.

I needed to talk to Jenny, my port in any storm. I half-expected to get her voicemail, but she answered on the second ring.

This was no time for chitchat. "You won't believe what happened this morning." I started telling her about Russo coming by, not sure what part of the story to tell first.

"Slow down. Tell me what happened." Jenny's calm voice was like a balm.

My mouth was dry. I reached for the water bottle on my desk and stared out at the gathering clouds. "We have a name for the guy who's been following Maddy. And get this—he claims she's his granddaughter."

She said nothing for a moment, then, "How does that make sense?"

"He says Maddy's the long-lost child of his dead daughter. That she's not mine at all."

She snorted. "Well, that's ridiculous. So who is this guy?"

I took a sip of water, forcing myself to swallow. "His name's Daniel Kazan." I summarized the story for her. "So he's not been following some random girl. He thinks Maddy belongs to him."

"Wow. No wonder you're upset." Her voice deepened. "But go back a minute. What does he think happened? How—?"

I blinked back angry tears. "I guess he thinks I stole her, or bought her or something. As a baby."

More silence. "What do the police say? Do they think there's any basis to that story?"

I leaned against the window, feeling the cool glass on my forehead. "I don't think so, but Kazan really did have a missing granddaughter."

Jenny's voice took on urgency. "Well, obviously it's not Maddy."

"Of course not. And I think the cops will try to convince him of that. I'll give Marie Boucher a call— you remember, she was the officer that came to interview Maddy and Emma when Kazan first followed them. Now that we have an ID for him, she can warn him off."

"That'll be a relief."

"It may not be enough. Russo—the officer who told me all this—said I should pull together documents showing that Maddy really is mine."

"And do what with it?"

"He didn't really say—I think he was suggesting I should have it ready in case it was needed."

"What about a DNA test to prove there's no relationship between him and Maddy? There are several private genetics labs in Ottawa—my neighbor had to have a paternity test done."

Whoa. A story for another occasion. "Yeah, that would settle the matter. But DNA tests take time."

"True. So the police are going to tell him Maddy is definitely yours and hope that convinces him to stay away?"

"Yeah. The idea is to dislodge his mistaken belief."

"Do you think that'll work?"

"I'm not sure." Actually I was far from sure, but I wanted to end on a positive note. "It's worth a try."

****

I went down the hall to Abel's office. He was the other psychologist on staff and my closest friend at work.

His office door was open, and he was alone, staring at something on his computer screen. Papers littered his desk. I knocked on the doorframe and leaned through. "Can I interrupt? I need to update you on something."

He looked up with a quick smile. "Susan! Certainly, come in, come in." He leapt up and moved a pile of books from a nearby chair, clearing a space for me.

Pushing up his glasses and tossing hair out of his eyes, he remained standing until I sat, then resumed his own chair. "What can I help you with? Is it something at the clinic, or something at home?" Abel's English was great but a little formal, still using constructions he learned at his excellent high school in Zagreb before his parents sent him to Canada in the 1990s.

I took a sip from the water bottle I'd brought with me, gathering my thoughts. "This is a crazy problem that's come up. I told you about the guy who was following Maddy."

A frown flashed across his face. "Yes, a very bad thing. Has something more—?"

"There's now an unbelievable twist to the story." I described Russo's visit that morning and the increased threat that Kazan now posed, in my opinion.

Abel leaned toward me, elbows on his knees, his eyes focused on mine. "This is terrible! What a big worry, to learn that this man has designs on your Maddy."

The warmth of Abel's concern comforted me, but

that wasn't the reason I was in his office.

"I should be on top of this, but I'm surprised at how much it's taken me aback. Do you have any thoughts or advice?"

"About your situation?"

"Yeah. Mainly...do you think that a man with that background, those losses in his family...would he be likely to form an obsession about Maddy? If the police tell him to stay away from her, do you think he'll follow instructions?"

Our clinic focused on child mental health issues. Both Abel and I studied adult psychology as part of our training, of course, but for me it was only theoretical. I knew Abel spent several years working with adult clients at the Clarke Institute in Toronto, though, so he'd have a better practical sense for the question I was groping to answer.

He frowned. "I can't really answer that, without knowing more about him. But you may be right to be concerned."

I'd hoped he'd dismiss my fears about Daniel, but apparently not.

"Do you think I should talk to Dorothy about this?" Dorothy Landis was our boss, the psychiatrist who headed the clinic.

Abel pursed his lips. "Of course. Did she already know about the incidents with this man?"

"I did mention about him following Maddy. Mainly to let her know that with driving the girls and so on, I might have some scheduling issues." I hadn't given her a lot of detail; our discussions were generally about professional issues, not our personal lives.

"So—certainly, keep her informed. And she may

have further insights to offer." He leaned forward then, a fierce glint in his eye. "But I think you should get rid of this man before he can cause more trouble, if you can."

I stared at him. "Meaning…"

"Your police officer is right. Best to persuade the man he's mistaken about Maddy, to remove his interest in her."

I wasn't fully convinced. "I'm just not sure how persuadable he is. If he's really obsessed…" I sighed and got up to leave.

Abel stood up too. "You don't need to rely just on the police. Have you considered consulting a lawyer?"

I hadn't thought that far. I didn't have a regular lawyer; the only time I'd used one was when I bought my house. But my friend Tom Pascow was a partner at a well-known law firm downtown. He and his wife, Amy, adored Maddy and had often gone hiking with us.

Though I'd never talked about legal things with Tom, I knew he'd handled some tough cases. Maybe it was a time to consult him.

****

That afternoon, in between appointments, I managed to get hold of Marie. I wanted to make sure Russo had briefed her.

"Yes, Susan," she assured me. "I did speak with Bob Russo, and I've also spoken to his RCMP contact in Edmonton, Corporal MacCormick. I'm up to speed on Daniel Kazan."

Good. That was Step One. "Have you gotten hold of him yet?"

"He's on my list. I left a message on his phone, but he hasn't called back."

I frowned. "Do you have his address? Can't you stop by his house?"

"I do have his Ottawa address. I won't have a chance to go by there until later, but I'll try to get to him today."

She didn't seem to think this was urgent.

Maybe I was expecting too much too soon, but I couldn't help worrying. Daniel Kazan was obsessed and unpredictable. A loose cannon—and he was aimed right at Maddy.

Abel was right. I didn't have to rely only on the police.

It was time to call Tom.

Chapter Nine

Tom arrived after dinner; I was waiting for him on the front porch.

A small-boned man with close-cut gray hair, he smiled as he bounded up the steps. He gave me a quick hug and followed me inside, hanging his coat on a hook in the entryway. "You said this was something serious, so I came as soon as I could."

I led him into the living room, fetching a couple of beers on the way. He sat on the couch, and I took the chair across from him. "Emma's mom drove the girls to dance class. I wanted to talk to you while Maddy's gone."

He nodded. "So it's something you don't want her to know about."

"Well, not yet. I will tell her, at least the bare bones of it, but I wanted to talk to you first." I took a sip of my beer. "I've never asked you for legal advice, but now that's what I need."

He sat up straight and put down his drink, his gaze focused and alert. "Shoot."

I told him everything, along with my concerns.

He listened without interrupting. "I'm sorry to hear all that," he said when I finished. "So the police are going to warn him off?"

"Yes, they say they will. But...I'm concerned that may not be enough."

He raised his eyebrows.

"If he strongly believes that he has a claim to Maddy, just telling him to stay away doesn't mean he'll actually do it."

Tom stood and began pacing. "All right. To be clear, we're now on a lawyer-client basis."

"What does that mean?"

"I mean you're asking my advice as your lawyer, not just as a friend."

"Of course, that's what I want. And I'm assuming your time is chargeable."

He waved his hand. "We'll deal with fees later. For now, let's just examine your situation. You're wondering if we can take legal action to protect Maddy?"

"I was thinking a restraining order or something—"

"There are a couple of options along that line we can consider. But they may be premature."

"What do you mean?"

"Your police officer suggested first trying to convince him that he's mistaken about Maddy. I agree. It's definitely worth a shot."

"Do you have something specific in mind?"

Tom leaned forward. "I think you and I should meet with Kazan. You've seen my firm's law office. It's in a prestigious office building downtown; our boardroom looks like something out of a Victorian courtroom movie. If we meet him there, I'm betting the atmosphere will make an impression on him."

I smiled ruefully. "You're hoping to overwhelm the country bumpkin."

"Something like that." He gave a small laugh. "Even if he's more savvy, I think meeting him in a formal setting like that will show him you're serious. If nothing else, it will augment anything the police will tell him."

"And what would we say to him there?"

"You should pull together all your documentation about Maddy." He started ticking items off on his fingers. "Her birth certificate. All the medical records you have for her. Photos, preferably with dates attached—starting with when you were pregnant, and showing Maddy from when she was born and up to, say, age four or five." He flicked his eyes to me. "So the continuity is clear, and it's obvious she didn't suddenly arrive in your life at the age when his granddaughter disappeared." Raising another finger, he added, "And put together a list of people who knew you during that whole period."

"I can get all that. Do you think those'll convince him?"

He grimaced. "We can't know what'll convince him. He doesn't sound like the most rational guy. You said he fixated on Maddy because she resembles his daughter. That's pretty thin reasoning."

"Yeah. That's my concern. He sounds deluded."

"He may be. But I think we can impress on him that the weight and power of the law is on our side. We'll make clear to him that your claim is solid, that you're Maddy's mother without question."

"Jenny suggested having a DNA test to prove there's no relationship between him and Maddy."

He pursed his lips. "She may be right. That's the gold standard, for sure. But to get to that step, we have to engage with him. So let's meet with him and see if we can convince him upfront. Maybe we can make this all go away."

****

Maddy stopped on her way up the front steps, waving to Emma and Emma's mom as they left. Dance class had been fun. The music still echoed in her mind. As she reached for the door, it suddenly opened to let someone out. She pulled back, startled, but relaxed when she saw who it was. "Mr. Pascow! I didn't know you were coming over tonight!"

He gave her a big smile, holding the door open for her. "I'm just leaving, but I'm glad to see you."

"Do you have to go?" Too bad he wasn't staying. He and his wife didn't treat her like a kid; they talked to her like an equal, a person with her own ideas.

"I do. We're going to see Amy's mom tonight."

"Okay. Say hi from me." She gave him a hug and went into the house.

Her mom stood in the hallway. "Maddy, come in and close the door. You're letting in all the cold air."

Maddy scowled. "I was just saying goodbye." She'd been about to shut the door—Mom didn't need to tell her.

After hanging up her coat, she went into the kitchen and started opening cupboard doors. There must be something to snack on. "Do we have any chips or anything?"

"Are you hungry? How about a banana?"

As if. "No, I don't feel like fruit."

Maddy expected her mom to recommend another "healthy alternative." But tonight was a surprise. "There's a bag of chips in the back of that cupboard, behind the oatmeal."

Huh? Mom hardly ever allowed chips in the house.

"And I'll make some hot chocolate."

Wow. The last time Mom did that, Grandpa was still alive.

Might as well push it. "With marshmallows?"

"Sure."

Maddy reached past containers of pasta and cereal. *Yes!* A small bag, but still—chips! She ripped open the bag. Something was going on.

"What was Mr. Pascow doing here?"

Her mom was busy at the microwave. "He's going to do some legal work for me."

"Really?" Maddy knew he was a lawyer, but she just thought of the Pascows as family friends. "What about?"

Her mom had her back to the room, getting mugs out of the cupboard, not saying anything. Maddy's good mood faded. She was old enough to be let in on things! But her mom liked to keep what she called "grown-up topics" to herself.

Maddy pushed back her chair. "Never mind. I'm going upstairs." She picked up the bag of chips.

"Wait." Her mom turned to her. "I need to talk to you about something."

Maddy sighed, still standing. "Okay."

The microwave pinged.

Maddy slid back into her chair, slouching with her head down. A mug appeared on the table in front of her, steam rising from the hot chocolate.

"You forgot the marshmallows."

"Right, coming up." Her mom added a handful to each mug, then sat in a chair across from Maddy. "You know the old guy with the dog who followed you to school last week?"

"Sure." The parents had sure freaked out about that. Maddy glanced at her mom. She seemed strangely tense.

"Apparently his granddaughter, Hannah, disappeared as a baby and has never been found."

So? Why was Mom telling her all this?

"And...he thinks you're that baby, now grown."

Maddy frowned. "What do you mean?"

"The baby's mother was his daughter. He says you look like his daughter did when she was a girl. So he's got it into his head that you must be his granddaughter."

Maddy stared. "But I'm not. I had my own grandpa."

"I know. But this man doesn't care about that. He thinks his daughter was your mother."

Maddy's stomach tightened. "Wait. So he says you're not my mom? That's stupid." Obviously her mom was her mom.

"It's ridiculous, of course. You're my daughter and always have been."

Maddy stared. Was that really in question?

"Mr. Pascow's going to be helping me prove the guy is mistaken so he'll stop harassing us."

"That's not harassing!" Maddy frowned. Her mom had been overreacting about the whole thing. "He just followed me and Emma that one time. You're making too much of it." But now she was curious about the story.

Her mom sipped from her mug and lifted her eyes to Maddy. "We don't need to argue about it. Don't worry, we'll be dealing with the situation. I just thought you should know what's going on."

But her mom hadn't explained anything. "How did

the baby disappear? Did somebody take it?"

"They don't really know what happened. Her parents were killed in a car accident, and the baby was gone when the police found them."

"Oh." She didn't know what more to ask. "Do you know the guy's name?" She'd google the story, find out more that way.

"His name is Daniel Kazan." Her mother leaned forward, her eyes focused on Maddy's. "Do you have any other questions?"

"No, I'm okay." Maddy'd see what she could find out online.

****

That night, she lay in bed thinking over what she'd found on the internet. It was a sad story, about the missing baby girl. How she'd disappeared from the car wreck and had never been found.

And now this Daniel guy claimed she was that baby? That he was her grandpa? That was crazy.

She missed her own grandpa a lot; her sadness over his death hadn't gone away. When she was younger, she'd often spent weekend afternoons with him. Sometimes Emma came too—he'd taken them skating and flying kites. But the best times were when it was just the two of them. They played checkers, and he'd been teaching her to play guitar. And she could tell him anything.

Maddy's throat swelled as tears filled her eyes. She rubbed them away with a corner of her pillowcase.

They'd talked about pets, about her wishing they had a dog. Grandpa was going to help her convince her mom to get one, but that wouldn't happen now.

Her bedroom door creaked open, and a minute later

a weight landed on her bed. *Oscar.* She pulled him up next to her and stroked his fur, his purring and familiar warmth comforting her. "Even if we got a dog, I'd still love you," she whispered. He pushed his nose against her face.

Her thoughts returned to that guy. He was stupid to think he was her grandpa. But her mind swirled with the story, the baby gone missing. She shivered.

And he thought she was that baby. Crazy idea. But kind of interesting, even so. Her skin prickled, and her heart beat fast.

She was important to him, somehow. She was suddenly curious, wanting to know more about him.

Maybe she and Emma could try to find him and follow him. The idea gave her a little thrill. It'd be tricky to do, since nobody was letting them roam on their own anymore. The only time their parents left them unsupervised was when they were in school. But maybe they could get away during school hours. Nobody would notice if they did something at lunchtime.

Chapter Ten

As Daniel worked at emptying Aunt Ruby's basement, he kept remembering the moment of finding the girl. Replaying the sights of her—swinging down the street, laughing with her friend, stepping into the schoolyard. Swishing through crisp leaves in the park.

Everything about her was so much like Kelly at that age. And that had been a great age, when he and Kelly still got along. Before their fights and disagreements began...and before she died.

The painful memories resurfaced, fresh as if they happened yesterday. Constable MacCormick—Mac, as they later came to call him—stamping snow off his boots at their farmhouse door, turning from him to Patricia. "I'm sorry to have to tell you this." Daniel had watched Patricia backing away, her hands raised as if to forestall the bad news that must be coming. The officer's mouth twisted, and he took a breath before continuing. "Your daughter and son-in-law were in a car accident last night. They were both killed."

Daniel couldn't take it in, but Patricia screamed, clapping her hands to her mouth, tears already pouring down her face.

Mac continued, "The evidence indicates they had a head-on collision. We think they died instantly."

Daniel was frozen. Patricia gasped, "And Hannah? Is she okay?"

Mac stared at her. "Hannah?"

Patricia's eyes widened. "Hannah! Their baby girl. She's just eighteen months—"

Mac shook his head. "There wasn't any baby at the crash scene. We saw a child's car seat in the back of the car, but it was empty."

Daniel forced himself to speak. "What do you mean, empty? Hannah was in that car seat when they left here yesterday."

Mac shook his head. "There was no baby in the car."

"What happened?" Daniel couldn't wrap his mind around it.

"We're not sure yet." Mac rubbed his hand across his mouth. "Their truck is deep in snow, off in the ditch. The snowplow operator found them this morning." He shook his head. "There's no sign of whatever they collided with, but almost certainly another vehicle. A hit and run."

Patricia wailed, "But what about Hannah?"

Mac's expression was grim. "I wish I knew the answer to that. The only thing I can think of is that someone took her."

Daniel had grabbed Patricia's arm then, breaking her fall as she collapsed.

And the next day, after viewing Kelly's and Jacob's bodies at the morgue, Patricia had said, "I don't know what's worse. Imagining Kelly and Jacob lying in that ditch dead, or wondering where Hannah is and who has her." Daniel had been expecting her to blame him for Kelly and Jacob being out in the storm, but instead what she said was, "That has to be our priority now. Finding Hannah."

Mac had taken the search for Hannah to heart, pressing his team to put in extra time, and keeping him and Patricia informed. After a year or more with no progress, he stopped coming by as often. But they made a point of staying in touch with him to keep the investigation alive.

Since Patricia's death, Daniel had pressed even harder for continuing the search. The need to find Hannah had kept him awake many a night. He'd finally had to ask his doctor for a prescription for sleeping pills so he could get any rest at all.

And now he'd found her, without Mac's help. Daniel had no doubts—this girl was their Hannah. He was sorry that Patricia had died too soon to share in this discovery, but now it was up to him to bring Hannah back. She was the only family he had left, dammit!

He needed to get closer to her. Let her know who she really was. Get her used to being his granddaughter.

Then he could bring her back to Alberta, back to the farm. The rest of the family was gone now, but the two of them could be together again.

He gazed around the now-empty basement with satisfaction. Good progress this weekend. He'd start on the upstairs bedrooms next.

****

This was Maddy's second day of watching for the man. *Daniel Kazan*, that was his name. Yesterday at lunchtime she'd gone to the park section where they'd first seen him. Today she was at the opposite end of the park, on the other side of Bank Street.

Sure, the chance of him being here was slim, but it was worth a try. He'd need to walk his dog, and a park was a logical place for that. And if he lived nearby, th·

might be his closest park.

That could be why he had been there in the first place.

She was on her own. Emma had refused to come with her, pointing out that they needed permission slips to leave school. Maddy waved that excuse away; she was sure they could slip off without anyone noticing. As it turned out, it wasn't that hard, but Emma refused again today. She didn't see any point in looking for Daniel.

Maddy went down the steps into the park, scanning the grassy field ahead of her. She froze. Up ahead there was a man with a dog. Could she have already found him?

Her heart beat fast as she slipped behind a nearby tree. It wasn't wide enough to hide her, but at least she was less obvious than standing on the path.

She peered out at them. Across the park, the man threw a ball. The dog ran to catch it and returned, dropping it at his feet. They repeated this several times, taking turns throwing and retrieving the ball. She could tell they were having a good time.

And it was definitely the same guy. She recognized the dog.

A man playing with his dog. All at once this made him seem like a real person, somebody with a life, with habits and things he liked to do.

Now they were moving away, the dog trotting beside the man, the two of them heading toward the other end of the park. Maddy sighed, disappointed. She wasn't ready to let him go—she wanted to stretch this out, whatever "this" was.

She decided to follow.

The man and dog were leaving the park at the far end. A few minutes later, when she reached that exit, they were still in sight, turning at the next corner.

She stopped, not wanting him to notice her. Carefully leaning forward to peer around a bush, she watched him walk up the steps of a yellow house, his dog at his heels. He pulled a key from his pocket and reached for the front door.

That must be his house.

Suddenly he turned and faced in her direction. She jerked her head back. Had he seen her?

She heard the footsteps resume, coming toward her.

"Hannah?" he called. "Is that you?"

Maddy turned, running back into the park.

"Wait," the man called. "I just want to tell you something."

Nearing a park bench, Maddy's feet slowed. She *was* curious. What might he have to say?

She rested her hands on her hips, waiting for him to come closer but ready to run again at a moment's notice. Her heart was pounding, with excitement rather than fear.

He pulled up a dozen feet away, the dog at his heels. He didn't look terrifying—just an old guy, short white hair, bushy eyebrows, deep lines on his cheeks.

"Don't be scared," he said. "I just want to say hello."

It'd be rude not to answer. "Hello."

"I don't know what anybody's told you—" He stopped, watching her.

Maddy waited.

He started again. "You may not believe it yet.

But...you need to know, you're my granddaughter."

Maddy stared at him, shaking her head. "That's impossible."

"No, it's not. You've been missing for years, and now I've found you."

Maddy shivered. This was what Mom said he believed, but it was too weird. She didn't want to listen to any more. She took two steps backward, keeping her eyes on him. "I have to get back to school now," she said, then whirled and ran.

Heart pumping, feet flying, she raced back to Bank Street and turned toward the school. At the traffic light she caught her breath, bracing her hands on her knees.

Was he still behind her? She wasn't sure if she was scared or fascinated. Now she had another problem—getting back into school without getting in trouble.

****

That afternoon, Emma turned to Maddy as they waited outside the school for Emma's mom to pick them up. "I can't wait for Halloween, can you?"

Maddy gave her a high-five and did a little dance. "I know--I can't believe it's next week!" She and Emma even had costumes that went together. Emma was going to be a ladylike spaniel, and Maddy's mom had located a furry brown "mutt" costume for her, complete with pointed dog ears on a hairband. They'd be a pair.

Emma frowned. "But I hope this thing with that Daniel guy isn't going to spoil it."

Maddy stopped dancing. "Why would it?"

Emma stared at her. "Do you think our parents will still let us go out on our own, like we planned?"

Maddy blinked. "Oh my God. They have to."

This year, she and Emma had special Halloween plans—they'd been talking about it for weeks. Together with friends from school, they were going trick-or-treating as a group. This was likely their last dressing-up year, and they wanted to make the most of it.

They'd gotten their families to agree. They could go on their own, without parents.

It would already be dark. They'd roam up and down streets, moving fast, loading their bags with candy. And maybe play a few tricks. Some of them had heard of Halloween pranks played by their older siblings or, sometimes, their dads. Evan's dad once threw a live chicken into his teacher's house when he was a boy—"but don't you try anything like that," he'd warned. No worries there—how would they get a live chicken, anyway?

Now Emma was shaking her head. "If our parents won't even let us walk to school on our own, do you really think they'll still let us go out at night?"

Maddy shivered. "But there'll be a whole bunch of us! We'll be fine!"

"I don't think my parents will see it that way."

"Oh my God." Maddy's face flushed with anger. "My mom either. She's so overprotective—"

Emma frowned at her. "Well, it's their job to keep us safe."

Maddy groaned. "Maybe, but my mom won't let me do anything anymore since that guy showed up. It's not fair!"

"Well, we'd better find out about it, anyway. Whether they'll let us or not." Emma hitched her backpack higher on her shoulder as her mom's car pulled up.

Maddy had a bitter taste in her mouth. She had a sinking feeling that Emma might be right, that Halloween would be wrecked.

Chapter Eleven

Tom and I sat side by side at a polished mahogany table in his law firm's boardroom, facing the door. Heavy drapes framed the tall windows behind us, while outside a cold rain lashed against the panes. Sconces glowed softly above the portraits of elderly white-haired men that lined the paneled walls. Lamps suspended from the high ceiling cast pools of light down the long center table.

My stomach was churning. Tom said meeting in this room would lend gravitas to our position, that this formal setting would project power and authority. I hoped it'd work. If we could get this guy to concede that he was mistaken about Maddy, that might end this nightmare.

Tom straightened the pile of file folders he'd placed beside him. I was curious—the papers and photos I'd given him wouldn't have been enough to fill them. He must have added extra material as window dressing.

The door opened, and a man entered. Tom rose. "Mr. Kazan?" he asked, extending his hand across the table.

I held my face still, trying not to show any expression. I didn't want to appear concerned, but my breathing quickened as I got my first close-up look at the guy who'd been causing all this trouble.

To control my anxiety, I made a point of noting details. He was taller than Tom, about five-ten or eleven. I guessed he was past middle age, but I wouldn't call him elderly. He strode vigorously into the room and seemed energetic, not at all frail. He was wearing jeans, a tan bomber jacket, and a black shirt buttoned to the throat. My eyes shifted to his face. With high cheekbones, a weathered complexion, and neatly barbered white hair, at first glance he reminded me of my dad. But I shook off that illusion. This man had a fiery expression in his eye—quite unlike my dad's reserved demeanor—and an air of confidence that took me aback.

He took Tom's hand. "Call me Daniel."

"I'm Tom Pascow." He turned. "And this is Dr. Koss."

I smiled inwardly. My official title was part of the formality Tom was projecting.

Kazan tilted his head in my direction. I smiled coolly but didn't reach out my hand. *No way.* I wasn't playing nice with this guy.

Tom gestured to a chair across the table from us. "Please take a seat. Would you like coffee? Water?" He pointed to a tray in the middle of the table.

Kazan shook his head. "Nothing for me, thanks." He slipped out of his jacket, hanging it on the back of his chair, and sat, placing his hands on the table in front of him.

Tom leaned forward. "I'd like to start by stating what this meeting is about," he said. "We want to understand what your position is, Mr. Kazan. And we want to make our position very clear."

Kazan lifted one hand from the table, then let it

fall. "Okay."

Tom coughed. "The police told Dr. Koss that you have certain beliefs about her daughter."

I watched Kazan.

He nodded and spoke firmly, with no apparent hesitation. "When I first saw the girl, I recognized her right away. That's Kelly, I thought. Kelly's my daughter. But then I realized she couldn't be Kelly. Kelly's been dead for eleven years, and she was twenty-four when she died."

Tom moved his hand, interjecting. "We're sorry to hear about your loss. Losing a child must be devastating."

I shot him a glance. I could pity the guy too, but let's not overdo the sympathy. That's not why we were here.

Kazan—*Daniel*, as he wanted to be called—continued without acknowledging Tom's comment. "At first I thought I must be imagining things, but she's like a carbon copy. And who could look just like Kelly? Her daughter, that's who. Her baby daughter, Hannah, who's been missing for those same eleven years."

He cleared his throat. "So I phoned Mac, the RCMP investigator. He's been searching for Hannah since she disappeared. I told him I'd found her."

He glanced at me but spoke to Tom. "I don't know how my granddaughter ended up in Ottawa, at Dr. Koss's, but...well, that's where we're at."

I had to force myself not to erupt. I swiveled my eyes to Tom. *Tell him!* I didn't trust myself to speak.

"You're mistaken," said Tom. "Maddy can't be your granddaughter, because she's been Dr. Koss's daughter since birth." He patted the pile of folders beside him. "We have documents here proving that. We'll be pleased to show you all the evidence."

I swallowed; a sharp taste rose in my mouth. *Here we go.*

****

Daniel watched the woman as the lawyer spoke. So she was a doctor. That didn't make any difference to him; he already called her *Susan* in his mind, the name the neighbor had given him.

She didn't shake his hand. Couldn't she even be polite? Her clothes looked expensive but plain. A blue sweater with pearl buttons, a silky white blouse, small gold earrings. Definitely a city woman. Some wrinkles at her eyes, tight mouth. Fighting middle age, was his guess. And she had dark hair. Not blonde like Hannah.

He could see her draw in a breath. "Mr. Kazan," she began.

"Daniel," he repeated. "Let's keep it friendly." He wanted to cut through all this formal talk and get down to business.

She shook her head. "We're not friends. You've scared my daughter. You're annoying me with your ridiculous claim. Maddy is my daughter. She's always been my daughter. I have her birth certificate and her medical records. I also have photos showing that I gave birth to her in the hospital, and that she's been the same baby and toddler into childhood. And I have a list of friends and neighbors who've known her since she was born."

Daniel watched her, unmoved. "Maybe," he said. "But those could all be faked. Photos don't prove much. None of that changes what I know—your so-called daughter looks and acts exactly like my Kelly." He

63

gazed coolly at the lawyer, then back at the woman. "And she doesn't look anything like you."

The lawyer leaned forward. "You must know that resemblance isn't proof of anything. We'd like you to examine these documents. Once you've inspected them, we think you'll realize that you're mistaken." His voice deepened. "If you'll agree to stop harassing Dr. Koss and her daughter, we won't need to take further legal steps."

Daniel fought down a rising anger. They were trying to warn him off. But that wasn't going to fly. They didn't realize how sure he was, or how determined. Now that he'd found Hannah, no way would he simply leave her!

This meeting was a waste of time. Patricia's voice echoed in his mind.

She was right. He might as well take off—this wasn't going to lead anywhere. He half rose in disgust.

But maybe he should hang in a little longer—since he was here, he might as well see if there was anything more to learn from these two.

****

Giving Tom a pointed glance, I raised my eyebrows.

He leaned forward. "Mr. Kazan, I'm sure our documents will prove to you that you're mistaken. Maddy is Dr. Koss's daughter and has been since birth." He pulled the pile of folders toward him.

But I'd been watching the guy. *Daniel*, I told myself again, happy to mentally reduce him to a first name.

I could tell that our documents weren't going to make any impression on him. He didn't care about our evidence.

"Tom," I said, shaking my head. "None of these documents are going to convince Mr. Kazan. Let's move on. We need him to take a DNA test." Tom had called DNA the gold standard. I could see that all this other stuff was a distraction.

I turned to Daniel. "If you were Maddy's grandfather—which you are not—a DNA test would prove it. So I'm sure you'll be willing to provide a sample for the test."

I still didn't know what his game was, but this should call his bluff.

But he didn't seem fazed. "I'll take any test you want. What do I have to do?"

Tom shuffled his papers, wearing a disgruntled expression. "I believe all that's required is a scraping from the inside of your cheek."

"Fine. Let me know when and where." Daniel reached for a piece of paper and wrote a note, handing it across to Tom. "Here's my phone number so you can reach me."

Tom nodded to me. "You're right, Susan. A DNA test will prove whether Mr. Kazan is related to Maddy...or not." He turned to Daniel and scowled. "But let's get one thing straight. You are not to be following Maddy, or visiting their neighborhood or school, or interfering with the family in any way."

Daniel watched Tom coolly and shrugged. "Okay."

To me, that looked like perfunctory assent, not a commitment. I leaned forward, gazing directly into his face. "The police will be monitoring to make sure you stay away from her."

He stared back at me, unsmiling. "No need to raise

your voice. I get the point."

The meeting didn't last long after that. After Daniel left, I let out a deep breath and turned to Tom. "What did you think?"

Tom reached for a bottle of water. "Well, I guess we learned that he's a tough nut. Interesting that he agreed to a DNA test, though."

"I hope you didn't mind my leaping in to propose that," I said. "It just seemed the logical next step."

He smiled. "No, I think you were right. I was going to show him all your documentation, but he'd already said he didn't believe in it. At least we know that a DNA test will eliminate him." He shuffled the pile of folders. "Do you want to see if your police contact can arrange a test?"

I leaned back in my chair. As Abel said, I didn't have to rely solely on the police in dealing with Kazan. "Maybe not. I know there are private labs in the city. It might be quicker to deal with one of them."

****

Friday afternoon at the clinic was hectic, so I didn't get a chance to research DNA labs until the end of the day. Abel poked his head in my office as I was staring at a screen filled with Google results. I explained what I was doing. "And now it's Friday evening, so I won't be able to reach anyone until Monday."

"Oh," he said. "I can help you with that. I know someone who works at a DNA testing lab downtown. I have her cell number, so you can phone her now if you wish." Her name was Aisha Kouri; he'd met her at a friend's party, and she had made an impression. "She seemed intelligent," he said. "I liked her, and she kept me interested in DNA for close to half an hour."

She answered on the second ring. I introduced myself, mentioning the connection through Abel and explaining why I was calling.

"Of course I remember Abel," she said. "Yes, our lab does that kind of testing." She had a faint accent, one I couldn't place.

"Can you tell me a bit about how we'd proceed? We want to compare DNA between a child and a man who claims to be her maternal grandfather."

"You want to test the grandfather, not the father?" She sounded dubious.

"Yes. I'll tell you the circumstances. The child is my daughter. And the man is a stranger who's shown up out of the blue, claiming she's his granddaughter, his daughter's daughter. Clearly he's wrong, and I want to get this test underway so we can prove it."

Aisha didn't comment on the circumstances.

"Well," she said. "We do test for grandparent connections, but it's more usual to test a parent of the father, not of the mother. Testing for a male relative on the mother's side is trickier."

"Will it be a problem?"

"Not necessarily, but we won't know for sure until we examine the samples. Will you want your own DNA compared as well?"

Of course—why didn't I think of that? "That's a great idea. To compare hers and mine and prove she's my daughter. Yes, we'll do that." This sounded like exactly what we needed. "Can we get all three of us tested at the same time?"

"Certainly." She said that once we'd submitted the samples, the results would likely be ready in three to five business days.

Chapter Twelve

At dinner, I explained the test process to Maddy, and that we'd try to get it done early in the week. I had braced myself for an argument, but that wasn't where her mind went at all.

"Oh, I know about DNA," she said.

I was a bit surprised to discover she'd heard the term. "Did they teach you about it at school?" I hadn't realized DNA was on the curriculum at her grade level.

"No, but on TV they test DNA to see if someone's a criminal, or if their blood is on a body or something."

I laughed, though it wasn't actually funny. "We're not testing for anything like that. We're having this done to prove that Daniel Kazan isn't your grandfather, and that I'm your mother."

She turned back to her dinner, pushing carrot sticks around on her plate. I couldn't tell what she was thinking.

****

Maddy felt a warm glow, surprised; her mom was treating her with some respect today. Explaining about the DNA test and everything, almost like she was talking to Jenny or another adult.

Maybe this was a good time to raise the next topic…

"Mom," she began. "Can we talk about Halloween?"

Her mom, who had pushed back her chair and started clearing dishes from the table, gave her a sharp glance. "What about it?"

Maddy took a breath, willing her voice to stay level and calm. "It's still okay for Emma and me to go trick-or-treating with our friends, right?"

Her mom put their plates in the sink and leaned against the counter. "Maddy, you know that makes no sense now."

"What do you mean?" Maddy's stomach churned.

"That plan's not safe anymore. Out in the dark, without adults."

Maddy groaned. "I'll be perfectly safe—there'll be twelve other kids!"

"No, Maddy. I know I agreed to this earlier—"

"Yes, you did! You can't go back on your word!" Maddy could hear her voice turning shrill, but she couldn't help it. "You promised!"

Her mom crossed her arms. "That was before Daniel Kazan showed up. We just can't risk it now. He could well take the opportunity—" She stopped.

Maddy's forehead felt tight. "To what? Just what do you think he's going to do?"

Her mom's eyes bored into hers. "Well, for instance, he could follow your group in the dark and grab you when he saw a chance."

"He's not going to do that!"

"How do you know?"

Maddy couldn't tell her mom she'd seen Daniel in the park, that she'd talked to him. If he was going to grab her, he could have done it then. "I just don't think he's that dangerous," she muttered.

"Nicole and I have talked about it. We think it's

69

best if we all go together. You and I will go with Emma's family, including Andrew."

"Andrew! He's a little kid!"

"Yes, and you could be very helpful with him. Help him have a nice time trick-or-treating."

Maddy was aghast. This was going to ruin everything. "Come on, Mom. Even last year Andrew didn't come with us." Last year Mr. Obata had taken Andrew out alone right after supper, and Emma's mom had walked later with the two girls, staying well behind so they hardly even noticed her there.

"I know it's disappointing, but we all need to stay together this year." This was Mom's *I've made up my mind* voice.

Maddy's face flushed, helpless rage flooding through her. It was always like this. Once Mom laid down the law, there was no reasoning with her.

She whirled and left the kitchen, stomping loudly on the stairs as she ran to her room and slammed the door. She flopped onto her bed and buried her head in a pillow. She felt like screaming, but there was no point. Nothing was going to change her mom's mind.

Catching her breath, she turned to her closet and eyed her dog costume. The one her mom had picked out. The one Mom thought was so cute.

Leaping forward, Maddy pulled out a box from the back of the closet. It was full of things that were supposed to go to Goodwill. Digging to the bottom, she pulled out the costume she'd worn last year at Halloween.

The vampire's black cape and blood-red mask were a lot better match for how she felt at the moment.

Chapter Thirteen

Monday morning, I came out of the play therapy room with five-year-old Adrienne and handed her over to her mother. This was Adrienne's sixth session with me, and it had gone well. I was happy with the progress we were making.

As I returned to my office, Dorothy strode toward me down the hall. Director of our clinic since it was founded, she was an imposing woman, stocky but not fat, slightly taller than my five-feet-six, with excellent posture and a sharp gaze. She was wearing a two-piece blue wool dress and black pumps, her glasses hanging on a cord around her neck and several file folders under one arm.

I smiled and moved aside to allow room for her to pass, but she stopped me and rested a hand my arm. "Susan, how are you doing? Have the police resolved your situation?"

My cheeks flushed. I couldn't tell if she was being sympathetic or critical. "Well, they're working on it," I said, hoping this would satisfy her.

Her eyes were fixed on my face, a concerned expression on her face. "I've been worrying about you. This must be causing you a lot of anxiety."

I blinked. She'd been worrying about me?

"That's kind of you," I said, not sure how to respond. I'd seen her be empathetic toward the children and families who were our clients, and even toward other staff members, but she'd always seemed a bit cool with me. When I first told her about Daniel, she hadn't shown much reaction. I'd wondered if she thought my telling her about it was an imposition, intruding a personal issue into our professional roles.

That wasn't the feeling she was giving me now, though. She leaned forward, her hand tightening on my arm. "You'll tell me if there's anything you need," she said, her voice warm. "If I can help in any way, just let me know."

With a final squeeze to my arm, she hitched up the file folders she was carrying and continued down the hall, my stunned glance following her.

****

Daniel walked in the front door of the lab Tuesday morning, closing it behind him. He gazed around the waiting room, expecting to see Hannah and that woman. *Susan.* Weren't they all providing samples together?

He'd been looking forward to seeing Hannah again. Their short encounter in the park had ended before he'd had a chance to say much—she had run away too quickly. He wanted a chance to make a better impression on her. He'd practiced in the mirror that morning, making a friendly smile. It took effort—he was a bit rusty at smiling these days.

But he was the only person in the room, other than a young redheaded woman with frizzy hair and no makeup working behind a counter. She lifted her eyes from her computer as he approached.

Leaning one elbow on the counter, he announced his name. His voice came out louder than he intended, but she didn't seem bothered.

"Mr. Kazan?" She turned to a sheet of paper beside her and ran her finger down a typed column of names. "Yes, you're scheduled. Do you have your photo ID with you?"

She took his driver's license and stood, going through a door he hadn't noticed. He heard the whirring sound of a photocopier. She returned and handed him his license, clipping the copy to another paper, and picked up her phone. "I'll call the technician."

"Wait. What about the girl being tested with me?"

She glanced at him and back at her typed list. "What name?"

Drat, he knew the name, but for a minute he couldn't remember it. Then he had it. "Koss."

She ran her finger down the column again. "Yes, they're coming later this afternoon." She spoke into her phone, then returned to her computer.

Deep disappointment washed through Daniel. He wouldn't be seeing Hannah today.

But that wasn't the main reason he'd agreed to this test. If it proved he was Hannah's grandfather, that'd be worth it. There'd probably be some paperwork, but once he had proof—

That's what we want, whispered Patricia's voice in his head. *Proof she's ours. So we can get her back where she belongs.*

A thin young woman in a lab coat picked up the papers from the woman at the desk. "Mr. Kazan? Come with me, please."

Giving the sample was simple, just a quick swab of his cheek. The technician signed the photocopy of his driver's license as well as the vial holding the swab.

"Hold on," he said. "Can you tell me how this DNA stuff works?"

She sighed and rolled her eyes. "This brochure explains everything." She handed him a stapled booklet along with a separate piece of paper. "Your results will be available in three to five days. You can access the report online."

With that, she led him back to the waiting room. It was all over so fast. Daniel blinked. Was that all? He flipped through the brochure; he'd have to study it. Maybe then he'd understand more.

He folded the brochure and the paper with the password and put them in the inner pocket of his jacket.

But don't count on that. Science isn't everything. They might make a mistake.

Patricia's doubting voice could be annoying.

She had another piece of advice. This one he agreed with. *Go see the girl. Talk to her again. Let her see who you are.*

Chapter Fourteen

"You're letting Daniel spoil everything!" Maddy yelled, shoving the half-empty milk carton back into the fridge and slamming the door. She was supposed to be clearing the table, but she didn't feel like it.

Halloween was finally here, and Maddy was trying one more time.

This was the same argument they'd had last week. Her mom wasn't giving an inch. She still insisted that they'd all go trick-or-treating together, including Andrew. They'd had supper early today so they could finish before his bedtime.

Maddy knew she had to stop yelling, though it was hard. She took a breath and lowered her voice.

"We'll be really careful. We'll stay close to the group, I promise!" She carried the dinner plates and glasses over to the dishwasher, leaning over to cram them in.

Her mom squeezed out a sponge and began wiping the counter. "I'm not going to argue about this again. You and Emma will be sticking with us, and that's the end of it."

Maddy's composure vanished. "It's just not fair," she shouted.

Her mother didn't reply.

Maddy stormed up the stairs and into her room, pulling out her phone to text Emma.

—No—
—No what?—
—We have to go with them—
—I knew that—
—Its not fair—
—Its fine—
—No its not—

Trick-or-treating with their parents, like little kids! Maddy had to swallow hard and blink to keep the tears back.

—I dont even want to go—
—Sure you do its halloween—
—Its ruined—

Maddy flung herself on her bed and slammed down her phone. She pulled her pillowcase over to wipe her face.

Half an hour later Emma knocked at her door. "Can I come in?"

Maddy sighed. "Sure."

Maddy was at her desk, pencil in hand. She usually liked drawing, though today her mind wasn't on it. She'd been working on a sketch of Oscar; there was something about the shape of his ears that she couldn't quite get right.

She kept working on the drawing, resolutely not looking at Emma.

Emma sat on the bed and stared at Maddy. "Your face is red."

"Big whoop." Maddy rolled her eyes.

"Come on." Emma patted her shoulder. "Put on your costume."

Maddy threw down her pencil. "We were supposed to meet up with everybody and hit a ton of houses."

Emma was decked out in her spaniel costume, the long floppy ears hanging down, a black nose and whiskers painted on her face. She nodded. "Yeah, but it's not the end of the world if it doesn't happen."

Maddy glared at her. "No, but it's not fair either. And my mom thinks if that guy Daniel shows up again, *that's* the end of the world."

"Well, they're worried about us. Especially about you."

"I know, but I don't like it. My mom won't let me do anything anymore."

Emma took a breath. "I don't know why you're so mad at your mom all the time."

Maddy flounced out of her chair and stomped to the window. "She always wants to be the boss. Like I can't decide anything for myself."

"Well, be real. They're our parents, and we're still kids."

"I can't wait to be older!" Maddy choked back a sob.

Emma leaned forward and stared at her. "Do you really want to spend Halloween in your room?"

Maddy sighed. "No."

"So come on. Get your costume on. We'll make sure Andrew gets to a lot of houses. It'll still be fun."

Maddy lifted her shoulders. "All right." She wiped her eyes and went to the window, pulling the curtain aside. It was already almost dark outside, with streetlights glowing and shadows gathering. Despite everything, she felt herself being drawn into the magic of the evening.

She dragged out her dog costume, the companion to Emma's—then threw it back in the closet.

Emma stared at her.

With her chin set firmly, Maddy grabbed the vampire outfit she'd dropped on the floor earlier and pulled it on.

Chapter Fifteen

Two mornings later, a horn tooted out in the street. "Nicole's here!" I called.

Maddy's answer wafted down the stairs. "Be there in a minute."

Halloween had been okay after all. Daniel didn't show up, and Maddy and Emma had seemed reconciled to making sure Andrew got lots of candy.

I frowned, annoyed that Maddy wasn't ready yet. She'd insisted on joining the volleyball team, but that meant early practice every Tuesday and Thursday before school. *Shouldn't keep them waiting.* I grabbed a jacket off the rack in the hallway and trotted out to the car. There'd been a frost overnight, leaving a thin white coating on the grass.

Waving to Emma in the shotgun seat, I went around to the driver's side. Nicole rolled down her window, and I leaned toward her. "Maddy'll be here in a second." She nodded. "I feel bad," I added. "You've been doing more than your share of driving them."

She smiled. "I don't mind—I can fit it into my day. And I know you have a lot going on."

Maddy came running down the steps, coat and backpack flying, and hopped into the back seat. Nicole put the car in gear and sped away.

Back in the kitchen, I fed Oscar and stashed the breakfast dishes in the dishwasher. With Maddy gone, I could leave for work early too. Maybe I'd be able to finish a couple of reports I had fallen behind on.

As I was putting on my coat, the doorbell rang. I looked out the window.

What the hell?

Daniel Kazan stood on my doorstep.

I went cold. *How dare he?* I flung open the door. "What are you doing here?" I exploded.

Confronting him, I saw that he was a few inches taller than me and exuded a tense energy that raised my hackles. He raised his hands, palms out, a placating expression on his face. As if he were trying to calm me down or reassure me.

"I just want to talk to Hannah. I came early to catch her, before she leaves for school."

I squared my shoulders. "Get out of here! You've been told to stay away from us!"

His face was in shadow. "I think it's fair to want to see Hannah. I've waited a long time."

The guy is nuts. "She's not Hannah—she's my daughter. Maddy."

"You're keeping her from me." He was leaning toward me, and I had to keep from falling back. I couldn't let myself seem weak. If he thought he'd intimidated me, what would be his next move?

My heart pounded. My hands were curled tight, my nails biting into my palms. "Damn right I'm keeping her from you. Now get off my porch before I call the police!"

What if he wouldn't leave? I should call for help—but my phone was inside, and I didn't want to leave him on the porch unattended. My breathing was fast and shallow. I debated whether I could slip inside and lock the door, but I was afraid he'd push past me into the house. I forced myself to stare directly at him.

He stood there, glaring at me, his face reddening. In my peripheral vision I saw his hands clenching and unclenching. Despite the chill in the air, my whole body flushed hot. I fought my fight-or-flight instinct, determined to stand my ground.

After a long minute, he stepped back, turned, and left the porch.

As soon as he was off the step, I spun into the house and slammed the door, swallowing tears of relief. I watched him stride down the sidewalk and disappear into the park.

Shaking, I pulled my coat around me. Time to call the police.

I tried to phone Marie, but she wasn't available. Impatient, I went to my desk to dig out Russo's card.

He answered right away. Throwing my coat across a chair, I filled him in. My chances of getting to work early were vanishing.

"Did he threaten you or Maddy?" he asked.

I poured myself a glass of water at the sink. "Luckily, she'd already left. But yeah, just having him looming over me on our porch felt threatening. And he wasn't making sense. He insisted he wanted to see 'Hannah' as he calls her, and said he'd 'waited long enough.' "

"That's crazy. Mac called him to tell him he was wrong about Maddy. Mac thinks Kazan is actually an okay guy; he just wants him to stay out of trouble." So Russo had called his RCMP friend Mac. That was reassuring.

I sank onto one of the kitchen chairs. "He doesn't

seem to have absorbed that message. Even though he told my lawyer and me that he'd stay away—"

"Oh? I didn't know you'd had a meeting."

I realized I hadn't shared that step. "Yeah, we met with him to try to convince him that he's wrong about Maddy."

Russo made a sound that could have been a cough. "And how did that work out?"

I could feel a tightening behind my eyes. "Not the way we'd hoped. He didn't care at all about my having her birth certificate or medical records, any of that. He didn't even look at it."

Silence. "Did he really agree to stay away?"

Hah. "Yeah, but he obviously didn't mean it. Since he showed up here today. But we did get him to take a DNA test—that should prove he's not related to Maddy."

He was silent for a moment. "I'll stop by his house, tell him again to keep his distance. And a DNA test is a good idea. That should settle the matter."

By now I was pacing; a pounding had started at my temples. Reaching for my glass of water, I gulped down most of what was left in it. "You said your friend wanted to keep Daniel out of trouble. He'll be in trouble for sure if he keeps this up."

"I'll make sure to get that across."

****

Daniel strode along the sidewalk, his head down, gritting his teeth. He'd had to get away from there—if he had stayed, he would have punched that woman right in the mouth.

She'd deserve it. Daniel sucked in a breath. Patricia was never mean like this when she was alive, but lately her comments had been getting downright vicious.

All his life he'd been prone to sound off about things, to act first and think later. But that had often gotten him into trouble. He was trying to be more careful now.

This time he'd walked away instead of giving in to his impulse. *Instead of giving that woman a good pasting the way she deserved.*

But despite his good intentions, his gut agreed with Patricia. He wished he had barged into the house. That woman—Susan—said the girl wasn't there, but he was sure she was lying.

He'd tried to be reasonable, to ask politely. All he wanted was a chance to meet the girl, to talk to her. That wasn't too much to ask. But Susan just turned him down. Shook him off like dirt on her shoe.

He was a reasonable man. Of course the girl thought of herself as "Maddy" and thought Susan was her mother. She'd been raised to think that. He just wanted a chance to explain the real situation to her.

But that's what Susan wouldn't allow.

He had to find a way around her. A way to get to the girl, get her away from Susan's influence. He needed a plan. Or a miracle.

Hannah needed to be with her real family.

Chapter Sixteen

Jenny hopped out of her little silver SUV in front of our house. "Are the girls ready?" It was a sunny Saturday afternoon, and she had volunteered to take Maddy and Emma to a movie.

I leaned my rake against the porch railing. Clearing up leaves is not my favorite chore, and Jenny's interruption was welcome. "They're in Maddy's room." I stepped forward. "Listen, do you have a few minutes?"

She nodded. "Sure. We don't have to leave yet."

I sat on the step facing the street, gesturing to her to join me there. "Thanks for taking the girls to a show. They always love going places with you—it's not like going with a parent." Jenny called herself Maddy's honorary godmother, but she was more like a big sister. "What movie are you taking them to?" Normally I'd have checked reviews, but I figured I could trust Jenny to choose something appropriate.

She sat down beside me. "It's a few years old. *Wonderstruck.* I thought they'd enjoy it—I saw it when it came out, and it has a couple of kids Maddy's age in it."

"I'm sure they'll love it." I stretched my legs out in front of me, relishing the afternoon sun. "Guess what happened here yesterday morning." She turned to me, eyebrows raised. "Daniel Kazan showed up and wanted to see Maddy. Or Hannah, as he calls her."

Jenny clapped her hand over her mouth, her eyes wide. "Oh my God. What did you do?"

"I was terrified, but I stood my ground. I told him to leave, and he did. I called Bob Russo right after—you know, the cop." I filled her in on his intervention. "It's so frustrating that the police don't seem able to do much, other than tell him to stay away. I think he's really unpredictable, and I'm scared of what he might do." I brushed my hand across my mouth. "When he showed up here, he actually acted kind of crazy. Like he thought he had a right to see her."

Jenny leaned forward and put a hand on my knee. "I totally get it. It's nerve-wracking. You must feel vulnerable."

Tears pricked the backs of my eyes. "Especially for Maddy. She's the one who's exposed."

"What can I do?"

"You're already doing it. But I guess just keep a sharp eye out this afternoon. Make sure the girls stay with you."

"Of course."

"Maddy doesn't seem to be taking this seriously. I tried to tell her to stick with you, and she yelled at me that they're not babies."

Jenny made a wry face. "Maybe she has a point."

"What do you mean?"

"She's almost a teenager—not a kid anymore."

"I know, I get it." I swallowed. "I mean, I understand that. But...she *is* still my baby. And please—with Daniel out there somewhere, we have to stay vigilant. I don't want Maddy wandering off in the theater, going to the washroom by herself or whatever."

Jenny shushed me. "Okay. I know you want to be extra careful right now. I'll keep her close."

Abashed, I touched her shoulder. "I'm sorry. You've been my rock. I know you'll take good care of her."

"I will." She stood up and struck a dramatic pose, one arm in the air. "Now I should take my young ladies off for their afternoon at the cinema." With a smile, she added, "And I'll stay watchful, I promise."

Chapter Seventeen

On Sunday morning I had no trouble finding street parking. I grabbed my purse and headed toward Genetic Test Services, the lab where we'd submitted our DNA samples. Though the sky overhead was blue and the sun was shining, the weather had shifted. A chill breeze had sprung up—a sudden change from yesterday's warmth—and the smell of snow was in the air.

When Aisha phoned the night before, I thought she was calling to give me the DNA results, but she said no, they were still completing the tests. She said she had a few questions, though, that she'd like to discuss face-to-face, and asked if I could meet with her today.

I wondered why she wanted a face-to-face meeting—I'd thought they said the results would be made available online. And I didn't know why she'd want to see me on a Sunday. But if she needed anything from me to speed up the process, I was eager to provide it.

The low-rise office building was locked, but she had told me to knock on the door and she'd let me in. This would be my first time meeting her in person; she hadn't been there when we came to submit our samples. She turned out to be a smallish, slim woman with dark hair pulled back in a ponytail, wearing a pair of loose cream-colored pants and a blue top.

She unlocked the door to let me in, locking it again

once I was inside. She smiled politely and held out her hand in greeting. "Susan, I'm Aisha. Thank you for coming in this morning." She had a soft voice but a confident manner.

We were in the building's lobby, passing an empty security desk in front of a bank of elevators. "If you don't mind, we'll take the stairs," she said. "It's just one floor up." The stairway was utilitarian—unadorned cement—but the corridor upstairs was carpeted, and the walls were a quiet gray. She led me down a hall to a small meeting room furnished with a round table, four plastic chairs, and a whiteboard. The window overlooked a parking lot.

We each took a chair. Aisha didn't offer me any refreshment, though I would have welcomed something; I should have picked up a coffee on my way. She had no papers or files with her, which surprised me. After a moment's silence, I decided to get things rolling. "You said you don't have the results yet—so why did you want to see me?"

She appeared to hesitate. "You're Abel's friend, so I thought I should talk to you about this in person."

I raised my eyebrows, and she continued. "We haven't fully finished the analysis, but we do have a conclusion about the comparison between you and Madison."

I brightened. "Great!" This would resolve the whole dispute with Daniel right now.

Aisha frowned. "I should review a few basics first, about how DNA testing works."

I waited. *Okay.*

She sat back. "We inherit our DNA from our parents—half from our mother and half from our father.

88

We can't predict exactly which genes will be passed down to a child from each parent. And the combination from a given pair of parents is different for each of their offspring."

I nodded. *Nothing new here.*

She continued. "As humans, all of us share nearly identical DNA. But there are specific genetic markers where individual differences appear. Those are what we examine in relationship testing."

I smiled. "Yes, I get that."

Aisha carried on. "What we look for at those markers are correspondences between two individuals. There should be high correspondences between a parent and a child."

"Right."

"Well." I could see her drawing in her breath, and she stared directly at me. "When we compare your DNA with Madison's, we...don't see the level of correspondence we'd expect between mother and daughter. In fact...the test excludes that possibility."

I thought I must have misheard. I shook my head as if to empty my ears.

"What did you say?" My chest and shoulders suddenly clenched tight.

Aisha cleared her throat. "The test shows that...you can't be Madison's biological mother."

I stared at her blankly, blood pounding at my temples. "That makes no sense. I *am* her mother."

She simply stared at me, her hands clasped in front of her.

"That test is wrong," I insisted.

She shook her head. "We've double-checked the result."

My disbelief suddenly turned to indignation. I jumped from my chair, knocking it over behind me, and leaned over the table. "That's not possible! You must have mixed up the samples—"

"No." Aisha stared at me, shaking her head. "We took care to record each person's identity when we collected the samples, and we have followed chain-of-custody protocols throughout. We have not mixed up the samples. The test is accurate."

I swallowed, my mouth dry and my heart pounding. My back to the window, I glared at her. Finally I drew in a deep breath and returned to my chair. I had to make clear to her—this was unquestionably a mistake.

"Listen," I said, doing my best to speak calmly, "there is no possibility that that result is accurate. I gave birth to Maddy, right here at the Civic Hospital. I have all the records to prove it."

She said nothing, her expression unchanged.

I glowered. "There's simply no question. She's my child and always has been!"

Aisha leaned forward. "Susan. All I can say is your DNA and Madison's do not show that you are her mother. You do share some correspondences, but not enough to show parentage."

With great effort, I kept myself from shrieking. I was shattered. This was completely impossible. "So what does the test show about Daniel? Please tell me it at least proves *him* wrong?"

Aisha shook her head. "We haven't made that determination yet."

"What?" I was aghast.

"It's harder to draw conclusions when we only

have DNA from one grandparent. When we are trying to determine correspondences with a child two generations down, testing is more difficult. It can be inconclusive."

I gritted my teeth. "I can't believe this. You're telling me that this testing could end up concluding that Daniel Kazan is Maddy's grandfather?"

"We haven't yet ruled that out."

I glared at her. "So what happens now?"

"Nothing at the moment. We'll complete our report in a couple of days. Then we'll send you and Mr. Kazan a notice to access your reports online. How the two of you proceed with the results will be up to you."

"So he'll get the report as well?"

"Yes, you specified that on the order, that the results would be reported to each adult participant."

Back out on the street, the sun was still shining, but to me the day had closed in. I stumbled toward the spot where I'd parked my car but stopped before I reached it. I couldn't possibly drive—I was too distraught.

I continued down the sidewalk, passing a small coffee shop. Turning abruptly, I pushed open the door. A young couple was sitting at a far table, but no one was ahead of me at the counter, so I ordered a latte. I had to fumble for my wallet. I found an empty table in a corner by a window and sat down, wrapping my hands around the cup.

What could this mean?

A mood of despair fell over me. Daniel threatened to disrupt our lives—the life that Maddy and I had together—but I'd been sure that the DNA test would destroy his ridiculous claim.

Instead, it was about to make things worse.

If Daniel saw a test result that said I wasn't Maddy's mother, there was no way he would stay away from us. He'd be sure to proclaim the test result. He'd tell Maddy I wasn't her mother. I had to prepare her.

Though heaven knew what I'd tell her, or how I could explain it.

****

Maddy watched her mom in the driver's seat beside her as they pulled onto their street. They had taken Emma with them to the museum for the afternoon and had now dropped her off. She and Emma thought they lived close together, since their houses were just across the park from each other and they could run it in two minutes. But the driving route was farther, around several blocks.

When they got to their house, her mom stopped the car but didn't get out. "Let's sit here and talk for a minute," she said. Maddy glanced at her, wondering what was going on. Her mom had seemed distracted all afternoon, and now she looked tense, staring out the window. "I was downtown this morning and got a preview of the results of our DNA test."

Maddy hadn't thought much about the test since they gave the samples. Her mom had wanted the test and said it would solve their problems with Daniel.

Her mom fiddled with her key chain. "Well, there's a part of the test that's quite upsetting. I don't understand it. But I have to tell you about it." Maddy could see her mom draw in her breath, as if she had to force herself to talk.

Maddy's stomach tightened. Something about this was making her nervous. "What is it?" she asked.

Her mom's voice sounded hoarse. "The test

doesn't make sense. But what it supposedly says is...your DNA and my DNA don't match up."

Maddy was puzzled. "What do you mean?"

"Somehow, the test says that we aren't mother and daughter."

Maddy's eyes widened. "How can that be?"

Mom frowned and bit her lip. "It's impossible. You were my very own baby. As you know!"

Maddy stared at her mom. "But now DNA says I'm not?"

"Apparently."

Maddy blinked back sudden tears. "So what happened? Am I not your child?" She often thought her mom was a pain, but she hadn't expected anything like this.

Her mom's eyes flashed. "Yes, you are! The test is wrong! You're my child, no question."

Maddy shivered. "Maybe babies got mixed up in the hospital. I saw a movie where that happened."

Mom stared. "I didn't even think of that. But there's no way. I had 'rooming in.' You stayed with me in my room the entire time in the hospital. You never left my side."

"Unless...maybe someone switched me when you were asleep."

Her mom snorted. "Do you think I wouldn't have noticed a different baby? I had your face memorized from the minute you were born. You were my miracle. Nobody switched you."

Maddy rubbed her hand across her face; an empty feeling was filling her chest. She didn't know what to make of all this. "What about Daniel? What does his test say?"

"We don't know yet. They didn't tell me. They say it's more complicated testing for a possible grandfather."

"But he's not my grandfather."

"Of course not. But he thinks he is. That's what the test is supposed to disprove...though after these results, I'm not sure I'll believe those either."

Maddy closed her eyes and leaned her head against the car window. The cold glass felt good on her hot forehead.

****

Maddy went up to her room and threw herself on her bed, her thoughts swirling. How could a DNA test say she wasn't her mom's kid?

Other thoughts came creeping into her head. Thoughts she couldn't say out loud. What if it wasn't a mistake? Maybe the test was right?

All of this was hard to think about. How could she know for sure whether what her mom had always told her was right?

At school they were told to be critical thinkers. Start with the facts. Don't make assumptions. Don't just go along with what everyone thinks.

What facts do I know?

One. I've always lived with Mom. Since my earliest memories.

Two. I don't remember back to when I was a baby. Does anyone?

She remembered an early birthday cake and being excited about getting a kitten. *Oscar.* That must have been her third birthday.

So what I know from before is only what someone's told me.

Her real grandpa, her mom's dad, had told her about visiting them both in the hospital when she was born.

Tears filled Maddy's eyes. She could still feel the empty space his death had left in her life. *I can't ask him anything now.*

Daniel said she was *his* granddaughter—his daughter's baby, not Mom's. That was pretty unbelievable. But could it be true?

Suddenly her legs were hot, not cold, and she tossed her duvet aside. Everything solid she normally counted on was up for question. Her stomach was churning. She was going to throw up. She leapt off the bed and stumbled down the dark hall to the bathroom and leaned over the toilet.

And waited. Finally, after nothing happened, she sat on the floor, arms around her knees and her back against the tub.

She couldn't stop feeling like she suddenly had nothing to hold on to.

Chapter Eighteen

At school on Monday, Maddy kept thinking about what her mom told her the night before. That DNA test.

She almost told Emma about it but then pulled back. She wasn't sure what to say. Was it just a mistake, like her mom said? Or was there something to it?

Aloud she wondered, "Do you think Daniel might be right?"

Emma's eyes flashed in her direction. "What are you talking about?"

"Maybe...somehow...maybe we *are* related."

"Eww, no." Emma made a face. "Don't even think that."

Maddy ducked her head. "Yeah, you're right, I guess." But her mind kept going back to the thought. Not so much *could Daniel be right?* but *could Mom be wrong?*

Maybe her mom wasn't telling her everything.

The sick feeling in her stomach wouldn't go away.

****

After school, Maddy climbed into the back seat of her mom's car, dumping her backpack on the floor next to her feet.

She kept her eyes down but could tell that her mom had turned, a frown in her voice. "Isn't Emma with you?"

Maddy didn't feel like talking, but she'd better answer. "No, her dad came to get her." She bent to get her phone out of her backpack and added, "I think they're going to her grandma's."

"Oh. Well then, you might as well come and sit up front."

Maddy didn't want to do that. "I'm fine here."

Her mom shot her a sharp look, then shook her head and put the car in gear.

Maddy stared out her side window as they pulled away from the school. A tiny whirlwind picked up a handful of dead leaves and swirled them in the air.

Her stomach churned. She didn't even want to be in the same car with her mom. Blinking back tears, she tried to get her confused feelings under control, but it wasn't working.

Her phone beeped. It was a text from Emma.

—*Come to my house later?*—

Yeah. Anywhere but at home with her mom. Emma was being a bit of a pain lately but was still her best friend. "Can I go to Emma's after dinner?"

Her mom nodded. "All right, I'll drive you over."

Maddy's jaw tightened and her body tensed. *Enough!* She was suddenly tired of all this. Being driven around. Always under someone's eyes.

"Can't I just walk over? It's only a little way."

"You know I don't want you going out on your own right now. I'll take you."

A hot flush flooded Maddy's cheeks. "Stop!" she yelled, the word shooting out of her. The act of yelling felt good—so she did it again. "Stop the car! I want out!" She unbuckled her seat belt and lunged for the door handle.

"Put that seat belt back on!" Mom's voice was shrill, her head swiveling back and forth between Maddy and the road ahead. A moment later she slammed on the brakes, reaching backward to grab Maddy's arm.

Maddy's body smashed into the seat in front of her, her nose exploding in pain as it hit the headrest. "Owww!" she screamed. She clapped her hand to her nose and felt blindly for the door handle, wrenching her arm free from her mom's grasp.

Beeep! A brown van blared its horn as it swerved around them, the driver shaking a fist in their direction.

Maddy yanked on the handle and started pushing the door open. Their car had stopped at an awkward angle, wedged up against the sidewalk.

Her mom, now leaning into the back, grabbed Maddy's arm again and gave it a hard yank. "Listen, young lady. Close that door right now and put your seat belt back on."

Maddy's eyes flashed. "You gave me a nose bleed!" She wasn't sure it was actually bleeding, but it hurt a lot.

Her mom's fingers were digging into her arm. "That only happened because you undid your seat belt. Now close that door and fasten back up."

Reluctantly Maddy pulled the door shut. She was still boiling inside but also shocked. Her mom hardly ever shouted and had never grabbed her like that before.

She pressed on the bridge of her nose, trying to stop it from aching. Maybe it wasn't bleeding, but it sure hurt, and her arm throbbed where her mom's fingers had left an imprint.

Gritting her teeth, she did up her seat belt.

Her mom buckled herself back in too. She was breathing hard and was watching Maddy in the rearview mirror. "I don't know what's got into you."

Maddy cried, "I just want to walk to Emma's house. Is that a crime? I've done it a million times. What are you so afraid of?"

Her mom glared into the mirror. "We just need to be careful for now."

"It's not fair!" As her mom started the car, Maddy muttered, "I just wish we could go back to how things were before."

They were both silent the rest of the way home.

As they pulled into their street, her mom said, "Nothing's really changed, Maddy. It'll all be sorted out soon. We'll get everything straightened out."

Maddy's whole body was rigid.

Her mom was wrong. *Everything* had changed. She stared out the window, seeing nothing.

****

I dropped Maddy at our house and went to pick up a few groceries. I was still shaken by that scene on the way home—what had Maddy been thinking!—but I hoped it had blown over by now.

By the time I got back around six, it was already black outside. Daylight Saving Time was over. A cold wind swirled, driving sudden icy flakes into my face as I shifted the straps of both grocery bags into my left hand. I reached with my right hand to unlock the door but had trouble opening it. I stopped. Had I relocked it? Was it unlocked in the first place?

The light was on in the front hall, but the kitchen was dark. I flicked on the lights and dropped my bags on the counter. I had brought the makings for fish tacos and salad, one of Maddy's favorite dinners. Hopefully it would make up for the unpleasantness on the way home. It'd been a tough couple of weeks, actually. I hoped having a nice meal together would lighten the atmosphere.

I called up to her. "Maddy, dinner'll be ready soon. Would you come set the table?"

No answer.

I moved to the bottom of the stairs and called again. "Maddy, come and set the table, please."

Again, no answer.

This wasn't like Maddy. She might argue when I asked her to do something, but she wouldn't pretend she hadn't heard. I went upstairs and knocked on her door. It wasn't fully closed, so I pushed it open a few inches.

The room was dark. She wasn't at her desk or on her bed.

I opened the door wide and glanced around the room. Definitely not there.

I checked the bathroom. No Maddy.

My stomach was tightening. "Maddy," I called.

No reply.

Now I was feeling uneasy. I checked the other upstairs rooms—my bedroom and bath, the guest room. I even opened the linen closet door, though nobody could fit in there.

I ran back downstairs. Kitchen. Dining room. Living room. My office.

No Maddy.

I raced down to the basement, throwing open every door as I passed—the utility room with the furnace, the laundry room, the storage room under the porch. Maddy wasn't anywhere.

She wanted to go to Emma's. My breathing eased. That must be where she'd gone. Even though I'd told her I'd drive her after dinner.

I dialed her phone. The call went to voicemail.

Does she ever check voice messages? I didn't know, but I left a message anyway. "Maddy, where are you? I'm making fish tacos for dinner. I know you like them. Please call me right away."

She'd see a text.

—*Fish tacos for dinner. Come home.*—

But five minutes went by, and Maddy had not returned my call or my text. Was she deliberately ignoring me?

I called Emma's house. "Nicole, is Maddy there?"

Silence at her end. "It wasn't our turn to pick her up. Didn't she come home with you?"

A sudden chill ran through me. "Yeah, she did. But then I went to the grocery store, and now I'm back home, and she isn't here."

"Let me check with Emma."

Nicole came back in a couple of minutes. Long minutes. "Emma texted her after school, but Maddy didn't reply. Emma hasn't heard from her."

My palms were sweating. "Okay, thanks. Let me know if you hear anything."

"Of course! And let us know if there's a problem."

Hanging up, I was starting to feel sick. My twelve-year-old daughter was out in the dark somewhere.

On her own? Or did Daniel have something to do with this?

I remembered that the door might have been unlocked when I got home.

I need Jenny. Her calm support would help me now.

Barely two sentences into my story, Jenny said, "I'm coming right over."

It took her less than ten minutes to arrive, but it seemed like an hour. While I waited, I phoned every friend of Maddy's I could think of. None of them had seen her since school.

Jenny came straight in the door and gave me a big hug. "Hey," she said. "We can deal with this. Take a deep breath."

I complied, drawing air deep into my lungs and letting it out again. That helped clear my head, though it didn't reduce my growing fears.

She led me over to the couch and sat down with me, holding my hands in hers. "You're sure Maddy's not here?"

I grimaced, flushing. "Yes, I'm sure. I've searched everywhere. And she's not at Emma's either." I massaged my temples, trying to relieve the tightness.

"Have you tried her other friends?"

"I called everyone I could think of while I waited for you. None of them had seen her. And Emma's the most likely one anyway—they do almost everything together."

Jenny sat back. "Listen, she's twelve, and a resourceful girl. She's only been gone a short time."

I leapt to my feet and began pacing. It was time to put words to my fear. "If Daniel Kazan didn't exist, I wouldn't be worried. But what if he came here again? What if he took her?"

My eyes widened. *The DNA test*. Did Daniel know about that result? Had it emboldened him to come and grab Maddy?

I hadn't told Jenny yet about yesterday's conversation with Aisha, and it was too complicated to get into at the moment. I didn't want to get into a long discussion of why or how the DNA test was wrong.

The main thing right now was finding Maddy.

Jenny leaned over and grabbed my wrist. "If you think Kazan may be responsible, call the police," she said.

I gave her a sidelong glance. "It might be too soon." She was the one who said Maddy'd only been gone a short time.

She shook her head. "If you have the slightest suspicion that he's taken her, don't hesitate. You want the cops on this right away."

****

The doorbell rang just after 7:30 p.m. Russo was on the porch. When I called the police station, I'd asked for Marie Boucher or Bob Russo, but I was glad he was the one who showed up, as he was aware of the background issues with Daniel. I wasn't sure how fully he'd briefed Marie.

I opened the door. My eyes were probably red, but I tried to breathe deeply to calm myself. "Thank God you're here," I said.

He stepped in, bringing a blast of chilly air with him. "What's going on? Maddy's missing?"

I pushed hair out of my face, my hand shaking. "Maybe it's too soon to involve police, but I'm worried that Daniel Kazan may have something to do with it."

Russo gestured toward the living room. "Can we sit?"

I nodded and led him in, and Jenny introduced

herself. She was sitting in one of the armchairs, and he took the other. I sat on the couch under the window, staring at the cold fireplace.

He got out his notebook. "Let's start at the beginning. When did you notice she was missing?"

"I dropped her here around four thirty, and went to the grocery store. When I came back just before six, she was gone."

He looked at his watch, then sat back. "So she's been gone less than three hours. Why do you say she's missing? She could just be at a friend's house."

If only. "I don't think so. The most likely friend would be Emma, across the park, but I called, and she's not there. I called all the other friends I could think of, and she's not there either."

He leaned toward me. "What's the situation with her father? Could he be…"

"No." I had clarified this with Marie, but it hadn't come up with Russo. "There is no father. I conceived her by sperm donation."

He paused a second, then asked, "And you have no connection to the donor?"

"No, none at all." I saw no reason to explain further. I had chosen the donor from a database, based on my selection criteria. *I just wanted a baby.*

He glanced at me and then away. "All right, let's consider other possibilities. Would she go out to a store for something?"

"No, she never does that, not by herself. She always goes up to her room after school. There's just no reason for her to be gone."

He raised his eyebrows. "Was the front door locked when you got home from your shopping?"

104

I hesitated. "I thought it was, but I had a little trouble with the lock…"

He turned, his eyes searching the room. "Was anything disturbed in the house when you got back?"

"No, not that I noticed. There wasn't even any sign in the kitchen that she'd made a snack or anything."

He frowned. "What did she have with her when she came home?"

An image of her climbing into my car after school flashed into my mind. "She was wearing her green jacket, and she had her backpack. The one she takes to school."

"Are those here now?"

I bit my lip. "Usually she hangs her jacket in the hallway, and it's not there. She'd likely take her backpack upstairs."

Russo put his notebook in his pocket. "Okay, let's have a gander at her room."

I headed up the stairs, and he followed behind. Jenny stayed downstairs; from the sound of running water in the kitchen, I guessed she was putting the kettle on for tea.

Maddy's room looked like it usually does unless I've hounded her to tidy up—bed not made, clothes everywhere. The doors to her overflowing closet were ajar, and several dresser drawers were open. A pile of schoolbooks was on the desk, and a striped sock was draped over the headboard.

I forced myself to ignore the mess. I'd told Maddy to put her clothes away a hundred times, but that was now the least of my worries.

"I don't see a backpack," said Russo.

I gazed around the room and shook my head. "No,

I don't either." I walked over and inspected the schoolbooks. "These are this year's books, but I don't know if she had them in her backpack today."

He moved around the room, though I couldn't tell what he was expecting to find. "Can you tell if any clothes are missing?"

I poked at the clothing jammed in the closet, then shook my head. "I can't tell. Nothing obvious."

He edged toward the hallway. "It's not clear that she's actually missing. She may just have gone out, for some reason you don't know about."

I stared at him. "Even if she did, it's freezing out there tonight." I was trying to put words to the dark apprehension that was filling me. "A twelve-year-old girl alone in the dark in the city is not a good idea. Plus she's not answering her phone."

"It's not even eight o'clock, not late yet. Let's assume she's okay. I'll alert our downtown patrols to keep an eye out. I'll need a recent photo of her so they know what she looks like."

I opened my phone to find a photo. There were a couple from the summer that I thought would work. A sick feeling rose in my throat as I scrolled. *He's not taking this seriously enough.* "I think you need to check on Daniel Kazan."

He frowned. "I gave him a good warning on Saturday to stay away from her. Away from both of you."

"Yeah, but what makes you think he'd listen? He's obsessed with the idea she's his granddaughter. We know he's been hanging around the neighborhood."

He was watching me quizzically.

I wanted him to share my alarm. "He came banging

106

on our door just a few days ago, demanding to see her. What if he came again tonight? If Maddy opened the door, what would stop him from grabbing her?" I was a little out of breath after this speech, but I wanted him to realize that she could be in real danger.

He pursed his lips and frowned. "All right. Just to be sure, I'll go and check his house. But I'll also alert the patrols to watch for her."

We headed back downstairs. Jenny was standing in the hallway, holding a steaming mug.

She handed it to me once Russo had left, and I burst into tears.

Chapter Nineteen

After her mom left to get groceries, Maddy slipped out of the house. She closed the door, making sure Oscar was inside, but didn't lock it—digging into her bag for the key would take too much time. She wanted to be out of sight before Mom came home.

She didn't have any plan in mind; she just wanted to be gone, to get away from her mom, and to somehow silence the confusing thoughts and feelings that had been swirling through her head all day, and especially in the car on the way home.

She strode down the street, her jacket open and her backpack banging against her shoulder. The streetlights had already come on. Light shone in some windows, but many houses were dark.

At first it felt good to be out in the cool air, but soon she realized she was freezing. Tiny ice pellets were hitting her face, and she'd left the house without her mitts and hat. The wind was gusting, blowing sideways. She hunched her shoulders, trying to pull her collar up far enough to cover her ears. They'd started to hurt.

The sidewalks were nearly empty, with a few people scurrying along, huddled into their hoods and jackets. She imagined they were heading for somewhere warm. She couldn't stay outside in this wind much longer. The traffic light was green, so she crossed the street and realized she was almost at her school; her feet had taken her there on autopilot. Lights were on in the school, and people were going in and out. There must be some kind of meeting or event.

Nobody paid attention as she slipped inside and went to the girl's washroom. Taking a moment to check herself in the mirror, she patted her hair into place.

She walked up and down the hallway, checking rooms as she passed. The center of activity was in the gym. Chairs were grouped in several spots around the room, and people were moving from group to group.

She went back and hid in the girls' washroom until she heard people leaving. She pulled out her phone— she should tell Emma where she was. She typed a message but stopped before pressing Send.

Emma didn't understand Maddy's problems with her mom. Emma pretty much told her own mom everything. She wouldn't see why Maddy needed to get away right now. At all.

And if Emma told Nicole where Maddy was, Nicole would tell Maddy's mom.

Maddy wasn't ready for that yet. She wasn't ready to be hauled home. She lifted her thumb from the screen.

Once the noises ended, she found her way to the gym. In the dark, the school seemed like her private domain. It was like all the stress and hassle that had been bothering her had disappeared. In the back of her mind, she knew her mom would be wondering where she was and would be worried. But she pushed the thought away.

She knew where the gym mats were kept. She pulled one out and lay down on it.

Digging into her backpack, she got out her phone to check the time. She turned it on, but it turned itself off again. Tried again; it went off again. Oh, no—it was out of power, and she'd forgotten to bring her charger. Groaning, she lay back and closed her eyes. Just to rest them.

Later she woke to noises from the night cleaning staff moving through the building. She ducked into the cupboard where the gym mats were kept so the cleaners wouldn't find her.

Chapter Twenty

I paced the front hallway, trying to stay sane while waiting for Russo to return. The clock in the kitchen ticked the minutes. Bursts of wind swirled around the eaves and drove sleet against the front windows.

My head was pounding, and my eyes burned, my mind full of Maddy. What was happening to her right now? Did Daniel have her? Would Russo find her and bring her back?

And I was flooded with guilt about that disgraceful scene on the way home. I couldn't let her jump out of the car, but surely I could have stopped her without screaming at her or grabbing her so fiercely. And her nose getting smacked when I slammed on the brakes—it was her own fault, but it had added an ugly note to the whole episode.

That wasn't the kind of mother I wanted to be, or the relationship I wanted us to have.

Jenny came and put an arm around me. "Why don't you go and wash your face? It'll make you feel better."

I stared at myself in the downstairs washroom mirror. The dark green walls of the narrow room—the wallpaper I'd chosen for its quiet elegance—felt like they were closing in around me.

My earlier tears had left my eyes puffy. I splashed cold water on my face and rubbed it dry with the towel. That would have to do. Returning to the living room, I took a seat beside Jenny and picked up my cold mug of tea.

In the background I'd heard her phoning Nicole, Abel, and Tom to fill them in on the evening's events. I was grateful—I wanted my friends informed, but I was in no shape to make those calls. Now Jenny watched me carefully. "Listen, I'm sure she'll be okay. I know you're worried, but your police officer seems to be taking things in hand."

I nodded. "I hope so." But I was far from sure.

****

The doorbell rang an hour later. Though I'd been anxiously waiting for it, the shrill sound startled me. I peered through the small window next to the front door. It was Bob Russo.

He was alone.

I smothered my disappointment and opened the door. The porch light was on, but darkness pooled in the corners of the yard. There was no moon out tonight, and the icy wind blasted in, almost grabbing the door from me. I shuddered, trying to quell the fears that rose in my mind.

Russo faced me, unsmiling. "Hi. May I come in?"

"Of course." I stepped back to let him enter.

He gave me a searching gaze. "How are you feeling?"

"Not great, as you can imagine." I frowned at him. "So she wasn't at Daniel's?"

He tugged off his hat and unzipped his coat. "Daniel was home, but he didn't have Maddy."

I ushered him wordlessly into the living room and sat on the edge of the couch. Jenny watched from the doorway.

"How sure are you?" I asked. "Could he have hidden her somewhere?"

He shook his head and took a seat in one of the armchairs. "I don't think he had any opportunity to take her. I got to his place just before nine, and he had clearly just gotten in. I asked him where he'd been. He said he'd been bowling with the next-door neighbor. They arrived at South Park Lanes around five, bowled a few games, then had a bite to eat and a couple of beers at the Legion, and left just after eight thirty. I went next door and confirmed all of that with the neighbor."

He leaned back. "So Daniel was elsewhere at the time Maddy disappeared, and he spent all evening with a neighbor who vouches for him."

Nausea rose in my throat. "Did you tell him why you were asking?"

"I did, yes. I told him that Maddy was missing."

"What did he say to that?"

"Said he was sorry to hear it."

"Did you search his house?"

"I didn't have a warrant. But I asked if he'd mind if I looked around, and he said 'be my guest.' So yeah, I checked his house, including all the bedrooms and the basement. She isn't there."

My head swam. I'd thought that having Daniel take her was my worst fear. But now my imagination was filling with far more frightening scenarios.

"What about an Amber Alert?"

He shook his head. "We can only issue an Amber Alert if we're certain a child has been abducted and is in danger. We don't issue them for runaways, and that's now the most likely scenario here."

Fury rose inside me. "I can't believe she'd just run

away." I smothered my thoughts of our fight in the car. "She's not that kind of girl."

His eyes were in shadow. "I'm pretty sure Daniel couldn't have taken her. As far as we know, she left your house voluntarily."

"But—"

"The fact that she's not been seen since doesn't mean anything has happened to her. It just means she's been able to keep herself from being noticed."

I glared. "There has to be something more you can do. It's freezing out there. Where is she? And apart from the weather, she's a young girl alone at night in the city. I know this city is generally safe, but horrible things can happen here too."

Russo grimaced. "I can't tell you that there aren't any dangers out there."

I hugged my arms around myself. "You must have some ideas. If you think she ran away, where do you think she might go?"

"Most runaway girls end up staying at a friend's house. You've checked all her friends?"

I sighed. "Yes. I called every friend I could think of, but none of them had seen her. These kids are twelve—they're living with their families. It's not like they're going to have her couch surfing."

He leaned toward me, and I could see compassion in his eyes. "Listen, Susan—may I call you Susan?"

I nodded.

He flushed. "I'm sorry, I don't mean to be familiar. It just seemed like first names would be more comfortable…"

"Sure, that's fine. Bob, right?" First names *did* feel more natural. Somehow reassuring, under the circumstances.

He drew a breath. "So what I wanted to say is...I can only imagine how you're feeling right now, but driving yourself crazy with worry won't help anyone." He glanced at Jenny. "Are you going to be here with Susan for a while?"

She smiled. "Yes, I am."

"Good." He stood up, ready to leave. "I sent Maddy's photo and description to the station earlier tonight and had them send it out to all the patrol cars. We're already watching for her. And I've alerted our Missing Persons Unit. If we don't find her tonight, they'll be on the case in the morning."

After he left, Jenny led me into the living room. "I'm going to stay here with you tonight. You shouldn't be dealing with this alone." She gave me an appraising inspection. "You look like you could use a drink."

I longed for a stiff shot of something to blunt my rising fears—whiskey, maybe—but that was a slippery slope. "No, not tonight. I need a clear head."

She blinked, then gave me a hug. "Okay, I get it. I'll make some more tea instead. Why don't you try to get a bit of rest here?" She tucked a blanket around my knees and headed for the kitchen.

Chapter Twenty-One

I woke up on the couch in the living room, early morning light slanting in through the window. I sat up and rubbed my cheek, feeling creases from the cushion I'd been lying on. *What am I doing here?*

Then last night's events clicked into focus. *Maddy.* I hadn't left the front room, in case she came home.

I heard a rattling of dishes in the kitchen. *Was that her?* Then Jenny came through the doorway, holding a steaming mug and a plate. "I see you're awake."

My mood plummeted. "I thought you were Maddy."

She smiled ruefully. "Sorry." She set the mug and plate on the table beside me. Coffee and toast. "Try to eat something."

My throat closed. How could I eat with Maddy still gone? I gazed up at Jenny. "Could she have come home overnight without waking us?" Jenny shook her head sadly, but I ignored her and ran upstairs, stopping at the open doorway to Maddy's room.

The room was empty. That striped sock was still draped over the top of the bed, looking forlorn. Maddy had been gone all night. Pain hit my stomach.

Scanning the room again, I stepped over to her desk and did a double take. "Jenny, come here," I called.

She came racing upstairs. "What?"

I nodded to Maddy's desk. "I didn't notice last night. Maddy's phone charger's still here."

Jenny jumped to the same conclusion I had. "She can't recharge her phone. That could be why she hasn't answered."

Feeling sick, I dropped my face into my hands. "There's no way I can go to work today. I have to be here."

"Of course you do." She leaned over and gave me a hug. "I'm afraid I have to go, though—I can't stay with you today. I'll check in with you later and come back after work."

"I'll be fine. Thanks for staying over."

While she dressed and got ready, I texted Abel.

—I can't come in to work. Maddy still missing. Get Grace to cancel my appointments. Pls tell Dorothy.—

He probably wasn't awake yet, but he'd see my message before he left for the clinic.

Ten minutes later, I closed the front door behind Jenny, dimly noticing that the sun was shining and last night's wind had ended. I decided to call Russo. *Bob.* It was early for him too, but I figured a police officer should consider himself available.

He answered immediately.

"Bob," I started. The name felt a bit strange in my mouth, but I plowed on. "I had to call you. Maddy hasn't showed up here. Was there any sign of her overnight?"

"No, I checked with our central desk about half an hour ago. There's been nothing. Have you tried phoning and texting her again?"

"Yeah, but there's no answer." I drew a breath. "And I just noticed her phone charger is still here. If her phone battery has run out—"

"Hmm. That could be."

"What's happening today to find her? Will there be a search?"

"The Missing Persons Unit will take over now. It's headed by Staff Sergeant Bailey. He has two full-time constables working for him. They'll be in touch with you this morning."

"Will you stay on the case too?"

"Not officially, no. I'm not on that team."

A sudden hitch in my breath surprised me. *I just got used to working with you.* Almost immediately, though, that feeling was replaced by relief. I was glad to know that specialists would be looking for Maddy.

"What does 'not officially' mean?"

He coughed. "I'll stay in touch. I've been involved to this point, so I'm not going to just walk away."

I found that reassuring.

"In the meantime, all the officers on shift today will have her picture and description. And I'm meeting with Sergeant Bailey at eight to pass on everything I have."

I wandered the house, unable to settle to anything. My mind was racing. At eight thirty, my stomach rebelling from a third cup of coffee, I realized I had to call Maddy's school to explain her absence.

I shrank from it—somehow telling the school about it made her disappearance more real.

But it *was* real.

And presumably the police search would soon be public. They'd be in touch with the school even if I wasn't. So yes, I had to tell the school what was going on.

I took a deep breath, trying to overcome my sick, helpless feeling, and reached for my phone.

****

Fifteen minutes later, I was pacing the front hallway when Marie Boucher phoned. "Susan, I understand Maddy's missing. I'm so sorry."

My pulse quickened; I was glad to hear from her. "Bob Russo was involved overnight. Has he been in touch with you?"

"He briefed us this morning. I'm cross-appointed to the Missing Persons Unit, and my sergeant assigned me to follow up on Maddy's case. I need to come see you. Are you at home right now?"

"Yeah. I couldn't face going to work." An understatement. Maddy'd been gone now for over fourteen hours. My thoughts were circling, and my fears for her had nearly paralyzed me. But I was relieved to know that I'd be dealing with Marie rather than an unfamiliar officer.

"I understand. I'll be there shortly, with a colleague. We're not far away."

She arrived a few minutes later. Again, her confident manner calmed me down. A male officer was with her; she introduced him as Kevin Wheeler.

Taking charge, she headed for the kitchen. She waited for me to follow, then chose a chair, gesturing to me to sit across from her. "I need you to tell me everything that's happened."

My stomach sank. *Time's passing.* "Don't you already have all that from Russo?"

"He gave us a report, but please go through it again for me." She patted my hand. "We need to be thorough. I promise, this isn't a waste of time." With a direct glance, she added, "Maddy's young. She hasn't run away before, am I right?"

I flinched at the term. "I have a hard time imagining she ran away. I thought Daniel Kazan must have taken her, though Bob Russo doesn't think so."

She gazed at me. "Let's put it this way—she hasn't disappeared before?"

I shook my head.

"And she's not a kid who's used to roaming in the city."

I shook my head again. "Just in our neighborhood, and a bit downtown." Though I was starting to wonder how well I knew my daughter.

"So she's vulnerable. It's an urgent case. We want to find her as much as you do."

I doubted that but was glad to hear they were taking this seriously.

She took out a notepad. "While we talk, Kevin will have a look around your house and yard, if that's all right." She must have noted my puzzled expression. "I know you've already searched, but we need to do our own inspection. It's not unknown for a young person to hide in or around their own home."

Kevin had vanished; I could hear his footsteps in the hallway.

Sitting with Marie, I recounted the events of the previous evening. "I'm convinced Daniel Kazan is involved somehow."

"Yes, we'll be giving him another visit this morning. I know Bob checked on him last night, but given Mr. Kazan's interest in your daughter, we'll investigate again."

While we talked, I heard Kevin moving around the

house. Upstairs, the main floor, the basement. It sounded like he was opening and closing every door and cupboard.

Marie closed her notebook and stood up. "I'll need you to show me Maddy's room."

In Maddy's room I looked around helplessly. I didn't know what she thought we'd see here, but I pointed out the phone charger on Maddy's desk. "She usually charges her phone overnight, so it might be dead already."

"Can you tell if she took anything with her? Clothing, other belongings?"

I shook my head. "I don't see anything obvious. But if Daniel grabbed her downstairs, or off the street, she wouldn't have had a chance—"

She gave a thin smile. "We have to consider all possibilities."

Downstairs again, we met Kevin just coming in the back door. He turned to Marie and shook his head. "Nothing in the shed or the yard," he said.

She nodded and turned to me. "You understand that we had to do this search. We needed to rule out any possibility that she could still be in your home."

She'd said that before, but this time I realized with a pang that they might consider me a suspect in Maddy's disappearance. There'd been cases where a parent had harmed a child, then reported the child missing. Well, at least they now knew I didn't have her body hidden here somewhere.

Marie continued. "We'll canvass your neighbors to see if anyone saw anything unusual."

"In the meantime, we'll put in a request to track her phone. We may be able to ping it, to find her approximate location. And we can see if and when she's used it."

I pointed out again that Maddy's phone battery may have run down. Marie grimaced. "All we can do is try." She added, "We'll also put out a bulletin, with her photo and description, asking for anyone with information to come forward. If she's still missing by late afternoon, we'll likely have a press conference so the notice can get on tonight's news."

****

Daniel was putting his breakfast dishes in the rack to drain when Tucker barked and dashed into the hallway. Someone was knocking on the front door.

He grabbed a dishtowel to dry his hands and went to answer. Two police officers stood on the porch, a policewoman in front and a male officer standing slightly behind her. It was a different guy, not the one who came by last night, the one who said he'd known Mac back in Alberta.

Daniel's stomach tightened at the sight of them. What were they doing here? Could this be about the girl again? He didn't want them to see his agitation, so he made an effort to seem relaxed and polite.

They introduced themselves, but he immediately forgot their names. The policewoman spoke up, said they were from the Missing Persons Unit. They were searching for Madison Koss. "You know who we're talking about, right?"

Daniel nodded. "Yeah, of course. Another cop came by last night, said she was missing. Hasn't she shown up yet?"

The officer shook her head, her eyes fixed on him. "No, she's still missing, and we're anxious to find her.

We know you've been very interested in this girl."

He glared at her, then lowered his gaze. "I didn't even know she was missing until the officer came by last night. And he had a good look all through my house."

She moved forward, the other cop following. "We'd like to go over it again. Is it all right if we search your house and yard?" She must have seen doubt on his face, because she added, "We can get a warrant, but it would be simpler if you just give us permission."

He had no problem with them tramping through the house again; there was nothing for them to find, and if they were satisfied she wasn't there, maybe they'd leave him alone. "Go ahead." He stepped back to let them enter.

You're their obvious suspect. Patricia's voice grated in his mind. He guessed she was right, but it was annoying, even if it was logical from their point of view.

And if the girl's still missing…

For a second he couldn't breathe. Had he lost Hannah again?

The female cop asked him what he'd been up to last evening and night, at what times. He explained, the same as he'd told the other guy last night. He'd been bowling with Jim Trafford from next door, then they'd gone to the Legion for something to eat and a couple of beers, then he came home.

"You weren't in the Koss family's neighborhood at all yesterday evening?"

"No, I wasn't. You can ask Jim—he'll tell you how our evening went." He was sure they'd be checking with Jim anyway, just as the officer last night had done.

She wrote in her notebook, then put it away.

The two officers spent over an hour in the house, checking every nook and cranny, including the attic and the basement and the garage out back. They poked around the foundations and the supports to the back porch.

Before they left, the woman knocked on his door, gave him her card, and thanked him for his cooperation. "If you see or hear any sign of her, please call me right away."

"Sure." Hah. He wouldn't be doing that.

Closing the door, he sighed with relief. He'd passed their inspection; now they'd move on to look for the girl elsewhere.

But the whole thing left him unsettled. He returned to the kitchen and poured a cup of coffee, wincing as he took a mouthful of the now-bitter brew.

Where could she be? Maybe he should be out there searching for her too.

He bent to scratch Tucker's ears. Sometimes he talked to Tucker instead of to Patricia, laying out his thoughts and concerns. He could talk to Tucker out loud; conversations with Patricia were inside his mind. Though her presence felt real, more so all the time.

If you could find Hannah now, you could just pack her up and drive her home to Alberta.

Right. But he had no idea where she might be. Anywhere he'd think of, the cops would have already checked. No, it was better to keep his head down for now. Better not to attract attention. Surely she'd be found soon, and he could get on with his plans then. He whispered a promise. *I'll bring Hannah home, somehow.* A promise to himself, and Patricia.

Chapter Twenty-Two

Maddy woke when she heard the school's daytime custodian banging buckets in his utility room. The gym mat she'd been lying on hadn't been very comfortable, but she must have slept, since daylight was seeping in the high windows of the gym.

She didn't want anyone to find her there. It was too early for kids to arrive at school, and she didn't want to have to explain herself. She detoured to the girls' washroom to use the toilet and brush her teeth, hoping the sounds wouldn't carry too far. She splashed water on her face and rubbed it with paper towels. Digging out the small hairbrush she kept in her backpack, she neatened her ponytail.

She slipped out of the school, relieved that no one had noticed her. The morning was still cold, but the sun was shining, and there wasn't much wind. She zipped up her jacket and shoved her hands in her pockets.

She was hungry. Last night she'd found a protein bar and an apple in her backpack, but she'd had nothing else since lunch.

Bank Street was close. There were restaurants and coffee shops along there. She could get something for breakfast.

She wasn't ready to go home yet. There was something thrilling about being on her own, away from everything. It was too soon to give that up. She just needed a break. Time to think, without her mom always hovering.

She pushed away thoughts of what her mom would be doing right now. *If she's really my mom.*

Staying away was bad. There'd be "consequences"—her mom's word for punishment. She'd been away all night. She had no idea what consequence that might bring, but there'd be trouble for sure.

No point rushing home for that. For now, she didn't want her escape to end.

Her mind flashed to the movie they'd seen with Jenny on Saturday, to the two kids who set out alone, each of them wanting to find their own way. Pretty much like she was doing.

This was what she'd been wanting all along. A chance to make some decisions on her own, without someone running every second of her life for her.

But she needed to get off this street. Emma's mom or dad could be driving her to school, and this would be their route. They might see her.

Several restaurants she passed were still closed, but the coffee shop at Second Avenue was open. She ducked in and lined up behind a woman in an orange coat placing an order. There were people at a few tables, tapping at their phones or sipping coffee.

She pulled out her own phone and stared at it. It'd been dead last night and was still dead now. She looked around, but nobody was using a charger.

She went to the counter. "Does anyone have a phone charger back there?" she asked the young woman taking orders, who shook her head. Maddy grimaced, then placed her order—hot chocolate and toast with peanut butter.

Carrying them to a table in the back corner, she realized she couldn't go back to school either. Someone would let her mom know she was there, and her little break would be over.

I can stay here for now—but not for long. Where could she go?

****

When the cops left after searching his house, Daniel was relieved but unsettled. He'd decided to keep his head down and avoid any further police attention, but that left him frustrated. He couldn't see a way forward. How could he keep his promise to Patricia—to bring Hannah home—if he didn't even know where she was?

Restless, he decided to walk over to the Quickie Mart on Bronson to pick up milk and bread. The sun was warm on his shoulders; it had actually turned into a nice day. Striding along, he realized he'd left Tucker behind. He'd put the dog in the backyard when the police arrived, and hadn't given him a thought since.

Cement sidewalks are hard on an old dog's joints. Daniel decided to consider his forgetfulness an act of mercy.

When he got back to the house, walking along beside it to the back door, he heard a voice. A young voice, sounding excited. "Here, boy! Catch! Bring it back now. Good boy. You *are* a good boy, aren't you?"

He rounded the corner and stopped. A girl was in the backyard, playing ball with Tucker. Daniel was dumbfounded. It was...Hannah. Could it really be her? Almost as if his wish had made her materialize.

What was she doing here? If she'd showed up half

an hour earlier, the cops would have run into her.

Somehow, she was here now. It seemed like an omen—a sign that they were meant to be together. There was a way forward after all. He could keep his promise.

He was about to ask her if she knew the police were searching for her, when he stopped himself. *Go slow, don't make assumptions.* He didn't want to scare her away.

He bent to put his bag of groceries on the porch. Best to take a deep breath and talk to her easy.

"Hannah?" he said but quickly added, "Maddy?" Better to use the name she was used to, even though it came out tasting wrong in his mouth.

She turned, startled. "Oh. Hi. I saw your dog out here…"

Damn. She sure did look like a young Kelly. The turn of her mouth, the way her face lighted up when she glanced at Tucker…

"I don't mind," he said. "He likes to play ball."

They stared at each other, not speaking, and then Maddy dropped her eyes. She went over to the porch and put the ball down on the old wicker chair next to the door. Her backpack was leaning against the chair.

He smiled tentatively. "Good to see you again." He was hoping to put her at ease, but he sensed she was hesitant. So he tried again, smiling more widely. "You know who I am."

She ducked her head, then lifted it again, facing him. "Mm-hmm. You think I'm your long-lost granddaughter."

He swallowed. "I do. You're just like my daughter Kelly." He bit back the next phrase—"*your mother.*"

She gave him a shy look. "I knew where you live—I followed you and your dog that day."

Daniel nodded. "Yeah, I know. I'm glad you came."

She scuffed her feet against the step and ducked her head. "I'm skipping school today."

Daniel wondered what she was up to. "You were gone overnight too, weren't you?"

She shot a sharp glance at him. "How did you know that?"

He drew a breath. "The police were here earlier. They said you were missing. Did you stay out all night?"

She bent her head again. "I stayed at my school overnight. I was okay."

"The police came last night and again this morning. They searched the house to see if you were here. Susan—your...mom—supposedly thought I'd kidnapped you."

She frowned. "Nobody kidnapped me. I just wanted to be away from home."

Daniel climbed the back step. "Do you want to let anyone know you're all right?" He held his breath. He didn't want her contacting anyone, but it was smarter to let her think that was an option.

"No, not right now," she replied, moving aside. "Can't I just stay here for a bit?"

Daniel's heart leapt. *Yes!* Then he stopped. If the police found her here, he'd be in trouble for sure. But they'd already been here twice. Why would they come back?

The prospect of having Hannah to himself was thrilling. He certainly wasn't going to send her away.

"Sure," he said, opening the back door. "I was thinking of making grilled cheese and tomato soup for lunch. Would you like some?"

She stood up. "That's my favorite meal!" she said. "Thanks."

Food. Everybody likes to eat.

****

After lunch, Daniel cleared their dishes away. The meal had been quiet. The girl had eaten her soup and sandwich with her head down, occasionally glancing at him but not speaking.

She got up to gaze out the window, then turned to scan the kitchen. She seemed to be checking for Tucker, who was lying just inside the back door. She was silent, chewing her bottom lip, then raised her chin. "What makes you think you're my grandpa?"

Here was the chance to explain their connection. But he didn't want to overburden her with too many details.

He drew a breath. "My daughter, Kelly, had a baby girl, named Hannah. Hannah disappeared eleven years ago, when she was a baby, and we always hoped to find her. She'd be your age now. You look just like Kelly did when she was your age—you could be her all over again."

She stuck out her lower lip. "That doesn't mean I'm Hannah. Lots of girls look like me."

"No, they don't. I haven't ever seen anyone else that looks just like you, except Kelly." He'd been confused about that other girl—Nadine—but he'd been wrong about her. That had been a mistake.

She shook her head. "That still doesn't mean that I'm Hannah."

130

"It does, I'm sure of it. I've been searching for so long…"

Her expression was skeptical. "How old do you think I am?"

"Twelve. Isn't that right?"

"Yes." She frowned. "What was Hannah's birthday?"

"June sixth."

"Mine's April twenty-first. Not the same."

"Those details aren't important." He paused. His instinct told him not to directly challenge her relationship to Susan. Not yet.

He didn't want to tell her his speculations, how Hannah could have become the supposed daughter of a woman in Ottawa. A changed identity could include a changed birthdate.

If the DNA test proved he was her grandfather—as he expected—he'd be pointing the finger for sure. Susan wouldn't get away with claiming Hannah as hers.

He was enjoying this discussion. Other than that short encounter in the park, it was the first time he'd had direct contact with the girl. He liked her challenging attitude. That too was just like Kelly, who had fiercely defended her opinions and didn't accept any of his views as given.

She abruptly changed the subject. "Can I go play with your dog again?"

If she was in the backyard, could she be seen from the street? He decided it'd be okay—the house blocked the view into the back. Besides, it was best not to refuse. He didn't want her to feel she was being kept here against her will.

He'd have to find a way to make sure she didn't

leave, but he'd learned long ago on the farm that it was best to proceed slowly when coaxing an animal into a corral.

"Sure," he said. "His name's Tucker. Just keep him in the backyard. He's an old dog and gets tired easily."

He watched her head out the back door. He could hardly believe his luck. She'd come to him. It must be fate—it proved how right he'd been all along.

Patricia's voice murmured in his head. *Now make sure she stays.*

Chapter Twenty-Three

After Marie and Kevin left that morning, I found myself pacing between the kitchen and the hall, unable to sit still or focus. I was half-expecting Maddy to show up at any time. And fearing that she wouldn't.

Jenny texted me from work, asking for an update. There were messages from Nicole, Abel, and Tom as well.

I appreciated them all checking in, but I didn't feel up to replying in detail. I was in a holding pattern, where even forming words and sentences was a struggle. I just told them Missing Persons was involved, and there was no news yet.

I had to get a grip on myself. Heading upstairs, I decided to bring some order to Maddy's room. I stripped the duvet cover and sheets from her bed and dumped them in the hallway. Gathering up the clothes she'd left scattered on her floor—socks, underwear, two pairs of pants, a striped pullover, several long-sleeved shirts—I tried to sort "clean" from "dirty" but soon gave up. They might as well all go in the laundry. I took everything downstairs and put it in the washer.

Dusting, arranging books on the bookshelves, organizing things on her desk. Tidying the closet. Vacuuming. Every act was a prayer for Maddy's safe return. When she came home—"when," not "if"—I wanted her to have a clean, welcoming bedroom.

I moved on to her bathroom. Her not-too-tidy habits were on display here too, one towel crumpled in the corner, another tossed over the hook on the door. The counter was cluttered with hair bands, scrunchies, lip gloss. Even a tube of sunscreen—why was that here in November?

I set to work to clean and straighten the room. I changed the towels, scrubbed the bathtub, polished the mirror over the sink. As I wiped down the counter, I moved the red ceramic "bath accessories" I'd bought for her years ago—soap dish, cup, toothbrush holder. The soap dish was chipped. I moved it back into place; I should get her a new set. Maybe when she got home.

Then I did a double take. The toothbrush holder was empty. And she always shoved the toothpaste upright in the cup, but it wasn't there either.

Bob had asked me if Maddy had taken anything with her. Marie asked the same question. I hadn't been able to identify anything, but I hadn't thought to go through her bathroom. Now the empty holder and empty cup were staring me in the face.

I hadn't moved her toothbrush or toothpaste. Maddy must have taken them herself.

My head pounded. I had a sudden thought and whirled, heading into Maddy's bedroom where I grabbed the wooden money box that she kept on her top shelf. Why hadn't I thought to check this before? My dad made the box as a gift for her eighth Christmas. It was beautifully made, with a small padlock. She'd been keeping birthday money and allowance savings in it ever since.

I retrieved the key from her desk drawer where she kept it, and unlocked the box. The top fell open, revealing...nothing. It was empty. She had taken all her savings with her.

No! I had resisted the idea that Maddy could have left voluntarily, even when both Bob and Marie said that was the most likely possibility. But this evidence said I had deluded myself. She must have expected to be away long enough to need to brush her teeth. Long enough to need money.

She left deliberately, with at least some thought.

I sagged against the open doorframe, my hands pressing my midsection. Up to now I'd been imagining her taken by someone. Even after Bob had assured me that Daniel couldn't have done it, I had still clung to the idea that he was involved.

But now I had to come to grips with a different picture. Maddy had run away.

I was stricken, my mind filled with memories of the times we'd butted heads lately. Of her subdued reaction when I told her about the DNA test. And vivid images of the scene in the car on the way home from school the day before...just before she went missing.

Had I driven Maddy away?

****

It occurred to me Emma might know something about Maddy's whereabouts. She and Maddy lived in each other's pockets, after all. If Maddy'd been thinking of running away, surely she'd have said something to Emma.

I called Nicole's number but it went to voicemail. I left a quick message, saying I'd like to stop by when Emma got home from school.

****

It was early afternoon when Marie phoned. "I

wanted to let you know—we went to Daniel Kazan's house this morning after we left you."

I held my breath, hoping they'd found something.

"We inspected his house, his yard, his shed. There was no sign of Maddy."

"Do you believe his story about going bowling?" A cold dread invaded my mind.

"We didn't just check with the neighbor. We talked to staff who were on duty at both the Legion and the bowling alley. The neighbor is well-known at both places, and the staff remember him and Daniel being there."

I choked back a sob. "So where is she?"

"That's the question. We'll be mobilizing to find her. I need to come see you again—are you still at home?"

"Yes, I am."

"I'll stop by in a few minutes." She hung up, not waiting for me to say anything more.

She must have been around the corner. Five minutes later she was at my door, taking off her coat and seating herself in my kitchen. She pulled out her notebook and leveled her gaze at me across the table. "This morning you said you didn't think she had run away. But that now seems the most likely possibility."

My shoulders slumped. "I know. After you left this morning, I realized she took her toothbrush and some money. She put at least that much thought into it."

Marie regarded me; I read sympathy in her eyes. "I know this is all very upsetting for you. We're going to do everything we can to find her."

"Did you try pinging her phone?" I was grasping at straws, but this was an important one.

She shook her head. "We did try but had no success. You said the battery might be dead." She glanced inquiringly at me.

I reminded her that Maddy's charger was still in her room.

"Yeah, but we'll keep trying. She may find a way to get it recharged. And I'll need a list of the social media she uses."

I tried to marshal my thoughts. Maddy'd only had a smartphone since May, but she was already adept, though I insisted on monitoring her use. I knew of too many instances of cyberbullying to leave her at the unsupervised mercies of social media. "She's on Snapchat, Instagram, and TikTok. I'll give you her usernames." At least, the ones I knew about. I was starting to realize that I didn't know everything about Maddy anymore.

"Have you checked those accounts?"

"Of course. She hasn't posted anything since yesterday. And I tried texting and phoning her, but no answer."

"We'll check those accounts, and we'll keep trying to locate her cellphone." She made another note, then turned to me again. "You said you contacted some of Maddy's friends last night. I'll need you to give me their names--the ones you called, and any others you can think of."

I nodded, though this seemed like retracing steps already taken.

Marie leaned forward. "Is there anyone else she might have been in touch with? Did she have any contacts with older girls, girls not at her school?"

"What do you mean? What older girls?"

She set her shoulders. "I don't mean to suggest this is likely, but...we recently uncovered a group of teenage girls who were luring younger girls, recruiting them..."

"Oh my God." I remembered that being reported in the local press and on TV. The older girls were paid for bringing young recruits into what turned out to be a prostitution ring. "No! I don't see how—" I shrank from the thought.

Marie patted my hand. "Don't panic—I'm not saying that's what's happened with Maddy." But I could see her mind working. They had to consider every possibility. And those girls' parents had known nothing about what was going on.

I shuddered, my mind reviewing Maddy's recent schedule. Could anything like that have happened? Emma's parents and I kept a pretty close watch over the girls, but we had been giving them some time on their own recently. What about their trips to the mall?

Emma. Those girls were joined at the hip. If anything like this was going on, Emma would know about it. I'd find out when I talked to her later.

Marie gathered her coat and notebook. "We'll be doing everything we can to find your daughter. And we'll be holding a press conference later this afternoon. We want to get this into the media, to alert the public and ask for people to report any possible leads."

She stopped on her way out the door. "We're also producing a poster, asking people to watch out for her. It should be ready later today. We'll post them in our standard locations, but if you can get people to help put them up more widely..."

"Of course!" Putting up posters was something I could do.

****

Sitting on the back steps at Daniel's house in the afternoon, Maddy patted his dog, lying quietly beside her. Tucker, eh? He seemed like a nice dog. He didn't want to play anymore, but that was okay.

She shivered. She'd been warm enough while chasing Tucker around the yard, but now her hands and ears were cold, and she could feel a chill through the fabric of her pants.

She pulled her phone out of her pocket. There wasn't much point—it was still out of power. Without it she felt cut off, out of touch. She missed Emma, even though Emma had been a bit of a pill lately. But even if she could charge her phone, she couldn't contact Emma—she didn't want to answer a lot of questions. Emma would tell her parents, and they'd call her mom.

Giving Tucker another pat, Maddy wished she could at least check the time. Daniel had a clock in his kitchen; she'd look at it when she went in. Anyway, she guessed it was mid-afternoon. Not quite time for school to be out yet.

What were Emma and the others doing right now? Were they wondering where she was?

Chapter Twenty-Four

I headed for Emma's house just after 3:30. Nicole's car was in the driveway, and she and Emma were heading in the front door.

Nicole turned to me as I came up the sidewalk. "Susan, we've been so worried today! Is there any news?"

I shook my head. "No, there isn't." My throat caught. "I wish there were. But is it okay if I come in? I'd like to talk to Emma for a few minutes."

Emma looked at me warily.

Nicole put her arm around her daughter and brushed her hair off her forehead. "Of course," she said. "Come on in." She led the way to their kitchen, and the three of us sat around the table. Nicole sat next to Emma, watching both of us closely.

I did my best to mask my tension level as I turned to Emma. "Emma, have you heard from Maddy since yesterday?" I asked. "If you have, it's important to let us know."

Emma shook her head, her eyes glistening. "Uh-uh. I texted her last night, a bunch of times. And I tried again today. She hasn't answered." She wiped away a tear as I watched.

I squeezed her hand. "Emma, you're a good friend to Maddy. And you may think you need to keep her secrets, if she has any. But if you know anything about where she might be, you need to tell us. She could be in danger."

Emma gasped, and I could see pain in her eyes. "I know! I'm worried too."

I softened my voice. "Did you know she was going to run away?"

Nicole stared at me, and Emma bit her lip. Until then they'd just heard that Maddy was "missing." But this was no time for euphemisms.

Emma shook her head, her fingers twisting in her hair. "No! I had no idea." Lowering her head again, she added, "But she doesn't always tell me what she's thinking. Especially lately."

"Lately?"

She nodded. "Yeah. The last couple of weeks…"

"I thought you girls shared everything."

Her head was down, her black hair hanging in front of her face. Then she sat up and pushed it behind her ears. "Sometimes she just doesn't want to talk. Or I text her, and she doesn't answer."

I blinked. "So you have no idea where she might be?"

"No, I don't. Honest." Her chin quivered.

Try another tack. "When you two went to the mall the last few times, did you talk to any other kids?"

She shrugged. "We ran into a couple of girls from school one time. Megan and Alice."

"Are they in your class?"

"Uh-huh. They go to our dance class too."

"Did you talk to any strangers? Older girls? Or anyone else?"

"I don't think so. We just walked around and went into some stores and had a drink at the food court."

She shivered and leaned against her mother. Nicole turned to me. "What are you asking?"

"I wondered if they ran into someone who was trying to talk them into something." This sounded vague, but I didn't want to be more specific. I held my breath, afraid to hear any hint that Marie's speculation could apply to Maddy.

Emma looked puzzled. "No, we didn't."

Whew. She seemed honestly baffled at my question. Emma was generally truthful, to the point of being something of a goody-goody, so I figured I could rely on her denial.

"Can you think of anything else that I should know…?"

Her head was bent, but she gazed up at me through her eyelashes. "I know she sometimes wishes she was older and could make her own decisions, do what she wants."

I snorted without thinking. Maddy had been chafing at my rules more than ever lately. She'd thrown out "You treat me like a child!" more than a few times. So no surprise she'd complained about it to Emma.

Nicole leaned over, smoothing Emma's hair off her forehead. "I don't think Emma knows anything more." She added, "If she thinks of anything...you know we want to help any way we can."

I stood up, forcing a smile. "Thank you. I really appreciate it." I turned to Emma. "I know this is hard on you too. You're missing Maddy. We all want to find her."

She didn't answer, just leaned her head into Nicole's shoulder, her eyes filling.

****

Watching Tucker lying on Daniel's porch, Maddy tapped on the back door before opening it. Daniel was sitting at the table, reading a newspaper.

"Excuse me—do you have a cellphone charger?" she asked. "My phone's out of power."

He glanced up from his paper. "As a matter of fact, I do." He pointed to the counter. "It's over there."

Maddy pulled out her phone again and tried to insert the charger connector, but it didn't fit. Peering at it, she saw the connector was the wrong kind. She sighed.

"Do you need to make a phone call?"

She shook her head. "No, I just like to check things online." She wasn't ready to phone home, or to be home. Or to deal with her mom at all.

Though she hadn't spoken, Daniel must have read her thoughts on her face. "If you like, you could stay here tonight. I have a spare bedroom upstairs, and I can get you clean sheets and towels. I don't imagine you got a lot of sleep at your school last night."

Maddy suddenly realized she was exhausted. It would feel good to lie down. She looked at Daniel and nodded, "Okay, thanks."

Chapter Twenty-Five

As I returned home after talking to Nicole and Emma, Marie Boucher phoned. "I told you we were having a press conference. It'll be starting in about half an hour, in time to be broadcast on the six o'clock news. It'll hit tomorrow's newspapers too, and their online versions tonight."

The point of the press conference and publicity was to ask the public for help, but the idea of Maddy being "news" made me shudder. I texted Jenny; she came over so I wouldn't be by myself when the broadcast came on. She made me tea and held my hand as I watched, tears blurring my sight.

Maddy's face filled the screen, along with the number for the Missing Persons Unit and a toll-free number for Crime Stoppers. A police officer—Sergeant Bailey, head of Missing Persons—spoke, describing Maddy and the fact that she'd been missing since the evening before, and appealing to the public to watch for her and report any information or sighting of her.

When it was over, Jenny clicked off the TV. "They didn't mention Daniel, or abduction."

I swallowed. "They say Daniel couldn't have taken her. And she probably wasn't abducted." I stared at the mug in my hand. "I didn't want to think it, but it now seems clear that she ran away."

Jenny stared at me.

With a lump in my throat, I told her about the missing toothbrush and money. "It never crossed my mind she'd do this. I know we've been having battles lately—she says I have too many rules—but I didn't pick up any clues that she'd run away. Maybe I wasn't listening…"

Jenny's face had turned white. She put down her tea and leaned forward. "Oh, Susan, I'm so sorry."

I forced a smile. "Thanks." I appreciated her sympathy.

But there appeared to be more to her reaction. "No, I mean it. I really am sorry." She clutched her hands to her face. "I never told you—that movie. The plot. It didn't occur to me…"

"What are you talking about?"

"The movie I took Maddy and Emma to see on Saturday. *Wonderstruck*."

Why was she bringing that up now? "You said they loved it."

"They did. I thought they'd like it because it had a couple of twelve-year-olds in it. But—in the movie, both those kids ran away from home."

I stared at her.

She twisted her hands together. "I don't want to think the movie gave Maddy the idea. But maybe it normalized the concept in her mind, made it seem like something a kid her age could do."

I opened my mouth, about to ask what the hell she'd been thinking of, but then I choked back the thought. "Forget it. The movie didn't make her run away. If that was the case, Emma would be gone now too."

Jenny still looked uncomfortable, her face flushed.

"Well, I can't imagine that she'd run away just because you had a few arguments over rules."

"Well." My stomach twisted. "We had an awful fight in the car Monday on the way home from school."

"Even so…"

I drew a breath. "There's more. There was something else weighing on Maddy that day."

She turned to me; I had her attention.

"I told you we had DNA tests, right? With samples from Daniel, Maddy, and me."

"Right…"

"Last Sunday I got a call from Abel's friend Aisha. She works at that lab, and she said she wanted to give me a heads-up on the results."

"On Sunday? On the weekend?"

"I know, I thought it was strange too. But of course I went."

"What was the heads-up?"

"The test didn't show at all what we expected."

"I don't understand."

"You'll understand even less when I tell you." I took a deep breath. "The main report I was waiting for—comparing Daniel and Maddy—wasn't even ready yet. But Aisha wanted to talk about the maternal test, the one comparing Maddy and me."

"Well, that should be straightforward."

"It wasn't. It was horrible. I just don't understand it. It said they ruled me out as Maddy's biological mother."

Jenny's mouth fell open, her hand flying to her chest. "But that's ridiculous. I was in the delivery room. I saw Maddy being born." I'd been grateful to have her there. "And I've known her ever since. So that test has to be wrong."

"I know. The test *is* wrong. I just don't know how. I know she's my daughter, so how can a DNA test say otherwise? But Aisha swears the samples didn't get mixed up."

Jenny stared at me.

"Anyway, the point is that Aisha told me this on Sunday. I knew Daniel would get the report, the official one, and he wouldn't keep it secret. So I couldn't have Maddy hear about it from anyone else—I had to tell her myself. I did, on Sunday night."

"How did she react?"

"She didn't say a lot. I told her it was a mistake, that of course I'm her mother." Tears filled my eyes, and my mouth twisted. "But I'm not sure she believed me. She knew that DNA tests are considered accurate." I could scarcely force out the words. "She might have thought I was lying to her."

Jenny leaned forward. "Wow. But...I'm sure you were right to tell her."

I smiled at her through my tears.

"Listen." Her eyes drilled into mine. "This may be a stupid question, but...you used a sperm donor to get pregnant with Maddy. Could this DNA confusion have anything to do with that?"

I blinked. "No, it couldn't. It's not like she was a test-tube baby. She grew in my body just like any normal baby. It was my egg that was fertilized, inside me—the only difference is that the sperm was inserted by a doctor, not a sexual partner."

"Okay. I guess I knew that."

"Half of Maddy's genes came from me. So how can a DNA test not show that?"

Jenny placed both her hands over mine. "We'll figure this out. That test is wrong, and we'll find out why. Maddy will be back, and if she has any doubts you're her mother, we'll prove otherwise."

Brave words. But how?

****

Daniel turned on the TV to watch the six o'clock news, turning the sound low so as not to wake Maddy.

He expected her disappearance to be on the news, and it was. A middle-aged police officer stood at a podium. He had notes, but for the most part he looked straight into the camera as he spoke. The broadcast switched to a big photo of Maddy. It was a good likeness, showing her to be alert and friendly, with shining eyes and a bright smile. Kelly's smile, for sure.

The officer was asking the public to watch for her and to call in with any leads. He emphasized how young and vulnerable she was, and that she wasn't a streetwise kid. They were anxious to find her and urged everyone to be alert, to be good neighbors. To report anything that could help them find her.

Daniel groaned. This would make everything tougher. So far the girl had been willing to stay here—she'd even asked to stay—but he couldn't risk her seeing this kind of appeal. It might persuade her to go back to Susan. And with this amount of media coverage, there was a big risk someone would recognize her if they saw her.

Better start thinking of how to get her out of the city.

He had to ease her into the idea, get her used to him. She had to understand she belonged with him, belonged back on the farm.

148

In the meantime he should get rid of the TV. It was one of the few things of Aunt Ruby's he hadn't disposed of yet; he'd hung on to it so he could watch it in the evenings. But that was too risky now. He'd lock it away in one of the basement cupboards so she wouldn't see it.

Stay focused. Get Hannah home. Period.

Chapter Twenty-Six

Wednesday morning I woke early again, though this time I had at least made it to my bed the night before, and I'd managed to get a few hours' sleep. But on waking I was filled with fresh despair. Maddy had been gone for a day and a half. I was terrified for her.

Pulling on the same clothes I'd worn the day before, I stumbled downstairs. I roamed at loose ends from kitchen to living room, staring out windows as darkness faded to daylight. At least it looked like it would be a sunny day.

I desperately wanted to know if the police had made progress. But Marie hadn't given me her direct number, and I stopped myself from calling Bob; he was no longer on the case. They'd call if there was any sign of Maddy.

My body felt drained, every breath an effort. Despite having slept, my eyes stung, and my shoulders ached. I poured a glass of water in the kitchen and rinsed out my mouth, spitting into the sink. I refilled the glass and added ice. *I need to stay home again today.* In my current state, there was no way I could be of therapeutic help to anyone.

I tried once again to phone and text Maddy, though it seemed futile. The call went to voicemail, and there was no reply to the text. I needed to ask Marie if they had made more attempts to track her phone.

Then my phone rang—our landline, not my cellphone. It was Dorothy. "Good morning, Susan," she said. "I wanted to reach you before I head into the clinic."

I didn't know what Abel had told her yesterday. Surely she wasn't expecting me to come in this morning. I couldn't face it.

"I saw the news last evening," she said. "My heart goes out to you, my dear. How terrible that your daughter is missing! You must be at your wits' end."

Perhaps I made a sound, because she continued, "You don't have to tell me any details—I just wanted to let you know that you should take whatever time you need to deal with this. We'll handle all your appointments at the clinic, so don't worry about them. Just concentrate on finding your daughter."

****

Talking to Dorothy had given me a lift, but my mood was sinking again as my fears for Maddy returned. With nothing better to do, I headed into my home office and turned on my laptop. I'd already been watching for emails on my phone all morning. A new message had just popped in, this one from an address I didn't recognize. I was about to erase it, then hesitated. Maybe it was someone else reaching out as a result of last night's news.

It was from the DNA lab. But it wasn't from Aisha—in fact it wasn't very personal at all. It just said that the results of my recent test were available online. To access them I'd have to use the password they had given me at the time of testing.

Password? I didn't remember them giving me a password.

I reached into my top file drawer. Though I hardly remembered writing the label, here was a file marked DNA Test. Opening it, I saw I'd put in all the papers I received at the time of testing, along with the notes I took when I met with Aisha.

The paperwork confirmed the order I'd requested. A grandparent test and a maternity test. It also said I'd be notified by email when the reports were ready, and—hallelujah!—here was the password I'd need to access the report.

Back at my laptop, I clicked on the link to the lab's site. It said that the reports I'd requested were available. I carefully typed in the password.

I could hardly breathe as my fingers hovered over the keyboard. I was afraid to press Enter. This was the report Aisha had given me the heads-up for on Sunday.

CLICK.

The site loaded quickly, providing links to two reports.

Both were headed DNA Test Report. One was sub-headed *Maternity Test Report*. The other was *Grandparent Test Report*.

Both had columns, headings, and rows of numbers. Confused, I scanned the screen for cues. Focusing on the maternity report, I noted a boldfaced box.

INTERPRETATION: Alleged relationship is excluded.

In smaller type, the interpretation continued. "Based on the DNA analysis, the tested individual can be excluded as the biological mother of the tested child."

There was more, but my eyes went blurry, and I couldn't read any further.

It was just as Aisha had said. According to the report, my DNA and Maddy's did not match.

My stomach clenched. How was that possible? It was simply wrong, and I couldn't explain it. GTS was a reputable laboratory, and DNA testing was supposedly both routine and accurate. Yet somehow this test said I wasn't Maddy's mother.

I flipped to the second report, the grandparent report.

INTERPRETATION: Inconclusive.

My eyes stopped on the text below. "Insufficient data to determine whether the tested individual is the maternal grandfather of the tested child."

What did that mean? I was ruled out, but Daniel was not?

Does Daniel have these results now too?

My faced flushed with anger as I imagined a nightmare scenario—Maddy found, but Daniel still insisting he had a claim to her, while I'm unable to prove that she's mine.

If I didn't challenge that report, I'd be failing Maddy and failing myself.

Fighting nausea, I grabbed my phone and dialed Aisha's number.

Voicemail.

I left an urgent message for her to call me.

Chapter Twenty-Seven

While he waited for the girl to wake up Wednesday morning, Daniel went to check his email, thinking he might have something from his cousins or his neighbors back home. He'd left his laptop on the kitchen counter. He turned it on, waited for it to boot up, and clicked on Gmail.

There were a few new messages, though nothing much that drew his eye. Then one subject line jumped out at him—*DNA Test Results.*

A sudden excitement surged through him. This could be the answer he'd been waiting for! The message said he needed the password they'd they given him. He'd shoved the papers from the lab into one of the empty kitchen drawers. He shuffled through the pages and found it.

There were two reports. He clicked on the second one, the grandparent report. That was the one that interested him.

That's the one that'll prove Hannah's my granddaughter.

His eye was drawn to a box near the top of the report, with a heavy line around it and a heading in boldface.

INTERPRETATION: Inconclusive.

He read the text below. "Insufficient data to determine whether the tested individual is the maternal grandfather of the tested child."

Disappointment thudded into his midsection. What did "insufficient data" mean?

He didn't understand much about how DNA worked, or in fact what they were testing. He just knew the test was somehow supposed to prove identity.

He had been sure it would prove his relationship to Hannah. That's why he had gladly provided the sample.

And now it had proved nothing.

He got up and paced around the kitchen. He pulled a glass out of the cupboard and filled it with water, then took a deep drink. He watched Tucker for a minute, curled up in the corner under the window, one ear twitching in his sleep.

This was a blow. Not that he was discouraged—he didn't really need proof. He knew the girl was Hannah. But it would have been easier if the test had proved it.

Wait. "Inconclusive" doesn't mean "no."

It meant he hadn't been ruled out.

He returned to his laptop and stared at the screen. He still couldn't make any sense of the report, and the more he looked at it the more confused he felt.

Then he remembered the other report. Maternity report. He hadn't realized it at the time, but apparently Susan had been tested too, since she said she was the girl's mother.

A sinking feeling filled him. What if this report said she was right? He clicked on the report. Just like the other one, it had a boldfaced box near the top.

INTERPRETATION: Alleged relationship is excluded.

Below, it said, "Based on the DNA analysis, the tested individual can be excluded as the biological

155

mother of the tested child." Wait—what? He read it again.

Susan was not Maddy's mother.

This one wasn't "inconclusive." This one was definite.

This was vindication.

Susan isn't the girl's mother.

He could hear Hannah stirring upstairs now. She'd be down soon, and he'd make her breakfast. Something she'd like. Maybe pancakes.

The report changed everything. No way was he going to let her go back to Susan. This made it all the more clear—they had to get back to Alberta, to the farm. To her true home, where she belonged.

As Patricia had always said, the only thing that mattered after Kelly and Jacob died was finding Hannah. Satisfaction and relief filled him. *I'll bring her home as soon as I can.*

But he needed more time. She was willing to stay with him for now, but that willingness was still shaky. He needed time to win her over, get her to accept that she was Hannah and that she should come back home with him.

He couldn't risk her being found in the meantime.

The first thing was to gain her confidence. He'd start by making her a good breakfast. And he'd better find ways to keep her busy, keep her entertained. What did a girl her age like to do? Most kids these days were on their phones all the time, but hers was out of juice. That was just as well—she couldn't get calls or messages. Couldn't send them. He was glad about that.

He'd better hide this laptop too. There were already too many online references to her disappearance.

Couldn't have her seeing those.

****

Maddy woke with a start, confused at first about where she was. Feeling something warm, she turned over. *Oh!* It was Tucker, curled up sound asleep beside her.

She recognized the room; she was at Daniel's house. For a moment she was sorry about everything. Sorry to have left her home, missing her familiar room and the usual routines. And missing her mom. If she were home now, Mom would be making her breakfast. The thought struck her with a pang. *Mom must be so mad.*

Pushing the thoughts away, she swung her legs out of bed and reached for her backpack. She was feeling grungy, still wearing the same clothes she'd left home in two nights ago. She hadn't brought much with her, but she did have a change of underwear. And another shirt and a different pair of jeans.

Stepping into the bathroom, she found fresh towels folded on the end of the tub. *That was nice of him.* She brushed her teeth and washed her face, pulling the elastic out of her hair so she could smooth it out and redo the ponytail.

Finally she went downstairs, feeling more than a little awkward. Daniel was in the kitchen, standing at the stove. "I heard you upstairs, so I got breakfast started. I hope you like pancakes."

She had a flash of memory. *Grandpa used to make me pancakes.* The memory was bittersweet—she missed him, but the image also eased her discomfort. And she was definitely hungry; she hadn't eaten since the soup and grilled cheese at lunch the day before.

She'd been too tired to eat anything last night, had just gone to bed.

She sank into a chair at the table. Daniel put two pancakes on her plate and pushed the maple syrup toward her. "Was Tucker up there with you?" Maddy smiled. "Mmm-hmm. He was lying beside me when I woke up."

Daniel smiled. "He and I were out for a walk early this morning, but I guess he decided to join you after we got back."

When she finished the pancakes, Maddy took her plate to the sink and rinsed it off. She didn't know what else to do with it, so she left it in the sink along with her knife and fork.

She was restless. Scanning the room, her eyes fell on the dog's leash. "Could I take Tucker for a walk?"

Daniel stiffened. Seeing him frown, she thought he was going to say no, but he must have changed his mind, or maybe she'd misinterpreted his first reaction. "All right, but just a short one. Tucker's a bit tired this morning."

"I just want some fresh air. We won't be long." She didn't want anyone to notice her, but she thought a short walk wouldn't hurt.

She took Tucker down the block a ways. He didn't seem all that tired, in fact walked along briskly. The sky was blue overhead, and the sun warmed her shoulders. There wasn't anybody around that she could see. She let Tucker off the leash so he could run a bit, but when she had to retrieve him from somebody's backyard she decided it was time to go back.

Daniel was waiting for them on the front porch. "How was your walk?" he asked.

"It was good," she said. She didn't mention letting Tucker off the leash or the game of chase they'd had, in case Daniel disapproved.

He followed her into the kitchen. When she'd hung Tucker's leash back up on the hook where she'd found it, he said, "There's something we should talk about."

She turned to him. His eyes were in shadow.

"You know we gave samples to the DNA lab," he began.

Maddy nodded.

He was watching her. "They've sent the report."

Did it say what Mom said?

"They said they didn't have enough information to prove you're my granddaughter." He heaved a sigh. "They called it *inconclusive*." He gave her a glance. "Do you know what that means?"

Maddy raised her eyebrows. "I think so."

"It means they can't say one way or another whether I'm right or wrong." He shrugged. "So much for science; they haven't proved anything." He tightened his lips. "But I know I'm right."

Then he frowned. "But there was another report with it. This one compared you with Susan." He watched her as he spoke. "And it said that Susan isn't your mother."

Maddy said nothing.

He cleared his throat. "The report was definite about that. You aren't her child."

Maddy blinked. "I know," she whispered.

His eyes snapped wide open. "You already knew that?" He leaned forward. "What did Susan tell you?"

Maddy recoiled from his intensity. "Just that part. She told me Sunday night."

Lis Angus

Daniel's shoulders dropped. "Ah. The night before you left. Is that why you ran away?"

"I didn't run away," she protested. "I'm just...taking a break." *From my mother,* she thought, but she didn't want to say that out loud, in front of Daniel.

Sudden tears pricked her eyelids. She stood and went over to the sink, pouring herself a drink of water. She wasn't thirsty, but she didn't want to cry in front of him.

Her mom *had* told her about the report, but she said the report was wrong. *But how can it be?* DNA testing was always being used to prove things. It must be right.

If Mom isn't my real mom, who is she? Or...who am I?

And is Daniel my grandpa or not?

Suddenly everything she knew was in question. Maybe this was where she belonged, with Daniel. Maybe the life back with her mom—*or whoever she is*—was a lie all along.

Taking her glass of water to the table, she sat back down. There was something more she wanted to know. "How did Hannah disappear?"

He grimaced and turned his head away, staring blankly out the window. "There was a snowstorm. Kelly and Jacob—my daughter and her husband—were driving from our farm to Edmonton and got caught in the storm. They had a bad accident, and both of them died in the crash."

Maddy shivered. "Oh my God. So what about Hannah?"

"She was in her car seat in the back when they left our place. But when the police came to the accident—they weren't found until the next morning, when the

160

storm was over—Hannah wasn't there. The car seat was empty."

Maddy stared, not quite grasping what he was telling her. "Where was she?"

"We don't know. Somebody took her."

Maddy blinked. How horrible. That poor baby girl! Then she realized. "And you think I'm her."

"Yeah, I do."

She took a breath. She couldn't avoid it—she had to say something about the report. "But the test doesn't say I'm your granddaughter."

He frowned. "It also doesn't say you're not. It said *inconclusive*."

So...what if she *was* that baby. If she wasn't her mom's child, she had to be somebody's.

"If I was Hannah, how did I end up with my mom?"

"With Susan?" Daniel's shoulders raised and fell. "I don't have an answer to that."

"Don't you have some idea?"

"Not really. Somebody must have taken you away, removed you from the accident." He glanced at her. "And one way or another, you ended up with Susan."

Images swirled through Maddy's head, but none of them made sense to her. She couldn't picture her mom getting a baby passed to her, like a parcel. There had to be some other explanation.

She suddenly didn't want to think about this anymore or talk about it. She stood up. "Do you have a washing machine? I want to wash the clothes I wore yesterday."

He looked surprised at the change of subject but pushed back his chair. "Yeah, it's in the basement. It's

old and a little tricky. If you give me your things, I'll
wash them for you."

Chapter Twenty-Eight

After a shower I felt fresher, though still wobbly from reading the DNA report. When the doorbell rang, I was surprised to see Bob on my doorstep.

He took off his hat. "Can I come in for a few minutes?"

"Sure." I invited him into the kitchen. "Can I get you a coffee?" The pot was nearly full—I'd only had one cup so far.

"I guess I have time for a quick one." He'd moved into the kitchen doorway.

I filled two mugs and set them on the counter, gesturing for him to take one. "Are you here with an update?"

He stirred milk into his coffee. "No—Missing Persons is in charge now."

"I know—Marie came to see me yesterday. She had another guy with her, Kevin somebody."

"That'll be Kevin Wheeler. They got the investigation moving right away."

I nodded. "They seemed to know what they were doing. She called me again later, said they searched Daniel's place again and found no trace of Maddy. But I haven't heard from her since." He looked at me, eyebrow raised. I added, "I know her focus is finding Maddy, not updating me. But"—I could hear a hitch in my voice—"I want to know what's going on."

"I'm sure she'll keep you in the loop."

I turned away, shuffling some things around in the cupboard to mask the tears that threatened to fall. What was he doing here? He didn't have anything to report and wasn't even involved in the investigation.

He leaned against the doorjamb, sipping his coffee. "Have you had any result yet from the DNA tests you ordered?"

My breath caught. "No."

I was glad I had my back to him. I was sure my expression would have given me away. I didn't even regret the lie—no way was I going to tell him about that test result. At least not until I had an explanation.

"We may have another way," he said. "My buddy Mac called to say that the RCMP lab in Edmonton still has DNA from Hannah Byers. It's from hair and a few nail clippings left at her grandparents' house before she disappeared."

I swiveled, my eyes on him.

"It was never added to the National DNA Data Bank or the Missing Person's Index—they weren't set up yet when Hannah disappeared. But the lab can upload Hannah's DNA data now, so we can compare it to Maddy's."

My heart leapt. "And if Maddy isn't Hannah—which she isn't—the DNA won't match."

"That's right." He put down his mug. "He's going to do his best to fast-track the analysis. It'll come under his budget, since Hannah is still an open case on his docket."

A week ago this would have seemed like the answer to all our problems. But now... "We just need to find her. No DNA test is going to do that. Anyway, I thought you weren't involved anymore."

"I'm not part of Missing Persons; they're in charge. But I told you I'd stay in touch. And when Mac phoned me about this, I thought you'd want to follow it up."

He was right. Though for the moment I'd lost faith in DNA tests. "Still, the main thing right now is finding her."

"Sure, of course. But we can get this test underway at the same time we're searching for Maddy."

"I guess that makes sense." *We'll still need to get rid of Daniel.*

"We need something that has Maddy's DNA on it."

I rubbed my arms. "I think there's a hairbrush in her bathroom upstairs. Hair's a good way to get someone's DNA, isn't it?"

"Yeah, if the hairs have roots attached. And we have to be sure it's her hair—not yours, for example."

"I don't use her brush. We don't even use the same bathroom. And my hair's darker."

"Okay. Let's go look."

I started for the stairs but doubled over with a sudden cramp. A sob burst out of my throat. "This all seems so...what if she's..." I couldn't finish the sentences.

He lifted me by the elbow. "I know this is terrible for you. But we *will* find her."

"Alive?" I forced out the word.

His face darkened. "There's no reason to think otherwise."

I was doing my best to stay positive, to push away the dire possibilities that threatened to flood my brain. But it was getting harder.

Needing to tamp down the dread I was feeling, I

welcomed any kind of movement. I turned to lead him upstairs for Maddy's hairbrush.

****

Back downstairs, Bob stopped in the front hallway. "I've been wondering—if you don't mind me asking—have you thought about why Maddy would run away?"

I stared at him. Of course I had.

But I wasn't sure how much I was ready to share. "I don't know. I find it hard to accept that it happened at all." I dropped my eyes. "I *have* been thinking about it, though. A lot."

"So...what are your thoughts?" He didn't seem in a hurry to leave; now he was leaning against the kitchen doorway, his hands in his pockets.

I swallowed and sank onto the second-from-bottom stair, an ache rising in my throat. "She and I have had a lot of arguments these last few months—even more lately. Almost every day there was something. And that last day, we had a fight in the car on the way home."

His face was in shadow, so I couldn't read his expression. I continued, somehow relieved to be blurting this all out. "She wanted to walk across the park to her friend's house that night, and I wouldn't let her."

I drew a breath. "She didn't like the restrictions I'd placed on her to keep her safe. She was upset at Halloween, when she wanted to roam with her friends. I'd already said okay, earlier, but with Daniel in the picture, I changed my mind and said no."

He folded his arms. "So you think that's why she left?"

"Maybe." I eyed him speculatively. Up to now I'd only dealt with him as a police officer, but maybe he'd

166

have some comments as a dad? "You said you have kids. Are any of them teenagers?"

He nodded. "Yup, all three of them. Olivia's seventeen, and the twins are fourteen. Ryan and Ethan."

"Have any of them ever run away?"

"No, and as far as I know they haven't considered it. But they live with their mom, so I don't see them every day."

I grimaced. "So maybe you don't know what I'm talking about."

"Maybe not. But even though they don't live with me, I stay involved with them."

I rubbed my hands over my face. "I hate that Maddy would leave without talking to me. But...maybe I just wasn't listening." I glanced back at him, but he didn't say anything, just raised his eyebrows. "When I think about our arguments, they mostly consist of her wanting to do something and me saying no."

"Yeah, a lot of conversations with teenagers are like that."

I sighed. "I'm supposed to know all about kids. What they need at different ages. I can't tell you how many books I've studied about child psychology...but when it comes down to my own daughter, I'm at a loss."

"At least you come at it with some knowledge. Jessie and I were pretty much flying by the seats of our pants when our kids hit the teen years."

"So...did you figure it out?"

"Who knows? But our kids seem okay so far."

I watched him. He was staring at his hands.

He continued. "Jessie and I've been divorced since last year. But the kids were never the problem. We've stayed on the same page as to how we handle them."

"And how is that?" I wanted to know.

"Well, when they were getting to be teenagers, we decided we had to start holding back a bit. Let them decide some things for themselves. Not always put our own judgment first."

I groaned. "That's what I have trouble with."

"Jessie has a poster she framed and put up on the wall in the kitchen. It's a poem. I don't have it memorized, but its first line says 'Your children are not your children.' "

"I think I know that poem. By Khalil Gibran, right?"

He shrugged. "I didn't check out the author. But I think the message is that you can't live your kids' lives for them."

A sob rose in my throat. I choked it back down. "Right now I just want to know she *has* a life, that she's alive. I need her back home."

Chapter Twenty-Nine

After Bob left late Wednesday morning, I paced from room to room, my mind churning. Maddy had been away for two nights now. I felt helpless, my fears for her reverberating endlessly through my mind. I had to get out of the house.

Pulling on a light jacket, I plunged into our nearby park, striding across the grass and the fallen leaves toward the canal on the far side. The weather was milder than I'd expected, with the sun shining and very little wind. The fresh air was helping to clear my head. I breathed in deeply, absorbing the musky late-fall scents of damp leaves and dying grass. My cellphone buzzed in my jacket pocket. I pulled it out. The display said "Ottawa Police." My heart speeding, I swiped to answer it.

"Hi, Susan. It's Marie. I wanted to bring you up to date."

I was glad to hear her voice, anxious for any news. "You haven't found her?" The words tumbled out of my mouth—I couldn't help asking, though if that were the case, Marie would have already told me.

"No, I'm sorry. But we have a lot of activity under way—"

"What about the press conference? Did you get any calls from that?" Surely there had to be something…

"There were a few calls, but so far nothing has

169

checked out."

I clenched my fists in frustration and fear. "So nothing is happening."

"That's not true; we have many initiatives under way. We checked with all hospitals and walk-in clinics yesterday, and again today. We've briefed all our personnel at every shift, and all our patrol cars have her photo and description. We're checking again with all the friends on the list you gave us, and we've probed her social media contacts."

More nothing.

Marie continued, "Our youth officers have been circulating among homeless kids to see if any of them have seen her. And we've alerted shelters and other agencies that come in contact with street kids."

I protested, "Maddy's no street kid." She might be technically on the street, but I wasn't willing to define her that way.

She made a *pssh* sound. "We know. But we have to explore every possibility."

"Have you checked Daniel again?"

Silence. "No, but we've already been through his place twice, and we confirmed that he was otherwise occupied when she disappeared. We have to focus our resources where they'll be useful, not retrace steps we've already taken."

"But you haven't found any leads." I couldn't keep the frustration out of my voice.

"These are all important activities. And we're reaching out to the public, asking people to watch for her. We've started distributing the poster with Maddy's photo. You said you could arrange for further postering? The more widely it's distributed, the better."

"Yes, of course. Can you bring me the posters, or should I pick them up?"

"I'll drop them at your place at the end of the day."

Good. I'd call Jenny, see if she could help.

She continued. "We want to keep pressuring the public for help. CTV says they'd like to do a TV interview with you—I know we've been trying to keep the media from hounding you, but we think broadcasting a personal appeal from you would be a good idea." She raised an inquiring eyebrow.

"If you think it'll help—"

"It can't hurt. We'll be doing another press conference tomorrow, and if they have an interview with you to air too, that can really strengthen the appeal."

"Sure. When do they want to do the taping?"

"I think they want to do it tomorrow morning, if that works for you."

****

As Daniel wiped the table after lunch, he asked, "Do you like to play cards?"

Maddy glanced at him. "What kind of cards?" She sometimes played Go Fish and Uno with Emma, but she didn't know any other games.

"How about Rummy?" She shook her head. "I can teach you." He left the room for a minute, then came back with a deck of cards and sat at the table. He shuffled the cards without looking, like he'd had a lot of practice. "Come and sit down. I'll tell you how the game works."

They played three games. Maddy lost every time, but she was getting better at it. He was patient, pointing out times when she could have made a better move, and nodding approvingly when she made a good one. She had another memory flash, this time back to when Grandpa was showing her how to play chords on the guitar. He'd been patient too, just like this.

Partway through the afternoon the skies darkened, and it started to rain. A sharp wind blew around the house, rattling the windows—good weather for staying indoors. Daniel opened a bag of potato chips, and the two of them snacked as they played cards. At one point they noticed Tucker under the table, licking chip crumbs off the floor. That made them laugh.

"Do you want pizza for supper, or hot dogs?" he asked, as he packed the cards away in their box.

Wow—Mom would have a fit. Maddy's eyes widened, and she couldn't help but smile. Who cared about healthy meals? "Pizza, please. If you don't mind."

"Anything for my girl."

She watched him. She found herself wondering, *What if he's right? What if I am his?*

Chapter Thirty

After trying—and failing—to force myself to eat some lunch, I tossed my cheese sandwich in the garbage and grabbed my keys. I couldn't face more hours of staring out windows or waiting for phone calls. I had to move, to do something.

Knowing that aimless searching made no sense, I nevertheless drove up and down streets, examining the faces of pedestrians, peering into every laneway and recessed doorway. My fears and frustration mounted with every failure to see any sign of Maddy, but I kept going.

Luckily the mid-afternoon traffic wasn't heavy, because my attention was not on my driving. I had a couple of close calls and a few angry drivers blaring their horns at me.

Though the weather had still been clear when I left home, half an hour later big raindrops started falling on my windshield. The skies darkened, and wind was buffeting my car. By the time I reached Wellington Street, passing by the Parliament Buildings on my left, their stone walls were barely visible through the driving rain. Even leaning forward I could hardly see the top of the Peace Tower, and the few pedestrians on the sidewalks were scurrying to find somewhere dry.

I could only hope that Maddy wasn't out in this. It was hard to even pretend that I had a chance to find her.

All that this fruitless drive had accomplished was giving me the illusion of doing something. I headed down O'Connor Avenue, my windshield wipers valiantly working to give me a view of the street ahead. By the time I arrived home, I was wondering why I'd thought this trip made any sense.

****

Tom phoned around five. After asking if there was any news about Maddy, he asked if I'd had any result from the DNA test yet. "I thought the report was due by now."

I should have expected him to ask about it—he'd been there when I demanded the test, after all—but I wasn't ready with an answer. I realized I couldn't hide the result from him, though.

"Yes, it came through this morning."

"Well—?"

"It's not a good result."

"What do you mean?"

"The report on Daniel is inconclusive. Due to insufficient data, apparently." I drew a breath. "But the maternal test, the one comparing Maddy and me, is not showing that I'm Maddy's mother. It says—" I took a breath. "It says I'm excluded as her mother."

Silence. "How's that possible?"

"I don't know!" My denial suddenly seemed ludicrous. I was flying in the face of science; how could I counter the accuracy of DNA?

But Tom wasn't a lawyer for nothing. "Could there be a problem with the sample collection, or a mix-up in samples?"

All right. "That's the only explanation that makes sense. Because, believe me, I am her mother. But the

174

say there was no mix-up."

Another brief silence. "Will Daniel get those results too?"

"I assume he already has them."

"This isn't good. He'll latch on to that as proof."

My throat tightened. "I know."

Aisha still hadn't returned my call. I checked her number and phoned again. This one went to voicemail as well, so all I could do was leave another message. "Aisha, I need to speak to you. That maternal test is wrong. We need to figure out how that could have happened. I know you don't believe me, but...something is definitely not right with that test. Please call me back as soon as possible."

****

I called Jenny after talking to Tom. She asked how I was doing.

"I forced myself to have a shower and put on clean clothes this morning. But it somehow seemed wrong to spend any time on things like that."

"Don't be silly. Neglecting yourself won't help Maddy."

I sighed. "And then I spent the afternoon driving around like an idiot, telling myself I was searching for her. I'm lucky I didn't have an accident." I refocused. "But that's not why I'm calling. The police want to know if we can put up a bunch of posters about Maddy. Marie said she'd be dropping them off later. I was hoping to work on that tonight...but now with this rain—"

Jenny broke in. "Look outside—the rain has already stopped."

She was right; the sky was now clear. Just another

example of Ottawa's unpredictable November weather.

"Okay—assuming Marie does deliver the posters, would you be able to help me with them tonight?"

"Of course! And I'll see if we can get a couple of helpers."

Chapter Thirty-One

Daniel pulled the pizza from the oven and divided it up on two plates.

The card games this afternoon had gone well. He could see she was relaxing, getting more comfortable with him. That was the whole point.

Get her to like being with you.

He called up the stairs. "Hannah, supper's ready." He no longer hesitated to call her by her right name. That other name was from her life with Susan. That was over now.

She came downstairs, carrying one of the books he'd found for her earlier. They'd been tucked away in the basement—looked like old-fashioned books for girls. He didn't know if she liked to read, but she had seemed glad to get them.

"How's that book?" he asked. "Which one are you reading?"

She held the cover up. "*Little Women*. It's good."

"What's it about?"

She sat down at the table, laying the book beside her plate. "It's about some girls. They live with their mom. It's in olden times." She picked up her pizza and took a big bite.

Daniel nodded, chewing. He couldn't think of anything else to ask her about the book. They ate in silence for a few minutes.

177

Meanwhile Patricia kept whispering to him. *Start talking about going to the farm. Sell her on the idea.*

He knew they couldn't stay here much longer. Police were putting her photo out there, asking people to watch for her. And they might come back, check his house again.

Get her away from here. Don't let them take Hannah.

Staying in this area was a risk. Someone could recognize her, and he couldn't let that happen. They had to get on the road, get out of the city.

But he first had to get her thinking that way. "What would you say about going on a trip?"

Her eyes narrowed. "Who? You and me?"

"And Tucker."

She swallowed the bite she'd been chewing. "What kind of trip?"

"A trip in the truck. The weather looks good for a few days, and we could head out west."

She pushed the pizza around her plate. "Where out west?"

"I was thinking we'd head for Alberta. To the farm." Seeing her blank expression, he added, "Where I live."

She frowned. "I thought you lived here."

"No, this was my aunt's house. She died in the spring. I'm just clearing it out, getting it ready for sale." He reached for another slice of pizza. "My home's in Alberta. Our home. We'll go back there."

She didn't say anything, just took a bite of her pizza and chewed it, watching him.

Tell her about the farm.

"It's a grain farm, mostly…" He could see her

losing interest.

Don't be so boring.

What would grab her attention? "The neighbors raise alpacas—you know what those are. They're from South America? Look like llamas or little camels?"

She turned back to him, her eyes widening. So she was interested in animals?

Encouraged, he continued. "They're friendly and fun to watch—they race around like crazy sometimes. That farm has goats and sheep too."

She rubbed her hand across her mouth. "Do you have animals on your own farm? Like cows?"

Good—she was asking questions. "No, not anymore. We used to raise beef cattle, and we had chickens and turkeys, but we gave them up."

Too bad. That sounds more interesting than grain.

"But across the road there's a horse farm, with riding stables. Have you ever ridden a horse?"

She'd perked up now. "No, but I'd like to."

He went on. "And we do have wild animals. There are deer living in the woods behind our barn. They come right up into the yard sometimes, almost up to the porch. And there are beavers who've built a dam in our creek; they're pretty interesting."

He remembered something else. "There's a treehouse I built for Kelly. It's still in good shape. You could have fun up there."

She raised her eyebrows but didn't say anything. She'd finished her pizza, all but the last crust.

He watched her uneasily. He probably shouldn't push this too hard yet. That was enough for now, get her thinking. "We can talk about it more tomorrow. Would you like to play cards again tonight?"

"Okay." She pushed back her chair and took her plate to the sink, throwing her crust to Tucker on the way. He caught it before it hit the floor.

Daniel filled the sink with hot water and wiped the counter. Patricia always insisted on a tidy kitchen.

Maddy sat at the table, dealing out the cards after an awkward attempt at shuffling them.

He weighed the logistics of them leaving. They had to get out of the city without her being recognized.

Try to find a way to disguise her.

Could he cut her hair? Or maybe just cover it up. If it was cold, she could wear a toque. Or a baseball cap. And he'd have to get her another jacket, not the green one that was mentioned in the broadcast.

But he didn't want to tell her it was a disguise. She didn't know there'd been a citywide alert.

She didn't have many clothes with her at all, just what she was wearing. Maybe she had brought something else in her backpack, but it couldn't be much. She'd need more things.

He'd never shopped for a girl—Patricia had done all the shopping for Kelly, before Kelly started to buy her own clothes. But he supposed he could get her some clean underwear at least. Maybe a sweater or two. And some mitts.

He watched her sorting the cards in her hand. "You'll need more clothes for the trip," he said. "I'll get some things for you tomorrow."

She raised her eyes. "Can I come with you?"

"No," he said, "you need to stay inside the house while I'm gone." He could see she was about to object, so he quickly added the point she'd made herself earlier. "You don't want anyone to see you. Not yet anyway. Right? Isn't that what you said yesterday?"

She gave a small nod, looking uncertain.

He continued, "After a couple of days on the road, we'll find a place to do some more shopping. You can pick out what you like then."

"All right." She appeared to accept that. She gathered up the cards and reshuffled them.

Plans for the trip kept swirling in his head. He didn't think they could get away sooner than Saturday; he had to do that shopping, and there were still things to do around the house before he left. Besides, he wanted to get on the road early, and there'd be less of a morning rush hour on a Saturday. He'd have to let Gord and Pete know that he was leaving. There wasn't much left for them to do on the house, anyway.

Tomorrow he'd see if he could finish replacing the post on the back porch that he'd been working on. Along with shopping for Hannah's clothes.

****

Marie dropped off the pile of posters at my house around seven. Most were on letter-size paper, though a dozen or so were blown up to a bigger size. The poster was bilingual, with MISSING PERSON/PERSONNE DISPARUE in large print across the top, and Maddy's name underneath. An image of her smiling face was centered below that. It was the photo I'd given Bob the night before. The bottom third of the poster gave details about Maddy, in both English and French—age, height, coloring, when she disappeared, what she was wearing—followed by an appeal for anyone who had information to call the Missing Persons' phone number.

Staring at the poster, I felt a chill. Somehow seeing it in print solidified Maddy's absence, made it official.

But I squared my shoulders and turned to Jenny, who was standing beside me in the hallway. "Right. Let's get as many of these up tonight as we can."

She nodded. "Tom's wife, Amy, is coming to help, and so's my next-door neighbor Bonnie. They'll be here in a few minutes."

"You're great. Thanks." I could always count on Jenny to be practical, to get things moving.

And move we did, the four of us, putting up posters on both sides of Bank Street all the way from Wellington to the canal. Amy and Jenny took the west side of the street, while Bonnie and I did the east.

Bonnie proved to be a young mother in her thirties, energetic and cheerful, wearing a puffy jacket and toque against the cold. The two of us developed a rhythm as we moved down the street, one carrying our stack of posters, the other attaching them to poles. Amy and Jenny were using a similar routine.

By nine we were exhausted. I had imagined covering the city with posters. But it was going to take more than one evening to get posters distributed even in the main areas of the downtown, let alone farther out.

Much as I hoped the posters would prove unnecessary—surely Maddy would be back by tomorrow?—I couldn't keep dark fears from burying that hope. *What's she going through?*

Jenny and Amy crossed the street to join us. Amy said, "If it's okay with you, I'll post a copy of the poster on social media and ask people to repost. Hopefully we can reach a lot of people on Facebook and Twitter. And Instagram."

My depleted energy level must have shown in my face. Jenny took one look and said, "I think we've done as much as we can do tonight. We can come again tomorrow, and we'll get more people to help."

Part of me wanted to insist we should keep going. But she was right. It was time to call it a night.

****

After Hannah was in bed, Daniel locked the front and back doors, pushing the sliding deadbolts into place; these were positioned high enough that he didn't think she could easily reach them. From his earlier work at the house, he knew most of the windows were painted shut, other than a couple in the kitchen, which she likely wouldn't figure out.

He stared at the door of the room Hannah was using. It didn't have a lock, and it opened inward. He couldn't think of a way to make sure she stayed in there, but decided it'd be okay. She might need the bathroom in the night anyway.

And he was a light sleeper. He'd hear her if she left her room.

Chapter Thirty-Two

Marie phoned Thursday morning, just as the aroma of fresh coffee was filling my kitchen. "I'll be stopping by to see you shortly, if that's okay."

Her tone put me on high alert. "What's going on? Has something happened?"

A brief pause. "There's been a small development. I'll be at your place in about fifteen minutes."

"Wait! Can't you tell me now?" But she had already hung up.

My pulse was racing. What could a "small development" mean? Was it good news or bad news? On impulse, I lit a fire in the fireplace to take the chill out of the air. The kindling had just begun to crackle when Marie rang the doorbell.

She came in, shedding her coat in the hallway. She bustled into the living room and held her hands out to the flames that were now shooting up. "It's a good day for a fire." Turning, she added, "I have a few things to tell you. Shall we sit here?"

She moved to one of the armchairs, seating herself and pulling out her notebook, nodding to the mug of coffee I set next to her. She had a kind, almost motherly manner that I found soothing.

"The first thing is that there's been a possible sighting of Maddy."

My breathing stopped.

"It's not confirmed yet, so it may not lead to anything. But we got a call this morning from a woman who thinks she might have seen her in a coffee shop on Bank Street on Tuesday morning."

I breathed again. "The morning after she disappeared?"

"Exactly. The caller didn't pay a lot of attention at the time, but after she saw the news about Maddy being missing, she thought that a girl she'd seen in the coffee shop might have been her."

My spirits dropped; *nothing certain*. "Do you think it really was Maddy?"

"I spoke to the woman myself. She thinks the girl looked like Maddy. She's certain it was Tuesday morning, because she and a friend meet there for coffee every Tuesday. But they were in a conversation, not watching people in the room. So she didn't notice if there was someone else with the girl, or how long she was there."

I didn't know what to think. "So…"

"There's not a lot we can follow up from that, so you might think it's not useful information."

That's what I was thinking.

"But if it was Maddy, it does tell us a couple of things. First, she was still in Ottawa that morning—so she wasn't taken out of the city overnight." She shifted in her chair, her eyes on me. "And it tells us that she made it through the night without freezing and was warm and possibly getting something to eat on Tuesday morning."

My heart lifted. "Right. That *would* be a relief. It was awfully cold Monday night."

"So, assuming it was her, it means she must have

found somewhere to take shelter. Maybe with other homeless youth— that's why we've been questioning in those circles. She could have gone to the coffee shop with one of them."

I hated the way she said "found somewhere" and "other homeless youth." Thinking of Maddy in those terms turned my stomach.

"Listen," I said. "She ran away—I accept that. And she might have been okay Tuesday morning, if it was actually Maddy that woman saw. But it's now two days later. Who knows what's happened in the meantime? Somebody could have grabbed her…"

Marie rested her hand on my arm. "Don't let yourself dwell on bad things. She may have found shelter with someone who thinks they're helping her."

I shook her off. "That's still not okay. It can't be legal to hide a runaway."

"No, it's not. Concealing or harboring a minor is a crime. And she's under fourteen, so just keeping her away from the control of her parent or legal guardian is illegal, regardless of whether she consented or not."

"And what if—"

"The main thing now is to find her."

I nodded. Of course.

Marie continued. "We've been checking her social media accounts, but she hasn't posted anything since she disappeared. And we keep trying to get a location on her cellphone, but so far no luck. Apparently she hasn't found a way to charge her phone."

I picked up the poker to stoke the fire, rearranging the logs so they'd burn more steadily. Despite the radiating heat, I shivered.

****

Local CTV journalist Karen Dijksma arrived at my house an hour later along with a cameraman. She was dressed casually, in jeans and a gray turtleneck, her hair pulled back in a clasp.

While the cameraman was setting up his video camera and tripod in the living room, she sat down with me at the kitchen table. "We'll broadcast this later today, along with coverage from the police press conference," she said. "We hope the coverage will help, that it'll alert people to watch for Maddy."

I fervently hoped so too. "Do I look okay?" I asked. I had tried to dress simply for the taping, a pale blue pullover and black slacks; supposedly solid colors work better on TV. I'd brushed my hair back and put on a little lipstick.

Karen patted my hand. "You look fine. Very appropriate."

My stomach tightened. "How'll we do this? Will you be asking me questions?"

"No. You should speak directly to the camera. That way, whoever is watching will feel like you're speaking to them."

"I'm not sure what I should say." I'd been trying to rehearse in my mind, but everything felt wrong.

"Just relax. Speak naturally, from your heart. You're talking to Maddy, and to people in the public who you hope will help find her." She stood up. "And don't worry about being perfect. We can do multiple takes."

Seated in front of the camera, I was awkward at first, stumbling over my words and repeating myself.

After a few tries, though, I figured out what I wanted to say, and the words flowed more smoothly.

"Maddy, I miss you terribly. I love you, and I want you home very much. Home isn't the same without you. I'm very worried about you, and I need to know you're safe. Oscar and I are waiting for you at home."

The first time I mentioned Oscar, Karen raised her eyebrows questioningly. "Our cat. Maddy loves him." Karen nodded, and he stayed in the final version.

"I hope everyone who sees this video will watch for Maddy. We need your help to find her. She's only twelve, and she's been missing since Monday night. She needs to be home with me. If you see her or know of anything that could lead us to her, please contact the Ottawa Police right away."

Finally Karen seemed satisfied and let the cameraman know he could pack up. "That's great. You were choked up in the middle that time, and that was good too."

"I couldn't help it. I thought you'd do another retake."

"It's fine the way it is. People know you're upset. I'm glad you didn't control it too much." She picked up her belongings. "The interview will be part of our suppertime news show today."

Chapter Thirty-Three

Daniel stood in the grocery store aisle, staring at the selection of frozen meals. If they left on Saturday, they'd still need food for a couple of days until then. What do kids like to eat? She'd liked pizza last night—he'd get another of those—and he added a package of hot dogs. Sliced cheese for grilled cheese sandwiches. And milk. Chips. Maybe some cookies.

He didn't want to have to shop again. Leaving her alone at the house was risky.

When he left she'd been kneeling on the kitchen floor, petting Tucker, who was basking in the attention. "You should stay in the house while I'm gone," he'd said. "You don't want anyone to notice you." He was careful to pose it as her preference, not as pressure from him.

"No," she'd said, glancing up at him with a quick smile. "I'll just be here, if that's still okay." She seemed to think he was doing her a favor by letting her stay, and he was happy to have her think that way.

She'd still be thinking of Susan's house as home, even though she didn't show any sign of wanting to go back there.

Get her looking forward to being on the farm.

He'd told her he'd lock the door, saying it was for her protection. He didn't want her to think he was locking her in.

189

Her picture was everywhere—he'd seen a lot of posters along the street, and her photo was plastered across the newspapers in the kiosk out on the sidewalk. He couldn't risk someone seeing her.

As long as the police didn't come by again...

The grocery store had a clothing section. Nothing fancy, but serviceable. He searched the Girls and Women section for the things he thought she'd need, and added them to his cart.

As he made his way to the checkout, he tossed in a few odds and ends. At a rack of stationery supplies, he picked up a big pad of paper and flipped through it—blank pages, thick paper. Kelly had had drawing pads like this. Maybe Hannah would like this. He'd seen her drawing on the back of a flyer at the kitchen table this morning, sketching a picture of a dog. It was clearly Tucker. That made sense—Kelly was artistic, so Hannah would be too. He added the pad, along with some markers and pencils, to his cart.

****

Driving home, Daniel remembered Mac standing in their farmhouse kitchen long ago. Mac had come back a second time that day, after they'd insisted Hannah must have been in the car with Kelly and Jacob at the time of the crash.

"From marks in the snow, we can tell that someone else came by the accident before the snow stopped." he told them. "There are tracks around the truck, half filled with snow. And the pickup's back door wasn't latched. We're thinking someone walked around the vehicle, discovered the baby, unbuckled her, and took her away."

Daniel had protested. "Why would someone do

that? Where would they have taken her?"

"That's the question. Nobody reported the accident before the snowplow operator found it, and no one has reported a baby. We're checking hospitals and walk-in clinics, seeing if anyone brought in a baby girl without a health card."

Daniel shot a look at Patricia, who was barely holding herself together.

"Another possibility—I don't like to suggest it, but we have to consider it—is that she's been abducted. Kidnapped."

Patricia cried out, a sudden piercing wail. "No! Why would they do that?"

Mac glanced at her. "We don't know. Child abductions are rare in Canada, especially abductions by a stranger. But it can happen. There are cases of someone taking a baby from a hospital nursery because they want a baby of their own, for example."

Daniel had heard of worse possibilities, but he pushed the thoughts away. "You think someone took Hannah to keep as their own child?"

"That's possible. Be assured, we'll be pulling out all stops to find her."

Mac had come back week after week to give them updates. He even brought a team to search the scene of the accident again. But there was no sign of Hannah anywhere, and the updates gradually became less frequent.

It had been a heartbreak for him and Patricia, but she'd taken it especially hard. At last now he'd be able to bring Hannah home.

Chapter Thirty-Four

Maddy was reading in her room when Daniel came back from shopping; she could hear him stamping his feet by the back door. Tucker bounded down the stairs to greet him. "Hannah, I have some things for you," he called.

Daniel was calling her Hannah all the time now. It made her feel strange, but she hadn't corrected him. "I'll be down in a minute."

She brushed her hair and went downstairs. Daniel was in the kitchen. He'd emptied several bags of shopping onto the table. He turned toward her, looking proud of himself.

"First, a new jacket." He picked it up to show her—it was a parka, blue and black, with black fur around the hood. It wasn't what she would have picked out, but she supposed she could wear it. "And some mitts and a hat. Two hats." One was an ugly gray wool thing—she'd never wear that, unless it got really cold—and the other was a baseball cap. Blue Jays. Oh well.

There were also two pullovers, a pair of jeans, and some socks and underwear. The sizes seemed okay, and she liked the sweater colors.

He was watching her, and she tried to figure out what to say. The clothes weren't that great, but she couldn't expect him to know what she'd like. "Thank you. They're nice." She gave him a smile, trying to be polite.

"And I got you a surprise." He handed her a large flat bag, watching her as if expecting her to be especially pleased.

Reaching in, she pulled out a pad of paper and a selection of markers and pencils. These *were* a surprise, and she was happy to get them. She didn't have to force a smile this time. "This is great—I love drawing. Thanks so much!"

He smiled back at her and reached into yet another bag, bringing out a small box. "And here's something else," he said, handing it to her. She studied the box, turning it over. On the front it had a picture of a beautiful woman with swirling brown hair and sultry eyes. Superior Preference was printed across the bottom of the picture in big letters, covering the woman's shoulders. Other letters, across the top, said L'Oréal.

She blinked. "Is it hair color?" she asked.

He nodded. "Yeah. Anyone watching for you will expect a girl with blonde hair. This'll turn your hair brown."

She must have looked doubtful, because he added, "There are instructions. If you want, I can help you figure out how to do it."

No. She *was* hiding, but still—changing her appearance seemed too drastic, too big of a step away from being Maddy. Away from...her mom. Her friends.

But she kept the box and grabbed the paper and pencil crayons, heading for the stairs. "I'll come back for the other stuff in a minute."

"Don't take too long. Supper'll be ready in a jiffy."

Chapter Thirty-Five

Jenny arrived around four, rousing me from a fitful nap on the couch. "Get your coat on. I'm taking you out for an early dinner. We'll be back in time to watch the suppertime news show." When I hesitated, she pulled my red wool jacket from the hallway coat rack. "And brush your hair or something first, okay?"

I took the hint and made a quick stop in the washroom before slipping into my jacket. In the car, I asked, "Where are we going?"

She named a burger restaurant on Bank Street. "You need some protein." In the restaurant, we took a booth and placed our orders—two burgers with the works. The waitress asked what I wanted to drink. "Water's fine." Jenny stuck with water too. We usually had beers to go with this kind of meal, but that didn't seem right tonight.

She sipped her water. "I know how scary this is for you. And I do feel terrible that I took the girls to that movie."

I waved her comment away. What was the point?

The waitress brought our burgers and placed them in front of us. Big, meaty patties with tomatoes and pickles, and fries on the side. I stared at mine, my throat thick. How could I eat? I cut the burger in two, picked up half in both hands, and leaned forward, letting juice drip onto the plate while I bit off one end. I forced myself to chew. Usually these burgers are delicious, but this time I couldn't taste anything. I choked the bite down, following it with water. Looking at what was left on the plate, I pushed it away. "This was a good idea, but I just can't manage it."

Jenny cut off a quarter of the burger and put it on a side plate, added five french fries, and handed it to me. "Here, just try to get through this much."

I sighed. "All right, I'll try." I picked up one of the fries and bit off half. "It already seems like Maddy's been gone forever. I keep wondering what she's doing, what's happening to her. I'm almost afraid to think about it. I hope she's eating…"

Jenny nodded. "I know. But starving yourself will not feed her." She signaled the waiter for our bill and a to-go container. When he brought them, she gave him her credit card and packed the rest of my burger into the container. "We'll take this home, and maybe you'll feel like eating it later."

I made a face, but she ignored me. We collected our coats and went out to her car.

We got back to my house and were settled in front of the TV in time for the local news at six. After a few short items, they moved to the "journal" section of the broadcast.

A still photo of Maddy came on screen, while an announcer introduced the segment. "Twelve-year-old Madison Koss was last seen at home in the Glebe area around 4:30 p.m. this past Monday, November sixth. She's five feet two inches tall, weighs about ninety-five pounds, and has blue eyes and blonde hair that she wears in a ponytail. Ottawa Police released a bulletin on Tuesday asking for anyone with information to come forward. Today police held another press conference to step up appeals for help in finding her."

The camera switched to Staff Sergeant Bailey from Missing Persons. He stood at a podium, with Maddy's poster displayed on the front.

"This is a vulnerable twelve-year-old girl," he was saying. "Every hour that passes makes us more concerned about her safety. We think she may be with someone, as we don't believe she has the resources to be on her own for so long. Someone may think they're helping her by harboring her."

The broadcast switched to the video I'd recorded that morning. They froze the first frame while an announcer introduced it, then played the clip. I clutched Jenny's hand; it was like watching a stranger. The program returned to Sergeant Bailey answering a few questions from reporters, and the segment was over.

We had barely turned the TV off when Amy phoned. "Tom and I just watched the news. Your video was very good." She paused. "It must have been hard for you to record. And to watch."

I blinked back tears. "I'm all right—Jenny's here. I was glad to get it out there. I just hope it has some effect."

"That clip would make anyone's heart hurt."

My heart was hurting, that was for sure. Along with the rest of me—I arched my shoulders against the dull ache seeping through my bones, and the dread that was filling my mind.

Amy added, "Abel called me this afternoon—he's coming out tonight with some more friends. We'll get a lot more posters put up."

My stomach clenched. *I can't face leaving this*

couch.

She continued, "But you don't need to come along this time—you must be exhausted. You should take a night off. We can handle it."

She was telling me to stay home. But could I? Was I a bad mother if I didn't force myself to go with them?

Just then Jenny brought a blanket and tucked it over my knees. That simple gesture decided me. "Thanks, Amy. I think I will stay in—I don't have any more energy tonight."

Jenny, overhearing this, stared at me. "You weren't considering going out again, were you?"

I sighed. "I feel like I should. How can I take a night off while Maddy's still missing?"

"You need to conserve your energy. There's nothing more you can do tonight."

"The posters—"

"They're important, but you have friends to work on that for you."

****

Maddy finished putting away the things Daniel had bought her, and joined him in the kitchen. He'd set the table and was busy at the stove. She didn't wait for him to tell her where to sit. She knew her spot by now, the one next to the window, facing the hallway.

They were having hot dogs for supper. She watched him spear them from the pot he'd heated them in; buns were already on the plates. Mustard, ketchup, and relish were on the table. He gave her two dogs along with some chips and poured milk into her glass.

They ate in silence. Then Daniel set aside his second hot dog and looked at her. His thumb was tapping against the table, but he didn't seem aware of it.

"I said we'd talk some more today about going out west."

Maddy dropped the chip she was about to eat. He hadn't mentioned the trip all day, and she'd hoped he'd forgotten about it.

He continued. "I was thinking we'd leave Saturday. We can pack up tomorrow. There's not a lot we need to take."

Maddy's mouth fell open, and her stomach fluttered. She didn't know what to say. She hadn't thought he wanted to leave so soon.

He nodded. "There could be snow out west any time. We want to be home before winter hits, and you'll be glad to get to the farm."

He was acting like she remembered the farm—but she didn't. She wasn't convinced she was Hannah, but even if she was, Hannah was a baby when she disappeared. She wouldn't remember anything.

After supper they played cards again. It was kind of fun—she was getting better at it, and she almost won twice. Daniel was being nice. But the idea of going on a trip with him made her uneasy.

Upstairs later, she took another look at the box of Superior Preference. Changing her hair color still felt like a drastic step, but maybe she'd think about it again in the morning.

Lying in bed, she watched the moon shining in through the bare trees.

His farm must be far away—he'd mentioned being "on the road" for several days. And he said *Alberta*, and *out west*. She knew Alberta was one of the prairie provinces, and it had mountains. She wasn't really sure of much else, though.

She told herself a trip might be fun. She'd never been on a farm, and the animals sounded interesting. But the idea of leaving unsettled her.

Susan was the only mom Maddy had ever known. As long as they were in the same city, she could still feel the connection. Even if she was here with Daniel instead of at home—she was just taking a break.

Leaving the city seemed like a much bigger step.

Maddy swiped at the tears leaking down her cheek. She didn't know what to think. Did she belong with Daniel, or with her mom?

If only they'd never had the DNA test. Everything was simpler before.

****

Jenny brought me a mug of tea, and I leaned back against a cushion, my feet curled underneath me on the couch. I tried to think positive thoughts, imagining sunny pictures of Maddy home again—comfortably ensconced in the kitchen, or petting Oscar, or...then a shadow flitted across my fantasy as a darker image filled my mind. It was Maddy, saying, "But that test said you're not my mother."

I gripped Jenny's arm. "When Maddy gets back, I have to have an explanation for how that DNA test could be so wrong. I need a solution, an answer. Otherwise—"

She finished the sentence for me. "Otherwise, she might run away again."

The blunt statement hurt, but it only put my fear into words. "I can't...she needs to know she *is* my daughter."

Jenny gave me another hug. We were still standing in the hallway. "Of course she does. And you need an answer too."

"I've been leaving messages for Aisha—they must have made an error somewhere. But she seems to be avoiding me. She doesn't want to hear me say they got it wrong."

"So…" Jenny hesitated before continuing. "What if they didn't get it wrong?"

I stared at her. "What do you mean?"

"Is there any way the test could be right?"

"Jenny, you said yourself—you were there when she was born. You know I'm her mother! How can a test that says I'm not her mother be right?"

"I don't know…but what if there's some actual explanation?"

That same question had briefly popped into my mind after I'd sat with the results for a bit, but I'd pushed it aside as nonsensical. Now on an impulse, I got up and went into my little office, coming back with my laptop.

"Okay. Let's see what the internet has to say on that question." How stupid of me, that I hadn't done this sooner! But I'd been focused first on telling Maddy and then on dealing with her disappearance. Research had not been at the top of my mind.

I googled "mother's DNA doesn't match child."

And dozens of entries popped up.

The first one led me to a woman in the state of Washington. In 2002 she applied for enforcement of child support payments from her ex-husband for their three children. DNA tests of the whole family were required to prove his paternity. The test showed that he was indeed their father—but that she was not their mother. She was accused of fraudulently receiving welfare payments for someone else's children, or of running a surrogacy scam. She almost had her children removed by child welfare authorities. Nobody believed her, because everyone involved considered DNA tests to be infallible. When she was taken to court, she had trouble finding a lawyer, because no lawyer wanted to challenge the accuracy of a DNA test.

Finally a lawyer stepped forward to take her case. He knew about another woman, this one in Boston, who had had a similar experience. She needed a kidney donor; her children were tested to see if they could be donors, and in the process she was told that a DNA comparison showed she was not their mother.

Other entries led me further through these women's stories, and to other articles on a similar theme. And the sources seemed reliable.

By now Jenny had refilled our tea and was reading along with me. I could well understand the shock these women had experienced on receiving those test results— the same shock I'd been dealing with. Or not dealing with.

We read further. There was an explanation—a strange one, but an explanation. Maybe the same could be true for me. If—*when!*—we got Maddy home, this might cut through the confusion.

I turned to Jenny. "I think I'd better double-check these sources." She nodded. But further exploration appeared to substantiate the reports.

"Now I definitely have to talk to Aisha." I reached for my cellphone and dialed her number. This time, amazingly, she answered. I launched into my spiel. "Aisha, it's Susan. I've been doing some research. I may have found an explanation for how your test could say that I'm not Maddy's mother, when I know for sure that I am."

She sighed. "Susan, I told you, I've reviewed the procedures that were followed in your case. There was no error in handling your samples, and we stand by our results."

I squared my shoulders. Jenny was leaning forward, encouraging me. "I know that. But there's a possible explanation. There are at least two well-known cases of women who were found to have different DNA from their children."

Aisha made a scoffing sound. "Where did you find this? On the internet?"

I wasn't intimidated. "I started with a Google search, yes. But that led me to some reports in medical journals and also in the *New York Times* and the *Independent*, which don't normally carry stories without fact checking."

"So what did they say?"

I recounted what I had found. After a short hesitation, she agreed to check it out.

Later that evening, she called me back. "Susan, what you're talking about is a rare occurrence; it's far-fetched to think it could apply in your case. But if you're willing to pay for retesting, we'll do it. Come in tomorrow, and we'll take some more samples."

I sighed in relief. "Fine. I'll be in early in the morning."

****

My feeling of relief didn't last long. As I brushed my teeth and got ready for bed, I was overcome by the dread I'd been fighting since Maddy disappeared. It was now over three days that she'd been gone.

I couldn't imagine what she was going through. I pushed away the flickering thoughts—I couldn't stand the idea of Maddy in pain, or injured. Or abused. I refused to think about it.

But that didn't mean she was okay.

On impulse, I went down the hall to her room and leaned in, scanning the shadows cast by the hallway light. I was suddenly struck by how different the room looked from the way Maddy usually kept it.

My frantic cleaning efforts had imposed order—but it was my order. Not hers.

I'd thought I was tidying the room for her benefit, but maybe I was wrong. Maybe this was like a lot of the things Maddy and I fought about, when she'd want to do things one way and I insisted on a different way. My way.

Had I been quashing her efforts to find a way of her own?

Swallowing a sob, I crawled into her bed and pulled her comforter over me.

Chapter Thirty-Six

First thing Friday morning, I went downstairs to get coffee started before showering and getting dressed. When the coffee was ready, I filled a travel mug and took it with me out to the car, on my way to the DNA lab. The walkway was covered with frost, but it would soon melt in the sun that was already clearing the treetops.

An hour later I was back, having submitted samples for the retest Aisha and I had discussed. It had been more complicated than I expected, but we'd gotten it done.

I was determined to stay focused today, to rise above the funk I'd been in since Monday night. My concern for Maddy was increasing with every passing hour, but letting myself sink into anxiety and panic helped no one.

I opened the fridge door and scowled—it could use a thorough cleaning. I sighed. The effort seemed ridiculous at a time like this, but the mindless task suddenly appealed to me. It would at least give me something to do. I began removing bottles and containers, setting them on the kitchen table.

I had just pitched out a virtually empty mustard bottle when the doorbell rang. A glance through the window told me it was Bob.

When I pulled the door open, he gave me a

lopsided grin. "Hi—I'm just stopping by for a few minutes. Can I come in?"

I stepped back. "Sure—if you don't mind watching me clean my fridge."

He followed me into the kitchen and leaned against the doorjamb. I turned back to the fridge, pulling out several half-full Tupperware containers and inspecting them. Leftovers. I hadn't cooked since Maddy left, so these were long past saving. I scraped their contents into the green bin for composting and put the containers in the dishwasher. Bob said nothing, watching me.

Maybe I should be hospitable. "Would you like something? Coffee, water…"

"No, nothing, thanks. I won't stay long."

The fridge was empty now, all except the vegetable drawers. I pulled them out and began separating shriveled greens from still-usable garlic, celery, and red peppers.

He shifted position. "I have some news."

I looked at him sharply. "About Maddy?"

"Yes. Well, not about finding her. But it is about her."

My interest in vegetables vanished. "Well—?"

"I told you the Edmonton lab uploaded Hannah's DNA to the National DNA Databank. And I took in that hair sample from Maddy. Mac managed to light a fire under the lab here and got the comparative analysis fast-tracked—unheard of, but somehow they got it done already."

He watched me as he spoke. "He emailed me a copy of the report last night. I would have phoned you, but it was late…"

My breath caught, and I stared at him. "And?"

He smiled. "And the two samples don't match." He gave me a searching gaze. "This is the proof you were looking for. Maddy is definitely not Hannah."

I stared at him. "You could have told me that the minute you walked in. Or phoned…"

He flushed. "I wanted to see your face when I told you. And…I was enjoying watching you work."

I frowned, grabbing a dishtowel to dry my hands. "You think I'd rather clean my fridge than hear this news?"

"No. Sorry. You're right, I should have told you right away."

I waved that away. "Anyway." I leaned against the sink, suddenly feeling lighter as relief washed over me. "So that's the proof. Daniel's been wrong all along."

"Yes, it's definite."

"Does he know?"

"Not yet. I'll stop by his house later today and tell him."

I turned my eyes to the clutter I'd left on the counter, though not fully registering it. "When this all started, that's the only thing I wanted. To prove that he was wrong."

He nodded. "But now the problem's way bigger than that."

I choked back a sudden sob. "Now all I want is to get Maddy home safe." I'd make any bargain—with the fates, with myself, with Maddy—if I could just make that happen.

Chapter Thirty-Seven

On Friday morning, Daniel collected the tools he'd used to install the new post on the porch. That was the last of the house-rehabbing chores he'd be able to finish; he had to get organized and get on the road with Hannah. They should leave tomorrow.

Gord and Pete were looking forward to money from the house sale, and they wouldn't be happy when he left before finishing the work. But getting Hannah back to the farm was more important. He'd found her— he'd kept his promise to Patricia—now he needed to get her back home to complete the promise.

He set his toolbox on the floor inside the back door and refilled his coffee cup, sitting down at the kitchen table to complete his plans

The police hadn't come by again since Tuesday morning, but they could reappear any time.

If they do, it'll be game over. They'll take her away.

The two of them had to leave before that happened.

She seemed to be getting used to the idea of being Hannah. Even if she wasn't calling him Grandpa yet, though he'd suggested it.

But she wasn't Susan's, that was for sure. The DNA report made that clear. If the police knew about that, they wouldn't be trying to return her to Susan. In fact, Susan would have a lot of explaining to do.

Should he maybe report her? Tell the cops about that report?

No. Stirring up that hornet's nest could get into a lot of red tape. Better just to pick up stakes and leave. Get Hannah out of town without anyone noticing.

If he pushed with the driving, they could make it to Alberta in three days.

They'd have to be careful getting out of the city. People were watching for her, and alerts might be out across the country by now too.

He'd been thinking about ways to make her less noticeable. She was too old to disguise as a boy; she already had some shape and walked like a girl. But the bulky jacket and looser clothes he'd bought yesterday should help.

She hadn't applied the hair color last night, but he'd try to get her to do it today. That blonde hair featured in every description and photo of her and would be the first thing people would notice.

He didn't like having to disguise her. But he was justified—he had to get her back to their family's base. Once he had her at the farm, he was sure she'd love the life. How could she not?

Hannah would need to be in school. He'd gotten the laptop out again last night to check online for Alberta schools. The one Kelly attended was still operating. That'd be fine.

He imagined he'd have to go through some paperwork to establish that she was Hannah. He'd deal with that once they got home.

He worried about her reaction to the trip, though. She didn't seem warm to it. What if she refused to go? They had to leave, he had no doubt about that. She wasn't used to the idea, that was all. He'd see if she was readier to talk about it later today. If need be, they could wait until Sunday.

Patricia, we'll be there as soon as we can. He waited, but she didn't answer.

He grimaced, and pounded the heel of his hand against his head. *Straighten up, man!* Talking to a dead woman. Anybody would think he was losing it.

****

Patricia had blamed him for the whole thing.

He'd woken, a few months after the accident, to find her side of the bed empty. He could hear her banging pots in the kitchen.

What would she be doing with pots at this time of the morning? Struggling to clear his sleep-fogged mind, he stumbled down the hall. Patricia turned toward him, her eyes red. "You know what today is, don't you?"

He had tried to kiss her, but she pulled away. "It's Hannah's birthday. She's two years old today." Her voice rose in a wail. "I can't stand thinking of her, out there somewhere in the world. Where is she? Is someone looking after her? Has anyone hurt her?"

Daniel's throat tightened, and he forced himself to swallow. These were the same questions that kept running through his head.

She buried her face in a dishtowel. Her voice was muffled. "If you'd only had the sense not to get Kelly arguing. You just kept going and going at her! You should have known she'd blow up!"

Daniel's mouth was dry. "Are you saying it was my fault they were in that accident?"

"All I'm saying is, if they hadn't left that night, none of this would have happened."

209

Patricia never repeated her accusation. She didn't need to. Daniel had been blaming himself since the night it happened.

**** ✳✳✳✳

Patricia had brought out her grandmother's dessert plates and was offering slices of chocolate cake to Kelly and Jacob. They had come for the weekend with baby Hannah.

Kelly was glaring at Daniel. "You're a hypocrite," she said. "You never wanted me to study animation in the first place! And now you're saying I'm wasting my training!"

Daniel flushed but tried to keep his voice even. "I did think there were more practical things you could have studied." He winced; they'd had some knock-down drag-out fights over that. He and Kelly were a lot alike. They both had opinions and didn't hold back from expressing them. And neither of them ever backed down.

He could see Patricia watching him out of the corner of her eye. She hated it when he and Kelly fought.

She slid a plate of cake in front of Kelly. Kelly ignored it, jutting her chin at Daniel. "I never wanted to be an accountant, or a nurse, or whatever you thought was 'more practical.' " Her words spilled out as if she were tripping over them.

Daniel tried to keep his jaw from clenching. "You went through three years of high-tech training to end up back as a salesgirl?"

Kelly scowled. "That's temporary, I've told you! With Jacob on part-time hours, we can't afford daycare, so we have to work opposite shifts so we can take care of Hannah."

Jacob had been silent, concentrating on his slice of cake. But now he put down his fork. "We're just waiting for me to be called back full-time at the autobody shop. Kenny told me he thinks they'll reopen after New Year's."

Patricia broke in. "You know we love to have Hannah around. Why not leave her here with us for a bit?"

Kelly sighed, exasperated. "No, Mom. Hannah stays with us. I try to bring her out to see you as often as we can—I know you love her to bits. But my baby stays with me."

Daniel got up and went to the window, holding the curtain aside to peer outside. The sky was already turning dark, and the wind was howling around the house; he could see it swaying the tall poplars at the far edge of the yard. The CBC said there could be a heavy storm this evening.

He came back to the table. "I warned you—you'd end up with a husband who couldn't support you."

Kelly jumped to her feet, her eyes flashing. "That's too much! It's not up to Jacob to support me." She glared at him. "We support each other. And don't talk about Jacob as if he's not in the room."

Daniel turned to Jacob. "I'll say it to your face, then. You should get out there and find a better job. Let Kelly do the work she's trained for, not just whatever fits around your shifts."

Jacob sighed and ducked his head. "I've been looking."

Kelly slammed both hands on the table, hard enough to make the dishes jump. "We don't have to listen to this." She whirled to face Jacob. "I can't stay here another minute. Let's get Hannah and get out of here."

Jacob pushed back his plate. "All right," he said, standing up.

Patricia reached out a hand, her brow furrowed and her eyes full of concern. "Kelly, I wish you'd stay the night..."

Kelly sighed. "Mom, I can't." She flounced out of the kitchen and returned a few minutes later, holding a sleepy Hannah. Kelly could still carry her, though Hannah now weighed over twenty-five pounds. It wouldn't be long before she was too big to carry.

Hannah, who'd been napping, blinked at them all with a small smile. Her hair was matted against her forehead. She was wearing blue corduroy overalls and a pink shirt and seemed to take for granted that she was the center of everyone's attention. She opened and closed her hands in a little wave to her grandma.

Kelly shoved Hannah's limbs into her red snowsuit and boots and pulled on her hat and mitts. She grabbed her own coat and purse. "Bye, Mom," she said and headed out the door that Jacob held open.

Daniel swallowed, choking back the hurt. She'd been too angry to include him in her goodbye.

The snow swirled in through the door; the wind had picked up, and snow had started falling. Daniel worried about them driving in this weather. But if they left now, they could be back in Edmonton in an hour—they should beat the worst of the storm.

That night he and Patricia had slept soundly, tucked under their quilt while the storm raged outside. It was the last good night's sleep they ever had. The next morning their world slid sideways as they learned of the accident, the deaths. And Hannah's disappearance.

Daniel groaned now as his eyes returned to the kitchen window in front of him. He rubbed his forehead. All of that happened so long ago, but the images were as fresh in his mind as if they'd happened yesterday.

But he was finally going to fix it.

Chapter Thirty-Eight

After breakfast Friday morning, Maddy went back upstairs to the room she'd been using. Lying on her bed, she watched the bare treetops in Daniel's backyard waving in the wind outside the window. She could hear him hammering on something downstairs.

She let her mind drift, trying not to think about anything, though a few thoughts did float into view. Emma and the others would be at school right now. What was her mom doing?

People must be looking for her. She wasn't quite ready to be found, though.

For now, she liked having a hideaway here. This room had become her nest, her own spot. It was kind of bare, but she liked that. No clutter. The walls were a faded light brown, with blank rectangles of darker brown in spots where she figured there used to be pictures. There was a blind on the double window, but no curtains. The room smelled a bit musty, or maybe it was just Tucker's doggy smell; he'd been coming in several times a day, paws whispering on the wood floor, to jump on the bed and snooze. She smiled. She liked having him there.

The bed was narrow, with a standing lamp beside it. Daniel had brought the lamp so she could read in bed. Or draw. Her two main activities.

She tried not to think about her mom. *She's not my*

214

mom. The test said so. But those thoughts made her ache inside, and she had to bite her lips hard to keep tears away.

"You have a good imagination," Daniel had said at breakfast, when he saw the drawing she'd made. It was an imaginary scene this time—a castle hidden in a forest. She'd made the forest a thick, deep green. It was an enchanted castle. "And I'm not surprised you like drawing. Kelly was always artistic too."

She didn't know what to say when he mentioned Kelly. She didn't feel any connection to her.

Tucker was lying on the floor beside the bed, but now he raised his head. He got to his feet and headed down the stairs. She could hear him barking at the front door. What was he barking at?

Daniel came rushing upstairs, giving her urgent whispered instructions. "I'm closing your door," he said. "There's someone here. I'll get rid of them if I can, but just stay quiet. Be careful—don't make a sound until they're gone."

Maddy shivered, her throat suddenly tight. Was the outside world about to come crashing in?

****

Daniel made sure Hannah was settled upstairs before he opened the front door. His heart sank when he saw a police officer standing on the porch, and he suppressed a shiver. *Not a cop now, for God's sake.* They were so close to leaving. Another day and they would have already been gone.

He recognized this cop. He was Mac's friend, the one who'd searched his house that night when the girl went missing. Daniel tried to dredge up his name, but it was gone, if he'd ever remembered it.

The officer stepped forward. "Hi, Daniel. Remember me? I'm Bob Russo, with the Ottawa Police. May I come in?"

Daniel nodded. "All right, come in." He pulled Tucker back from the door. "Don't mind my dog," he said. "He barks to let me know there's a visitor, but he'll never bite. He's my pal, keeps me company."

His mind was working furiously. Had someone seen Hannah and called the cops? Was he here to look for her again?

She wasn't even hidden; the only thing concealing her was a door.

The cop turned toward the living room. "Can we sit down? I have something I need to tell you."

The living room was empty apart from one shabby easy chair that Daniel had hung on to so he'd have somewhere to sit and watch TV, back before he hid the set. "You can sit there," he offered, before bringing in one of the kitchen chairs for himself.

Tucker came and lay down on the floor alongside his chair.

Daniel was puzzled. This didn't seem like the lead-in to a search of the house; last time they didn't sit down for a conversation. He stayed quiet, waiting to hear what the guy—Bob, was it?—had to say.

"We talked before about Maddy Koss," said Bob. "You had an interest in her, before she went missing."

Daniel frowned. Was that a question? "I've seen the posters," he said. "She hasn't been found yet?"

"No, she hasn't. We're investigating, and we hope to locate her soon. But I'm here to talk about your original interest. You said you thought she was your granddaughter."

216

A muscle in Daniel's cheek twitched. He tilted his head.

I didn't just think it. I was sure.

Bob leaned forward. "Are you aware the police lab in Edmonton still had DNA from Hannah?"

Daniel stared at him. What was this?

Bob continued. "They've compared that DNA to Maddy's now. Do you want to know what they discovered?"

His mouth suddenly dry, Daniel fidgeted in his chair.

"There is no match." Bob's eyes bored into his. "Maddy is not Hannah. They're two different girls."

Daniel stared at him blankly.

Bob leaned closer. "Did you hear me? This settles the question. You've been wrong all along. Maddy is not Hannah. I have a copy of the report here for you." He held out some papers, but Daniel ignored him.

Daniel found himself on his feet, shaking and unable to speak. He fought to keep the words from penetrating. He turned and stared at nothing, his vision blurring.

This can't be. That report's wrong.

But Bob's words battered their way into Daniel's brain, insisting on breaking through. He staggered into the hallway and bent over, leaning his hands on his knees, his breathing fast and shallow.

He couldn't accept this. *Patricia, this can't be right!*

A sour fluid rose in his gullet, and he fought it back down. Everything was swirling, and his vision went dark.

****

Daniel was half-sitting, half-lying in the easy chair. He could hear Bob's voice, but it sounded hollow, as if it were echoing down a deep well.

"Daniel? I have a glass of water. Would you like a sip?"

Obediently, Daniel drank. A few drops ran down the side of his chin, and he struggled to sit up straight. Bob helped him, pushing a cushion behind him to keep him upright.

Daniel shook his head, trying to clear his thoughts.

Don't fall for a cooked-up document.

Bob's story had thrown him for a minute, but it was hogwash.

The cops are up to the same tricks as that Susan woman and her lawyer. Just trying to get rid of you.

He'd almost fallen for it, but now he could see through the ploy.

They couldn't fool him. He knew he'd found Hannah, dammit. He was about to bring her home to the farm so they could be a family again.

Don't let on, though.

Best if he pretended to be convinced.

Stalling for time, he reached for the glass of water. Bob was still hovering, a concerned expression on his face, and leaned over to help. "Are you okay? Would you like me to call a doctor?"

Daniel put down the glass and stood up. "No, don't bother. I'm fine now." His head spun, but he fought to get his balance under control. He had to get the cop out of here. "All right," he said, smoothing his hand over his forehead. "I understand. I must have made a mistake." He started toward the hallway.

Bob followed him. "I wanted to let you know," he

said. "I guess it was a shock."

Daniel straightened his shoulders. "I was just dizzy for a minute. I'll be fine." *Get him out of here.* "Thanks for coming to tell me. I'll let you get back to your duties now." How much more jabber was it going to take to get rid of him?

Bob moved toward the door. "Yeah. I have to get back out there." He left, closing the door behind him, shutting out the cold wind gusting across the front porch.

As the latch clicked into place, Daniel turned to lean against the door, his knees unsteady and his mouth dry. His splayed hands slid down the door's hard surface, his fingers lingering on rough spots and ridges they encountered on the painted wood.

Rhythmic ticks from the hall clock measured the passing minutes. In the kitchen, the fridge motor cycled on and off.

Tucker came up to him, head raised and ears alert, and pressed his head against Daniel's knee. Stiffly, Daniel bent to rub the dog's head, running his hand over the familiar bumps under wiry fur. Tucker's wet nose nudged his palm.

When did you last feed him?

Daniel shook his head. He couldn't focus on Tucker right now.

He pushed off from the door and stumbled back into the living room. Rubbing sweat from his forehead, he lowered himself onto the easy chair. The seat cushion sank under him and he leaned his head back, the rough upholstery pressing into his neck. He shook his head, doing his best to block Bob's words from memory.

After a few moments he sat up again, and his eyes fell on the papers on the floor where Bob had left them. With a small shiver, he reached over to pick them up. Two sheets of white paper, smooth against his fingers. A logo at the top. Black print, a bit smudged at one edge.

The pages were stapled together, the second page facing up, the first page folded to the back. Daniel flipped the first page to the front. It was a copy of an email message. Addressed to bobrusso99@gmail.com.

Daniel's eyes fell to the message.

—Hi, buddy. Here's the comparison from the National DNA Database. Note: Maddy's and Hannah's samples DO NOT MATCH. —

Stiffening, Daniel's sight dropped to the one-word signature.

Mac.

Below that name was an RCMP logo and a set of identifiers that he recognized. Name, address, and phone numbers.

That's our Mac.

Daniel stared at the message again. He flipped to the second page, the report. It confirmed what Mac's message said.

Bob's words replayed in Daniel's mind. "You've been wrong all along."

His mouth filled with a bitter taste. He swallowed twice, trying to get rid of it. He threw aside the pages, rising to his feet and stumbling out to the hallway. On the way he bumped his knee against a sharp corner by the stairs but scarcely registered the pain.

His head filled with a wordless wail.

He wasn't sure he'd ever known about the cops

having Hannah's DNA. They had come after the accident to collect things from the room that Kelly, Jacob, and Hannah had slept in. He hadn't paid much attention.

His vision blurred again.

Mac's name.

Mac's message.

He'd never known Mac to lie.

With a chill flooding through him, Daniel fell back into the chair. Tucker was staring at his face again, making a soft whining sound.

Daniel's throat clenched, and the muscles across his shoulders tensed. He felt hollow and cold.

The report was real.

He'd made a huge mistake.

****

Daniel stood in the kitchen, staring out into the backyard. He heard the girl's sock feet thudding softly as she came downstairs. She murmured something to Tucker in the hallway, then came into the kitchen.

"Who was that?" she asked.

"A policeman."

She went over to the sink and poured a glass of water. "Was he asking about me?"

Daniel turned to watch her. "Yeah, he was. He wanted to know if I'd seen you."

"What did you say?"

"I said no." He swallowed. "You didn't want him to find you, right?"

The girl gave him a sideways glance, then slid into one of the chairs and smoothed her pad of paper on the table. "I guess you convinced him, since he went away." She turned to a clean page and started drawing something.

The bitter taste rose in Daniel's throat again. She was carrying on as if nothing had changed—and for her it hadn't. But for him, everything was different.

Yesterday he'd taken her love of drawing as something she'd gotten from Kelly. Now he knew he'd been fooling himself. Yesterday he'd been imagining the moment when he got her home to Alberta, to the farm. Now that dream was shattered.

He closed his eyes. If she wasn't Hannah, he didn't want her here. He wished he'd never seen her, never let her stay.

He leaned over the sink, pouring himself another glass of water. He needed to stay calm, not give in to the rage bubbling up inside him.

It was the girl's fault! For looking so much like Kelly.

"That's what—" He bit off the sentence. He hadn't meant to speak out loud.

Turning from the sink, he realized the girl was watching him with an odd expression.

"Sorry, just thinking." He'd been about to say *that's what sucked me in.*

But what now? He couldn't just send her away.

Now that he'd hidden her for days and lied to the police, he'd be in for it if they found out. He didn't know what the penalty would be for concealing a runaway, but it'd be something serious. A jail term of some kind, for sure. He'd been willing to take that risk when he thought she was Hannah. Getting Hannah home was worth any risk, because the payoff—keeping his promise to Patricia, having a family life again—was all he had left to look forward to.

But this girl wasn't Hannah. He didn't want to go to jail for her. She was here because of troubles with her mother, but those were none of his business.

The thought gave him pause.

The girl shouldn't go back to Susan. That wouldn't be right. Susan wasn't her mom—that was what the other DNA test had said. So where could she even go?

Up to now he'd been working hard to persuade her that she belonged with him. She must be thinking they were heading out west tomorrow. Now they wouldn't be doing that.

He had to tamp down his anger again. *Be careful.* He could hear Patricia's voice. *She could get you into big trouble.*

He drew a deep breath. He had to give himself time to decide what to do. For now, he'd just try to act as if nothing had changed.

He went over to the fridge and opened it. With an effort, he smiled at the girl. "Are you ready for lunch?"

Chapter Thirty-Nine

After Bob left to go see Daniel, I found myself restlessly roaming through the house. At one point I washed my hands and inspected my face in the mirror; other than dark shadows under my eyes, the stress of the last few days didn't seem to have left an impact.

I stopped at Maddy's door but didn't enter. If only she were here—I'd never complain about her mess again.

Back downstairs, I wondered if I should think about lunch, but I wasn't hungry. I was staring blankly out the kitchen window when the doorbell rang. Who now?

It was Dorothy. What was she doing here? I opened the door, and she bustled in, bringing a gust of cold wind with her. Handing me a cardboard bakery box, she took off her coat and hung it on a hook in the hallway. She'd never been to my house before, but she headed unerringly for the kitchen.

"Come," she said. "Can we have tea?" She tilted her head to the box in my hands. "Those are cinnamon buns from my local baker. We'll have two now, and there'll be leftovers for your breakfast."

I was still taken aback by her showing up unannounced, but I didn't want to appear too witless. "Tea sounds good. Sit down. I'll make it." I filled the kettle and opened the box. There were six buns; two of them fit nicely on my grandmother's yellow cake plate. "Thank you for these. They look delicious."

She brushed away my thanks. "I wanted to come in person to tell you how sorry I am that you're going through all this. You must be devastated, to have Maddy gone so long."

Her kind words brought a warm flush to my face. "It's hard. The police are doing everything they can, but so far they have no leads. We're hoping the posters and appeals will help, that somebody may see her or know something."

I poured us each a cup of tea. I'd gotten out cups with actual saucers and matching side plates. Somehow giving Dorothy a mug didn't seem right, even though we were just sitting in the kitchen.

She picked up one of the buns and took a small bite, then set it on her plate. "As I said on the phone, take whatever time you need to deal with this. We'll handle your cases at the clinic in the meantime."

"I'm sorry to have my personal issues—"

Dorothy cut me off. "Personal issues! Your only daughter is missing! Don't be ridiculous. We'll divide up your clients among the rest of the staff. They'll be fine."

I took a breath. "Thanks for that. I appreciate it."

She gave me a penetrating glance. "How are you holding up through all this?"

Her concern warmed me. "I'm trying to stay positive. I have to believe Maddy'll be back, safe and sound." I decided to raise a further concern. "But after she's found, I'm going to need to spend more time with her. I'm wondering if I could work part-time, scale back my hours at the clinic."

She leaned over and patted my hand. "I'm sure we can accommodate that." She looked into my eyes. "You're a skilled clinician, an asset for our team. I want to keep you. If that means making adjustments, that's no problem."

I blinked, surprised that she'd agreed so quickly—and somewhat taken aback at her matter-of-fact praise for my work.

She smiled wryly and continued. "I know how hard it is to have a professional career and to also be needed at home." She tore off a piece of cinnamon bun but left it on her plate. "For now, you're likely right. Your daughter's needs can't be postponed. You're pulled in both directions."

Tears suddenly pricked my eyelids.

"But longer-term, I hope you'll continue the excellent work you're doing at the clinic."

I forced down a mouthful of tea, trying to dislodge the lump in my throat.

"So let's not make any hasty decisions. We can play this day to day, and week to week."

I choked. "I'm hoping this won't last for multiple weeks…"

But my defenses were slipping. Her kindness was overwhelming me.

Without planning to, I found myself telling her about my struggle to understand why Maddy had run away. "I always thought I was a good mother, but in the last while, to be honest, it's felt like she's been pulling away from me. We've had a lot of arguments." I paused. "Fights, really."

Dorothy was watching me. I couldn't read her expression.

"I feel like I've been floundering for at least a year." My face was warm. "I blamed the problems on Maddy, but now I wonder if I drove her away."

She opened her mouth to speak, but I cut her off.

"I used to think I was a natural mother. Caring for Maddy seemed to just flow, without my thinking too hard about it. But that hasn't been true for…"

She broke in. "Many parents find the teen years a challenge."

I winced. "I feel like there's a step I'm not taking. My 'natural mothering' isn't working anymore."

She leaned back. "You told me once that you lost your mother when you were young…"

The lump in my throat was back. "Yes, she died when I was eleven, and she was sick for a year before that."

"Were you close to her?"

"Until she got sick, yes. She was a wonderful mother."

A memory flashed into my mind. I was cuddling with Mom in a chair by the fireplace, my stuffed teddy curled under my elbow. Mom was holding a picture book and reading to me about three little kittens who had lost their mittens. I listened to her voice, rhythmic and soothing, while I traced the pictures with my hand. She'd read this book to me many times before, and I loved those kitties. On the next page, they'd soiled their mittens! Mom read it in that mother-cat voice she always used. "Meow meow meow, then you shall have no pie." I shivered at their punishment. But on the next page they got some pie after all.

Dad came into the room just then. Mom closed the book and gave me a squeeze. Dad said, "So would my little kittens like some pie? Or maybe some hot chocolate?" I squealed and jumped down to the floor. Dad picked me up, twirling me around. I repeated, "Meow meow meow" in a squeaky voice as he carried me out to the kitchen, where Mom poured hot chocolate for all three of us.

Did it happen that way? Was I combining events? It didn't matter—the core of the memory was that warm feeling, the sense of being their special girl.

Dorothy broke into my reverie. "So...you had a good model of what it meant to mother a young child."

"But then—"

"When she fell ill?"

I swallowed. "She spent her last months in hospital."

Dorothy watched me, compassion in her eyes. "And then she died, so you never knew how she would have adapted as you approached adolescence." She leaned forward. "So you're having to find your own way through this, without your mother as a model."

I nodded.

"What about your father?"

My throat tightened. "We were close earlier, but after Mom died, it was like he withdrew too."

Another memory surfaced. The visitors had all left after Mom's funeral. Dad and I were alone in the house; it felt empty with her gone. I found Dad standing at the front window, staring out. I went over and leaned against him, waiting for his arm to curl around me and give me a comforting hug. But instead he turned away and left the room.

Sometime later, another day. We were in the kitchen at supper time. The oven timer dinged. Dad reached in to pull out what had been a frozen meal, swearing under his breath when he burned his fingers. Without speaking, he scooped the food onto two plates and put mine in front of me. The meal was silent. When we were done, he took our plates and dropped them in the sink. "Do you have any homework?" he asked, without looking at me. I shook my head. I did have some, but I knew he'd already forgotten the question.

I raised my eyes to Dorothy's. "Dad made sure I was fed and had clothes and whatever I needed. But that was all." I grimaced. "He was probably depressed, dealing with his own grief. But at the time, it felt like I'd lost both my parents." Dad and I never regained our earlier closeness, though he adored Maddy from the time she was born.

Dorothy took a sip of tea, a thoughtful expression on her face. "From what you've told me—" She stopped. "No, pardon me. This isn't the time or place."

But I wanted to hear it. "Please...what were you going to say?"

"All right. I was just going to comment...here's how it seems to me." She put down her cup. "When Maddy was small, you were being a mother like your own mother was." Her eyes were steady. "In effect, you were recreating your own protected childhood. It was like you were mothering yourself, reliving an ideal time in your life."

I gulped. I hadn't quite gone that far in my thoughts.

She gazed into her teacup, a reflective expression in her eye. "But your early teen years were painful. You felt abandoned by both parents."

She didn't wait for me to nod this time. "As Maddy

approached that age, you unconsciously feared having to relive the emotions of those years. And maybe you were also trying to protect Maddy from similar pain, by continuing to treat her as if she were still at a younger age."

My eyes widened. "You think...I've been trying to keep her from growing up?"

"Not consciously, I'm sure."

I leaned my head on my hands. "I probably should have figured this out on my own, after all my training. But I guess I was blind to my own situation..."

Dorothy gave a little laugh. "Aren't we all. It's not easy to be objective about ourselves." I read empathy in her gaze.

Grabbing the teapot, I jumped to my feet. "Let me make some more tea." I didn't want more tea, but I couldn't sit still just then. As I plugged the kettle back in, Dorothy's words resonated in my mind. I waited for the water to boil, my thoughts turned inward. She watched me without speaking.

I turned back to face her. "In my work as a child therapist, I've always gravitated to younger children. I've avoided dealing with teenagers...other than one summer early in my training, when I had a practicum at a youth services agency."

She smiled. "And why did you choose to be a child therapist in the first place?"

Bringing the fresh tea back to the table, I shot Dorothy a look. This wasn't a question I'd asked myself.

"This may be presumptuous of me to say..." she said, "...but perhaps it was a way to recreate that close time with your mother?" Gazing at me, she added,

"That was the most important relationship of your life, made more important because it was taken from you."

Oh my God.

Maybe that was also why I'd felt such a strong need to have a child myself—so strong that I hadn't wanted to wait for an appropriate mate to show up, and chose the sperm donor route instead.

Dorothy picked up her bag. "That's enough of a deep dive for today—I need to get back. No more tea, thank you. I came by to say you needn't worry about us at the clinic. We'll be thinking of you and hoping all turns out well."

Fighting off a sudden weariness, I put the dishes in the sink; I'd deal with them later. Dorothy's insights were illuminating but exhausting to deal with. I didn't know where to go with these thoughts, but I knew that grappling with them had to be part of finding a new way forward with Maddy.

When—*when!*—she was home again.

Chapter Forty

Daniel was still reeling, not quite sure how to deal with the revelation of his mistake. The girl wasn't Hannah after all. So now what?

They'd gotten through lunch, no problem. He'd done his best to seem normal, setting out sandwiches and pouring milk, making small talk about Tucker and the weather. Until he decided what to do, he didn't want her noticing any change in him.

After lunch she'd gone upstairs to her room. Daniel paced around the kitchen, his mind working furiously. He had to find a way out of this.

Driving out west with her was out of the question now.

If she's not Hannah, she doesn't belong at the farm.

He fell into a chair at the kitchen table, his head in his hands. Patricia was right. He'd thought he was granting her final wish, but he'd failed.

He should have sent the girl away the day she showed up. Or if he could rewind events even further—he wished he'd never seen her. That day when he first saw her in the park, when he thought for a minute she was Kelly. That put everything in motion. If he could only have been somewhere else that morning, or just had not noticed her.

But there was no point in thinking that way. She

was here now. He no longer wanted her, but what should he do about her?

Maybe...just call the police, say it was all a mistake.

Don't be crazy. They'll arrest you. You'll go to jail.

He wasn't prepared to have that happen.

If this girl's not Hannah...

He swallowed.

...Hannah is still out there somewhere.

He couldn't go to jail. He had to be able to keep looking for her.

Maybe he could simply send the girl away. Open the door and tell her to leave.

That's no solution.

No, it wasn't. No matter where she went—back to Susan's or out on the street—they'd soon be asking her where she'd been all this time. And she had no reason not to tell them.

Then, no way around it. The cops would be here right away, and that would be the end.

What if he dropped her somewhere—the suburbs, or a small town outside the city? That might slow things down. It could be a while—hours or days, even—before the cops connected with her. That would give him time to get away.

But where would he go? He couldn't imagine himself going into hiding. He'd have to end up at the farm, anyway.

The farm is no secret. The cops know that's where you'd go.

Daniel continued pacing, pounding a fist into the other hand. There had to be a way out of this.

Patricia's voice was scratching at his brain.

Remember when Tucker got into my pills.

What was she getting at?

The vet said it could have been fatal.

No. She couldn't mean…

He shook his head, trying to knock the thought away. But…it couldn't hurt to know. Didn't mean he'd use it.

He rose and tiptoed up the stairs, careful to avoid the step that creaked. Her room was empty, but he could hear water running in the bathroom. Sounded like she was having a shower.

Turning, he went into his own room and pulled his suitcase out from under the bed. He zipped it open and dug out the bottle of sleeping pills he'd brought along in case of insomnia. He read the directions, the warning. Shaking the bottle, he guessed it was about three-quarters full.

That should be plenty.

****

Back in the kitchen, Daniel poured himself a glass of whiskey from the bottle stashed above the sink. He tossed back a measure, wincing as the liquid burned his throat, then bloomed hot in his chest. His eyes watering, he filled the glass again, the whiskey fumes filling his nostrils.

He couldn't believe he was thinking this way. But he had to get rid of her, and it had to be…permanent.

Pulling on his jacket, he tucked the bottle of pills into the pocket. He pulled a saucepan from the kitchen cupboard, and taking a flat-bottomed glass with him, he went out to the back porch.

He dropped six pills into the pan—three times the maximum adult dose—and carefully crushed them with the glass. She was less than half his weight, so that should be more than enough. He'd mix it in her food—or maybe in cocoa. That'd cover up the bitter taste if he didn't use too much. He couldn't risk her noticing anything strange.

In the kitchen again, he poured the powdered pills into the bottom of a mug and added a heaping spoonful of cocoa and three of sugar, mixing them all together. Ready for making the cocoa later.

Darkness was starting to close in. He made them a meal—the pizza he'd bought yesterday, heated in the oven—and called the girl down to eat.

As she entered the kitchen, she did a small twirl. "I used the hair color you brought me," she said, lifting a strand of dull-brown hair and pushing it behind her ears.

He glanced at her and blinked. "So I see." It definitely changed her appearance—though he no longer cared about disguising her.

"But don't worry, I cleaned up the mess in the bathroom."

He forced himself to smile. "Good for you." A mess in the bathroom was the least of his concerns.

They ate quietly, neither of them speaking much. Afterward he asked if she wanted to play cards; he figured that would pass the time until the pills took effect.

She reached for the deck of cards on the counter. "I'll try to beat you this time," she said, with a little laugh. Her laughter, so pleasing to him yesterday, irritated him today. But he tamped down his distaste. "I'll make some cocoa while you deal," he said.

He made cocoa the way Patricia had always done

it; he'd watched her many times over the years. Milk in the pan, heated slowly on the stove. Add cold milk to the already-mixed cocoa and sugar in the cup to make a paste. Of course Patricia's method didn't include sleeping pills, but he was glad to see that the powdered drug dissolved perfectly in the milk along with the cocoa and sugar.

When the milk started to steam in the pan, he added a little to the paste in the mug, then tipped the whole mixture back into the pan, stirring it in until the cocoa was smooth and uniform in color. He poured it into a fresh mug for the girl, then sat down to pick up the cards she'd dealt him.

"Don't you have any marshmallows?" she asked.

He shook his head. He wished he'd thought of that—it would have helped cover the taste. "No, sorry," he said.

"That's all right. It's just that my mom—" She stopped, glancing at him.

He nodded. He didn't care if she called Susan her mom. Not anymore.

She sipped the cocoa and played her hand. She was bright-eyed and eager at the beginning, actually playing quite well. She won the first game, and he dealt the cards for another.

But as the level of the cocoa fell in the cup, her eyes began to droop.

She jerked herself upright and stared at the cards in her hand. "Did...did I already dish...discard..." Her words were slurring. She reached toward the central card pile, but ended up spilling it. Cards fanned across the surface and several ended up on the floor.

"I'm sorry," she mumbled, putting her elbow on

the table and propping her head up. "I'm really…" Her voice trailed off, and a minute later she laid her head next to her cards. As Daniel watched, her body folded up, and she slipped to the floor.

Suddenly shaken, he dropped to his knees next to her. He frantically felt for her pulse.

Still beating.

He couldn't go on with this. Looking around for his phone, he fought down panic. He had to call an ambulance, get her to a doctor.

Don't do that. Patricia's voice was stern. *You have to follow through now.*

He turned back to stare at the girl, motionless with her legs crumpled under her.

She hadn't drunk all the cocoa, but it had knocked her right out. Was it enough to…finish the job?

He had to get her out of the kitchen, at least. He fit his arms awkwardly under her knees and shoulders and stood up, his knees groaning. She was heavier than he'd expected, and limp; her feet and arms bumped against the sides of the doorway and then the hall. He struggled to carry her upstairs; she was a dead weight, and the steps had never felt so steep.

A whisper in his mind said *you can still treat her decently*. He laid her out straight on her back on the bed, fully clothed, and covered her up with a blanket. He stood watching, listening to her faint breaths. Already they seemed quieter.

He pulled down the blind and went back downstairs.

Chapter Forty-One

Rolling out of bed Saturday morning, I stumbled into the bathroom and winced at my image in the mirror. My eyes had dark circles underneath, and my hair was tangled. Time for damage control—but all I had patience for was some moisturizer and a few swipes with a hairbrush.

Abel and Jenny had organized a postering blitz for this morning, but I wasn't looking forward to it. I knew it was important to get the posters distributed widely, but my energy was at a low ebb.

The sky was overcast, with flat gray clouds hovering low overhead as I locked my front door and headed toward the local church where people were gathering. I trudged along the sidewalk, the air cool on my face, my hands in my pockets.

I got to the church about ten to nine. A crowd had already gathered inside. People were standing around, chatting in small clusters, sipping coffees. More people arrived as I watched. Scanning the crowd, I saw that Jenny and Abel were at a table at the far end of the room. I tried to slip through the crowd to them, but people kept wanting to speak to me. Nicole introduced a group of friends from her gym, and she'd also brought other parents from Maddy and Emma's school. Some of our clinic staff had showed up, full of concern. Members of Jenny's book club had come, as well as several people from her office. Tom and Amy were there, with two of Amy's cousins and a few neighbors. Several had brought friends along.

I made a point of thanking everyone for coming out, but it took effort.

When I got to the front of the room, it was clear that Abel and Jenny had everything under control. They had set up a table, with piles of posters at one end and a city map laid out flat at the other. As people lined up, Abel assigned a neighborhood to each person or team, while Jenny wrote down their names and assignments and handed them a stack of posters.

I slipped in next to Jenny. "Do you really need me here?" I whispered.

She gave me a sharp glance. "No, we're fine. Why don't you go have a coffee, or take a walk..."

"Thanks, I think I'll just go back home."

I scuffed along the sidewalk with my head bowed, retracing my steps. Sudden wind gusts were lifting leaves from the gutters and sending them scudding along the sidewalks. A sense of dread was filling me, a sense that Maddy's time was running out.

Daniel was on my mind. I couldn't stop thinking about him. Somehow his alibi just didn't seem enough to eliminate him as a concern. On an impulse, I decided I had to go to his house and confront him.

I'd have to get his address from Bob.

Chapter Forty-Two

Daniel crept into the upstairs bedroom where he'd left the girl the night before. He expected—or dreaded—to find her lifeless.

He bent over the bed. She lay still, not moving. The blanket was tight around her, the way he'd left it. Her face was in shadow, hardly visible in the dim light seeping around the window blind. She must have shifted in the night—her body was tilted to one side, and he'd laid her out flat—but she was motionless now.

The tightness in his shoulders released. *Okay, it's over.*

He knelt and placed his fingers on her neck, then her wrist.

No pulse.

She felt cool.

But not cold.

Then something fluttered at her throat, just below the skin. So slight that he wasn't sure he'd seen it, until it happened again.

He reached forward, placing his hand in front of her face. A tiny whiff of air brushed his palm. A breath—almost not a breath at all, but a breath.

For a moment he was relieved. He jerked to his feet and stumbled out of the room.

His mouth dry, he paced up and down the short hallway. He peered in at her again, watching for any motion. None came.

He turned away from her doorway and bent over, bracing his hands against his thighs.

You still have the same problem as yesterday. If she can testify, that's the end for you.

There'd be criminal charges, jail time. And he wasn't willing to go to jail for her.

He stood up, rubbing a sore spot at his lower back. No, he had to carry on.

But maybe he hadn't waited long enough for the drug to finish its job. He'd give it a little more time.

Wiping his palm across his mouth, he headed downstairs.

****

I phoned Bob to get Daniel's address, but he wasn't eager to give it to me. "What are you planning to do?"

"I can't just sit around waiting—I need to do something. And I can't get Daniel out of my mind. I want to go see him myself, see if I can get a vibe off him."

Silence. "A vibe? What does that mean?"

I was impatient. "I don't know, I just want to see how he reacts if I show up."

"You know he had an alibi for the night she disappeared; he couldn't have taken her. And we searched his house. Twice."

"I know. But he's been so obsessed with Maddy. I still think—"

"—and he knows now that Maddy isn't Hannah. I told him yesterday."

"How did he react when you told him?"

"He didn't take it well."

"What does that mean?"

"He nearly passed out—I thought he was having a heart attack or something."

I snorted. "No wonder. You were undermining his obsession. Shaking his world."

"Yeah, I guess. But he seemed to pull himself together before I left."

"Anyway, I'm going to go see him."

"At least wait until I can go with you. And I can't get away right now—I'm with my boys at hockey practice. I'll have to take them home first."

"You don't need to come with me. Just give me the address."

Bob finally told me where Daniel was living. I was surprised to learn that it was only a few streets away from our neighborhood. Though it made sense—that explained how he'd come across the girls in the first place.

I jumped in my car and headed that way. I wasn't sure what I'd say to Daniel, but I couldn't let go of the idea that he was involved with Maddy's absence somehow, and that she was in dreadful danger.

I located his house and parked across the street, taking a minute to check the surroundings. The street—Renfrew Avenue—was a lot like mine, lined with mature trees and two-story older houses, each with a short walkway leading from the sidewalk to a front porch. Narrow driveways between the houses suggested backyard garages, though many residents appeared to prefer parking in their driveways.

Daniel's house was two stories like the others, with yellow siding and a small porch. A dark green pickup truck was parked in the drive.

Grabbing my shoulder bag, I got out of my car. A gust of wind took my breath away; the day was turning colder after all. I clutched my jacket more closely to me and crossed the street at an angle so I'd pass by that truck. I assumed it was Daniel's, and I wanted to get a look at it before I knocked on his door.

There wasn't much to see, though, either in the front seat or the extended-cab back seat. No garbage, nothing left in the footwells or on the dash. Beyond the truck, the driveway led to two garages, one behind Daniel's house and one in the next yard, the two houses sharing the driveway. I headed toward Daniel's front door.

There was no answer to my knock, though a dog started to bark inside the house. I knocked again, and the barking came closer, sounding like it was right inside the door.

I knocked a third time, my knuckles resounding on the wood. This time I heard movement inside and a man's voice, saying something to the dog. Then a click. He was unlocking the door.

Finally the door opened, and Daniel's face appeared. He seemed flushed, though I couldn't fully see his face; he was leaning over, holding his dog's collar. I tried to see over his shoulder into the house, but the hallway was dark. He and the dog filled the small entryway.

"Dr. Koss—Susan—what are you doing here?" Before I could answer, he added, "Wait a minute." He closed the door, leaving me on the porch. In a few moments he reappeared with a jacket on and came outside, closing the door again behind him.

He was upright now. As I'd remembered from our

last encounter, his frame was thin and wiry, his eyes a few inches above mine. "Tucker gets a bit excited. It's better if we talk out here without him." The dog had stopped barking. "So what can I do for you? Why are you here?"

My stomach clenched; my body remembered the terror I'd felt the day he appeared at my door demanding to see Maddy. I sensed the same coiled energy in him I'd felt then.

But this time I was on the offensive. "You know very well. Maddy is missing, and we're looking for her."

He nodded. "Yeah, I know. It's terrible." Then he frowned. "But I had nothing to do with that. The cops know it—they even searched my house. Twice."

I glowered at him. "I'm not convinced. She wasn't here when they searched. But you could have her someplace else…"

He backed away, his palms up toward me. "No!" His eyes were in shadow. "I had nothing to do with it," he said again.

I leaned forward, not bothering to mask my fury. "I find it hard to believe that. You were so determined to see her, to get to know her."

He squared his shoulders, his voice raspy. "I'm sorry to hear she's still missing. I'm worried about her too…"

I snorted. "If you're so worried, why haven't you been out searching?"

He wiped his hand across his face. "How do you know I haven't been? I've seen the appeals on TV. I've been watching for her any time I'm out."

I stared at him, my hands on my hips. "You

insisted she was your granddaughter. If you believed that, and you didn't have her, you'd have been doing more than 'watching for her.' You'd be frantic. Weren't you terrified something would happen to her?"

****

Daniel blinked at Susan, doing his best to keep his breathing level.

At least Tucker had stopped barking, though that had actually helped—it had kept Susan out on the porch. He couldn't let her in, of course. He was fairly certain the girl wouldn't stir, but she might have left something lying around downstairs that Susan would recognize.

Susan had her hands on her hips, glaring at him. He forced himself to appear calm. "I told you I've been worried. I wish I could help, but I don't know what more I could do."

She kept leaning into his face, wouldn't back up. "A lot of people who don't know her at all are out searching and putting up posters. They seem more concerned than you are."

He had to get rid of her. "The police will find her, won't they?"

Susan glared. "They haven't found her yet. Every minute she's gone, she could be in worse danger."

Daniel clamped his lips tight and reached for the doorknob. "I'll keep an eye out, like I said. And I hope she turns up." He turned and went inside, closing and locking the door behind him.

****

I stared at the door that had closed in front of me. What a terrible man! His protestations of concern didn't convince me.

Bob had told him that Maddy wasn't his granddaughter. So maybe he really didn't care what happened to her. But something about his reaction felt off. Phony.

I wished I had X-ray eyes to see into his house, but I had no authority to demand to be let in. There wasn't anything more I could do.

But he gave me a sick feeling. I didn't trust him one bit.

A burgeoning rage rose inside me. I could almost feel heat shooting up through my body and filling my head.

Maddy would never have run away if Daniel hadn't appeared in our lives. We would never have had that disastrous DNA test—that was the trigger for her to leave, I was sure. Yes, there were other issues between Maddy and me. But she wouldn't have run away without the disruption Daniel brought into our lives.

I wanted to explode, to do something violent. I felt a savage urge to pound at Daniel, do something vicious. To let out my frustration and anger.

I stepped back from the door. My car was across the street, but something in me rebelled against just driving home. I needed to do something to punish Daniel.

Eyeing his truck sitting in the driveway alongside the house, I glanced back and realized that none of Daniel's windows overlooked it. I stalked over to the vehicle and walked around it.

I wished I knew a way to disable it. Maybe…could I slash his tires? I reached into my shoulder bag to see if I had anything sharp enough. Wallet, Kleenex, my small cosmetic bag, hairbrush, nail clipper…I shoved aside my almost-full bottle of water to search farther, then stopped.

My dad said something once about water in the gas tank. "Make sure to close the gas tank after you fill it; you don't want water getting in."

I unscrewed the cap to Daniel's gas tank and emptied my bottle of water into it. Whistling, I walked to my car.

****

Daniel heaved a sigh of relief when she left. Now he could check on the girl, see if the drug had finished its job. And he needed to do a sweep through the ground floor, make sure none of her belongings were visible.

Turning, he saw a little stack of the girl's drawings on the hall table and scooped them up. *Whew*. Good thing Susan didn't see those. He'd have to burn them.

Before he could move farther, there was another knock at the door. Tucker barked again, three short barks.

Daniel opened the door cautiously. It was Jim Trafford from next door.

"Hi—I just wanted to let you know I'm taking off now."

Daniel gave him a blank look.

"For my fishing trip."

Daniel dimly remembered him mentioning it. "Oh, yeah. Well, the best of luck. Enjoy the peace and quiet, and catch lots of fish." Jim had been good company these last few weeks; he'd taken Daniel to the Legion and helped fill some evenings, playing cards or going bowling. And that had accidentally given him an alibi for the night the girl went missing.

Jim started to tell him the details—his driving route, the things he had to stop and pick up on the way, the best time of day to fish. Daniel wanted to be civil. He was grateful, after all, but would the guy not shut up? If he was leaving, why not just get under way?

Jim reached into his pocket and pulled out a key. "I was hoping you'd feed my cat, Josie. She shouldn't be any trouble. Just needs to be fed once a day, and pet her a little if you've got time. Her food and water dishes are in the kitchen beside the stove, and I left the bag of dry cat food there too. Just fill up the water dish and the food dish. She nibbles at it all day. It's not like feeding a dog."

Daniel was about to refuse. How could he agree to feed a cat—he wouldn't even be here! He'd be long gone before Jim was back from this fishing trip.

Wait—this could work out in your favor.

Having a key to an empty house might be just what he needed.

"Sure, of course," he said, forcing a smile as he took the key. "I'll be happy to do that."

If he had to leave the cat unfed, so be it. He could always leave a big bowl of food and water to last until Jim got home.

Chapter Forty-Three

After Jim left, Daniel dashed upstairs to have a look at the girl. He'd heard nothing from her. Surely by now it'd be over?

On entering the room he thought she was finished. Tucker pushed his way in too, sniffing around the girl. Daniel felt a pang on the dog's behalf—Tucker had liked her, and she'd been good with him.

Coming closer, though, Daniel could see that she was still breathing, her breaths shallow but faintly visible.

Daniel fought down his impatience. Now that he'd decided to go ahead with this, he wanted it over. Somehow those sleeping pills weren't doing the job. Despite the amount he'd given her, they weren't finishing her off.

He could give her a second dose, but he wasn't sure how to get her to swallow it. Maybe try something else?

His mind flashed to the kitchen, to the sharp knives in the drawer. But he recoiled from that idea. He'd butchered pigs and chickens in his day, but he'd always found the actual killing hard to do.

And anything that left blood would be a problem, would leave traces. If anyone investigated, it would tie him to her.

It had to be a cleaner method.

Use a pillow.

He blinked.

It wouldn't leave blood. She was asleep, so she wouldn't struggle. And then it'd be over.

It'd be quicker than the sleeping pills.

But the idea—the image of him pressing down on her while she died—made him queasy.

And he wasn't in that much of a hurry. The pills were just taking longer than expected. It would still happen.

What if somebody comes here while you're waiting?

His mouth was dry. He couldn't risk her being found, now more than ever.

He had Jim's key; he could move her next door. It would give the pills time to work and give him a breather, time to figure out what to do.

He stood beside the bed, staring down at the girl. As far as he could tell, she was in a stupor, and her breathing was getting shallower. It was just a matter of time now.

But depending how long he had to leave her, it was possible the drugs could wear off instead of finishing her.

He couldn't risk her getting loose, not now. He was going to have to tie her up. He groaned inwardly; he didn't have any ropes or straps here—when he packed his tools at the farm to come here, it hadn't occurred to him he'd need restraints.

Duct tape. He had a roll of that. He headed downstairs and found the toolbox where he'd left it by the back door.

Upstairs again, he taped her ankles together. He

considered taping her hands behind her but decided to tape them in front so he could still lie her on her back. No reason to make her too uncomfortable, even though she was out cold.

He gathered her belongings and shoved them in her backpack.

First he should scout out his route. Leaving the girl where she was, he went downstairs and out the back door, making sure he had Jim's house key in his hand.

He crossed their shared driveway; he'd have to carry her across to Jim's side door. He couldn't risk being seen from the street. His truck, parked between the two houses, blocked most of the view, but there was still a gap. He'd have to be fast when he brought her.

He unlocked Jim's side door. It opened into an entryway with two steps leading up to the main floor. Living room on the left, kitchen on the right.

In the kitchen, a black and white cat raised its head and looked at him. It had been eating from its food bowl beside the counter and didn't seem either surprised or alarmed to see him. After a moment it bent its head back down and resumed its meal.

Walking through the kitchen, Daniel found a mudroom at the back. It was a small room with two high windows and a door into the backyard. A row of jackets hung on hooks along one wall. He made sure the back door was locked.

He'd bring her in here, where no one would be able to see her.

Returning to the kitchen, he scooped up the cat and moved it, along with its food and water dishes, into the downstairs washroom. He couldn't have it escaping from the house while he was bringing in the girl.

No time to delay now. Back upstairs in Aunt Ruby's house, he wrapped the blanket around the girl to mask the contours of her body. If anyone were to catch a glimpse of her, they'd just see an oblong shape. He lifted her, straightening his shoulders against the weight. She was awkward to carry—he had to turn her and edge sideways down the steps to keep her legs from catching on the stair rail.

As he exited the house, the girl in his arms, he thought he heard a car door. He stood still, ready to retreat, but heard nothing further. Glancing toward the street to confirm that nobody was walking by, he hurried across the driveway and in through Jim's side door, nudging it closed behind him. He maneuvered the girl up the steps and through the kitchen to the mudroom, laying her on the floor under the row of coats.

Should he put something under her, something softer? No, that made no sense. But he reached for one of the jackets, folded it and placed it beneath her head.

He checked to see if the coast was clear before crossing back to his own house. Once inside, he retrieved the girl's backpack and double-checked to make sure there was nothing of hers left lying around, either upstairs or downstairs. Couldn't leave any sign there'd been a kid in the house. He took the backpack with him as he returned to Jim's house and looked in on the girl once more. She hadn't budged.

Chapter Forty-Four

I was home again, fuming after the unproductive confrontation with Daniel, when my phone rang; it was Marie. "Susan, I'm sending you a video. Can you tell if that girl in the background is Maddy?"

A moment later a video popped up on my screen. In the foreground was a group of four young people— twenty-somethings—standing outdoors, laughing and joking together. Blue sky told me it wasn't taken today, but they were wearing warm jackets, so it was recent. They were in someone's backyard; lawn was visible, along with the corner of a shed, a leafless bush, and a chain-link fence behind them.

Marie had said there was a girl in the background. The screen image was so small, and the video was over so quickly, that I wasn't sure what I'd seen. I played it again, this time ignoring the group in the foreground and focusing on a figure visible behind the chain-link fence, in another yard beyond.

There was a girl, all right, but I strained to get a clear view of her face in the tiny image. She seemed absorbed in whatever she was doing, moving back and forth in a kind of dance. She was partly blocked by the bush in the foreground, disappearing and reappearing behind it. A moment later a dog leapt into view, then vanished again. They were obviously playing chase or some kind of game.

My breath caught. Could it be? The girl's blonde hair was in a ponytail, and her figure was thin and wiry like Maddy's.

The image was small and blurry, but my heart leapt. *Yes! It's got to be her.*

I called Marie immediately. "Marie, it looks like her. What is this? When was it taken? Where is she?"

"We got a call this morning from the guy who took it. He says he took it Wednesday morning; some of his friends were helping him move stuff, and he'd recorded them goofing around. But this morning he was watching it again and noticed the girl in the background. He thought it might be her, so he called it in."

"Where were they when—?"

"He took it at his parents' house. They live on Powell Avenue."

I frowned. "Where's Powell?"

"It's over toward Bronson," she said. "And get this. Powell is one street over from Renfrew—their yards back on each other."

Wait a minute—I just got back from Renfrew. "That has to be Daniel's backyard!" I glared at the phone, even though Marie couldn't see me. "And you told me he had nothing to do with it!"

"I'm way ahead of you. We're already on the way to his house."

"Great. I'm coming too."

I could sense her disapproval. "I can't stop you. But you'll have to wait on the street. If we find her, we'll bring her out."

I grabbed my jacket and purse and slammed out of the house. Good thing there wasn't much traffic; I scarcely noticed anything between my place and Renfrew Avenue.

Two police cars were pulled up in front of Daniel's house. I parked on the opposite side, the same spot I'd parked in earlier. It gave me a good view of his house and driveway. His truck was still there, right where it had been earlier. I waited for nearly half an hour, impatiently tapping against the steering wheel. Then Marie came out and came across the street to my car. I rolled the window down.

Marie leaned over. "There's no sign of her in the house. Or in his garage or truck. No sign she's ever been there, so—"

I had to interrupt. "But I saw her on the video! In the backyard!"

She grimaced. "I've just checked with the guy who took the video. His parents' house is farther down the block. The yard backing on that property is not Daniel's yard."

I felt sick. "Whose yard is it?"

"I'm heading there now to find out."

I watched Marie and Kevin drive down the street, stopping halfway down the block. The officers in the other police car followed them.

Marie knocked on the door. There was no answer. She knocked again. Still no one came to the door. She disappeared around the side of the house, Kevin at her heels.

Minutes later she returned to the street, facing in my direction. I started my car and rolled toward her.

She leaned into my window. "There doesn't seem to be anyone home. I'll find out who lives here, and we'll come back later."

I wailed. "Later! We know she was seen in their yard…"

"You're not positive it was her. And it was two days ago. We have no reason to think she's still here."

"Can't you break in?" She looked shocked. "Or get a warrant or something?"

"Susan, I said we'll be back and check it out."

Chapter Forty-Five

Maddy couldn't make out where she was. She couldn't see a thing, and there was an odd smell, like old running shoes. Moving her head from side to side, she realized she was lying on something hard. Had she fallen out of bed?

Her head hurt, and her thoughts didn't seem to flow. There was a terrible taste in her mouth.

Darkness. She was gone again.

****

Something soft brushed against her face. It was bothering her nose, making her want to sneeze. She shook her head, trying to move away from it. It came again, a hard push this time. A purring sound.

Oscar? What was he doing here?

The cat kept rubbing against her, making a *mmmrr* sound.

She tried reaching out to it, to push it away. Her hands were stuck together; she couldn't separate them. And everything was so dark.

****

The next time she woke, there was no cat. She still couldn't see anything, and her head felt thick, woolly.

Think. But thoughts wouldn't come.

****

She tried to sit up, then fell back. Tried to roll over, but her feet seemed caught, tangled together somehow.

Lis Angus

Tried to call out, but couldn't open her mouth; something held her lips closed.

Bringing her hands up to her mouth, she could feel something flat and smooth stretched across it, something thin but firm. Like...it was some kind of tape. She reached her hands to her eyes. Tape covered them too.

She tried to separate her hands but couldn't. And she couldn't move her legs apart either; when she stretched one, the other moved with it. A jolt of fear shot through her, as she struggled to get loose from whatever gripped her.

She had her first clear thought. *I'm tied up.*

Someone had done this to her.

Her throat tightened, and she fought down her panic, trying to get rid of the muddy feeling in her head. She tried recalling her last memory. It was...having supper. Pizza. And cocoa. And playing cards...

She couldn't remember anything since then.

Lifting her hands to her face again, she scraped at the tape over her eyes. Her thumbnail caught under one corner, and she managed to pull it back enough to partly see something out of one eye.

It's daylight! That was a surprise. But...it was dark when they were playing cards. So this must be another day. What had happened to the night?

She didn't recognize where she was. This wasn't any room in Daniel's house. She was on the floor in some strange house, tied up.

Her breaths were coming fast and shallow now, puffing in and out through her nose. She reached to loosen the tape at her mouth, then jerked back as she heard steps. Instinctively she relaxed her hands and lay

258

still, doing her best to control her breathing.

A door creaked open, and the steps came closer. She could see a sliver of the room at the side of the loosened tape.

And a face appeared in that sliver.

Daniel.

Relief flooded through her. *He'll get me out of this!* But something about his movements made her wary. She lay still. His footsteps came closer, then moved away.

He must have seen her, but he wasn't doing anything to rescue her.

She risked another peek; he was at the doorway, heading down a hallway. What was he doing?

She'd thought he was a nice man. Yet...he didn't seem surprised that she was lying here, tied up.

Was he the one who did it?

The thought chilled her.

He'd been talking about a trip out west. He'd said they'd leave on Saturday. *But today must be Saturday.* He'd been talking about it like something they'd do together. Not something he'd force on her.

Why did he tie her up?

She suddenly longed for her mom. Mom would protect her. She might be bossy, but that wasn't the worst thing. Maddy ached to be back in her own house.

But her mom wasn't there. Her instinct said *lay low*; *don't let on you're awake.*

****

I was barely home from Daniel's when Bob showed up on my doorstep. "Hi, hockey practice is over. I thought I'd stop by, bring you a coffee." He held out a cup with a cardboard sleeve around it.

I accepted it and stepped back to let him in, and we headed to the kitchen.

"Did you go to Daniel's house?" he asked.

"Yeah, I did." I glanced at him; he didn't say anything, but I could tell he wanted to hear more. I sat across from him, fidgeting. I took a sip of coffee but could hardly taste it. "I have a bad feeling about him. He opened his door but didn't invite me in. He came out onto the porch to talk to me."

He cocked his head. "That's not surprising. When he came here, you didn't invite him in either."

"Well of course not!" I'd been terrified; I certainly couldn't have Daniel in my house. But I did see Bob's point. Daniel and I weren't exactly on visiting terms.

"I was over there just now a second time, while Marie and some other cops searched his house."

He raised his eyebrows. "Again? Why?"

"Somebody had a video with a girl, looked like Maddy. She was in a yard that had to be on Renfrew. Daniel's street."

"But they didn't find her—?"

I shook my head. "No. And it turned out that the yard in the video wasn't even Daniel's."

"So…"

I slammed my coffee cup against the table. "There's something not right about him." I turned my eyes to Bob's. "If he thinks Maddy is his granddaughter, wouldn't he be as distraught as I am about her being missing for so long?"

"Susan, he knows now that she isn't his granddaughter. I told him yesterday."

"Well, in that case you'd think he'd apologize for all the trouble he's caused. But he wasn't apologetic in the slightest."

"He doesn't seem like the apologizing type."

"What if Marie and the others missed something?"

He frowned at me. "They know how to do a search."

"They might not recognize something of Maddy's. Just because she's not there now doesn't mean she never was. What if there's something that I'd spot as hers…"

"What are you saying?"

I jumped to my feet. "I'm going back there. I have to check for myself. I won't let him keep me out this time."

Bob rose with me. "That's not a good idea."

"You can't stop me."

"Maybe not. But if you're going, I'll drive you. I don't think you're in any condition to drive safely."

****

His heart pounding, Daniel closed and locked the front door, taking a quick glance around the front hall as he headed back to the kitchen. Thank God he'd moved the girl and her belongings out of the house before the police arrived.

But they could come back any time. And having the girl stashed next door was too close for comfort. It was time to get her out of there.

There wasn't much left to do. He'd tossed his clothes into his suitcase earlier, and his tools were already in the truck.

Moving steadily, he emptied the perishables from the fridge into a garbage bag and dashed upstairs to grab his case. Back in the kitchen, he crushed several more sleeping pills and dumped them into a bottle of water, shaking it to dissolve them. If she was still alive, he'd get a last dose into her before they left.

As an afterthought, he wiped down the counters. He grabbed his suitcase and opened the back door. He let Tucker out and locked the door behind them.

That's goodbye to Aunt Ruby's house.

Next door at Jim's, Daniel filled two large bowls with dry cat food and water and took them into the downstairs washroom. The cat was no longer there; it must have nudged the door open and had gotten out. But here it was again, pushing against his ankles. Daniel put the dishes down, and the cat began to pick daintily at the dish of food. He closed the door, making sure to close it tightly this time, and headed to the mudroom.

The girl wasn't moving and looked out of it, but she was still breathing.

Get that last dose into her.

Kneeling beside the girl, he uncapped the water bottle and pulled the tape off her mouth. She made a sound, and he thought she might wake. But it was a false alarm. She was still limp and unresponsive.

He put an arm under her head to lift it so he could pour water into her mouth, hoping that she'd instinctively swallow. Her mouth filled with water, and then she choked, convulsing against his arm. Water flowed down her chin, but he thought most of it went down her throat.

That should do it.

He laid her head back on the floor while he cut another section of duct tape and applied it to her mouth. Then, wrapping her in the blanket and picking her up— hooking a finger through a strap on her backpack, so he wouldn't have to come back for it—he moved to the side door.

Now the riskiest part. He opened the door and peered toward the street; he didn't see anyone.

He got her in the cab of the truck and laid her in the footwell behind the front seat. He tucked the blanket over her, blocking her from view. She didn't stir.

As he climbed into the front seat, he paused. Had he forgotten anything?

He got out again, made sure Jim's door was closed and locked, then left the key in Jim's mailbox.

Putting the truck in gear, he pulled out of the driveway, heading toward Bronson Avenue. He could get onto the Queensway from there. That'd be the quickest way out of town, out to the countryside. He'd find someplace out there to get rid of her.

****

As we pulled up to Daniel's house, I peered up and down the street. There was no vehicle in the driveway or parked at the curb. So Daniel had left. I leapt out of the car and slammed the door, striding up the front walkway with Bob close behind.

Standing on the front porch, I grabbed the door handle and tried to turn it. It didn't budge; the door was locked. I glanced at Bob over my shoulder. He shook his head. "We can't go in."

I snorted. *Try and stop me.* "You may have rules, but I don't." I reached into my purse and pulled out a credit card. Turning to the door, I inserted the card into the doorjamb, swiping it down as I'd seen on TV.

Bob loomed over my shoulder. "You can't just break into his house."

I continued wiggling my card. "Why not? If he has

my daughter…as an illegal act, I'd say that trumps my entering his house."

He leaned in, closely watching my fruitless efforts with the credit card. "You have no proof he's got her. What do you think you're going to find in there, anyway?"

I was gripping the card so hard my fingers hurt. "I don't know. I just want to see if there's any sign that she's been staying here. And any clues about what's been going on."

Bob looked skeptical.

I kept wiggling the card. "We have nothing to lose by trying." But I was having no luck; the card just stuck. It wouldn't slip down beside the lock, no matter how I jiggled either the card or the door.

He sighed. "Let's see if there's a back door."

I followed him around toward the back of the house. As we rounded the corner, a dog started barking.

Bob raised his hand. "Hold on—that's Daniel's dog."

Peering past his shoulder, I could see a yellow Lab standing in the middle of the backyard, watching us. Barking, but not approaching.

"Do you think he's dangerous?" I asked.

"No, I saw him with Daniel before; I think he's pretty tame. Just barking because we're here." Bob turned to me. "But if Daniel's left his dog here, he won't have gone far. He'll be back."

"Right. So no time to lose. I want to get in there while he's gone." I ignored Bob, who was rolling his eyes. By now I suspected he was as interested as I was in what we might find.

Two steps led up to a back porch with a railing

running the width of the house. Beside the steps were three trash cans, lined up in a row.

I started up the steps, but Bob stopped to lift the lid off one of the trash cans, revealing a tightly filled black plastic garbage bag. He undid the twist tie and peered in. "This looks like food and stuff from the fridge."

I watched him check the other two trash cans. They were similarly full, though their contents appeared to be more like junk.

My chest tightened. "If he cleaned out his fridge, that seems like he's not planning to be back." Bob frowned, his eyes in shadow.

He joined me on the porch and reached to wiggle the back door handle. No surprise, it was locked.

I pulled out my credit card again. There was a bigger crevice in this doorjamb. The card slipped down more easily, but I still couldn't get the lock to open.

Bob shifted his feet. I could see him square his shoulders. "Let me try."

I smiled wryly. *So much for Mr. Upstanding.*

The door slipped open. Bob stood back. "I can't go in there." The unspoken postscript: *but you can.*

I crossed the threshold without hesitating. The door opened into a tidy kitchen. The counters had been wiped and the sink was clean. The fridge held a bottle of ketchup and a jar of pickles, nothing else. I checked a couple of cupboards, finding only a few dishes, some canned items, and a package of dry pasta. And a half-full whiskey bottle in the cupboard over the sink.

Bob was still outside, leaning against the railing of the back porch, though he'd been watching me through the open doorway.

"I'm going upstairs," I said. He shrugged, having

apparently given up on telling me what I could do or not do. I moved through the house, checking the downstairs rooms as well as the three bedrooms upstairs.

I checked each bedroom, opening the closets and bending to peer under the beds. I was about to leave the third one, near the back of the house, when I backtracked to look under the bed a second time. There was a scrap of something near the wall, at the back. I got down on my stomach to reach for it, and as I pulled it out, my heart rose in my throat.

It was a sock. A sock I'd held in my hands, along with its mate, every time I did laundry for the past six months. I pressed it to my face, tears streaming down my cheeks.

Stumbling downstairs with it in my hand, I flung myself toward the open back door where Bob still waited, leaning against the porch railing. "This is Maddy's," I cried. "It was in one of the upstairs bedrooms."

Bob stood up straight. "You're sure?" His eyes searched mine, then he nodded. "Yeah, you're sure." He moved forward. "I'll just have a quick look around." Ducking his head under the low doorframe, he went upstairs.

Shortly he returned. "I checked the rooms again. There wasn't much, but I found a couple of hair elastics in the bathroom. Do you recognize these?"

I inspected them. "I can't be sure—but that's the kind she uses."

"There's something else. There were strips of crumpled duct tape in the garbage too."

"Duct tape?"

"It works quite well as a restraint. If that's what…"

My eyes widened. "Are you suggesting he tied her—taped her up?"

"Maybe. While I was waiting for you, I checked that garbage can again, found this on top." He showed me an empty prescription bottle. "The label says it's for something called Zolpidem. Not sure what that is, but he may have drugged her too."

Just then the dog gave another short bark.

We both turned to look at him. He was still standing in the center of the yard, watching us.

"So why would he leave his dog behind?" I said.

"Yeah, that's weird. That dog's like part of his family."

"I can't think of a reason…unless—" Goose bumps rose on my arms. "He obviously left in a hurry— Marie and her crew were here less than two hours ago. I wonder if he just plain forgot his dog in the rush."

I turned to Bob, a sick feeling rising in my stomach. "If he's that confused…it makes me all the more worried for Maddy."

My head was pounding. I ran to the driveway, staring at the spot where Daniel's truck had been this morning. *He's taken her. And drugged and bound her.*

I had to do something, but I had no idea what. My fear was almost incapacitating.

Bob was behind me. I could hear him on his phone, calling Marie to update her on this development.

He turned to me. "She's putting out an alert on Daniel's license plate."

"Does she know his plate number?"

"Sure, she noted it this morning when she was here."

I swayed, suddenly feeling dizzy. "Oh my God. He's got Maddy."

"… It looks that way."

"We have to find them." My heart was racing, and my palms were sweating, despite the cold air. I stared around me, more frantic by the minute.

Bob took my arm and guided me to Daniel's front step. "Take a seat," he advised. "You're hyperventilating. Try and catch your breath." Reluctantly I sat down, my legs stretched in front of me and my head between my knees. After a minute my light-headedness lifted, but I could still feel adrenaline-fueled energy pulsing through me, demanding that I do something, anything.

Just then Bob's phone rang. He stepped away to answer it. "Great," I heard him say. "That's him." He turned to face me. "That was Marie. Daniel's truck has just been spotted on the Queensway, heading west."

"How did they find him so fast?"

"An officer in a patrol car equipped with automatic license plate recognition saw him. Unfortunately the officer was driving east at the time. With the median in between the east and west lanes, they couldn't turn and follow him."

I jumped to my feet. "Well, let's go!"

"Marie and Kevin are already on the way."

"Come on—we have to get moving." I was sorry I'd come in Bob's car; if I had mine here, I wouldn't have to rely on him.

Bob looked doubtful. I glared at him, my hands on my hips. "He's got Maddy—we can't sit here doing nothing!" What was wrong with him? "I know it's your day off, but you're still a cop."

He gave a wry grin. "Yeah, I am." As I dashed toward his car, he followed, pulling his keys from his pocket.

Chapter Forty-Six

Daniel pulled onto the Queensway, heading west toward Highway 17 and the Trans-Canada Highway. This was the reverse of the route he'd followed on his way to Ottawa; he could follow this highway now all the way back to Alberta. As soon as he got rid of the girl.

And he didn't have much time. He needed to get out of the city and find a place to dispose of her before an alert went out.

Taking a quick glance over his shoulder, he could see that she was still lying motionless where he'd put her, in the footwell behind the front seat. He hoped that last dose he'd given her had done the trick.

Wait. Where's Tucker?

Daniel caught his breath. Tucker wasn't in the back seat.

He'd meant to put the dog in the truck before getting the girl from Jim's house.

But he hadn't. He'd left Tucker in the backyard.

He gasped, his stomach clenching.

Too late now. You can't go back.

His eyes stung. What had he been thinking?

Don't lose focus now. You have to take this to the end. Get rid of the girl and move on.

He swallowed and sped up, his hands gripping the steering wheel tightly. There was a lot of traffic, more than he liked. A sudden pain pounded his temples, and his vision dimmed. The pain soon passed, but he'd almost clipped the car next to him. He couldn't slow down now, though—he had to put as much distance behind them as he could.

A wailing siren shrilled, making his heart pound. His rearview mirror showed flashing lights racing toward them on the paved shoulder. A police car. Daniel's heart raced, and his breath came fast. Could they be after him already? His palms were sweaty. He wiped them one at a time on his pants leg, doing his best to stay in his lane and maintain speed while watching the image in the mirror.

The police car was soon abreast of them, driving on the shoulder. Daniel concentrated on the highway and the traffic, his eyes now focused straight ahead. "No, Officer," he imagined himself saying, "I didn't see you there..."

He hoped the blanket he'd covered the girl with hadn't slipped, but it wouldn't fool a cop for long.

The police car kept on going, still flashing, still sounding its siren It pulled away from them and was now well ahead.

He's not after you. Chasing someone else.

Daniel exhaled. It took him a few minutes to calm down, concentrating on taking deep breaths. The truck was driving a bit sluggishly, so he pressed harder on the accelerator.

His mind spun; he needed a plan. As soon as they got out of the city, he'd pull off the highway and move onto side roads. He had come past a lot of wooded areas and farm country along there on his way into Ottawa; he'd find a spot to hide or bury her. Once that was done, he'd get back on the highway and keep driving west, go back to the farm.

A momentary desolation washed over him. He'd imagined returning to the farm with Hannah, but that wasn't going to happen. It had been fool's gold, a dream best forgotten.

****

Vibration. A side-to-side motion, and a rumbling sound. As her body swayed to and fro, Maddy kept bumping against something on either side of her. She was woozy, sick.

How long had she been out of it?

Something was scratchy against her face. The dank, woolly smell was familiar; it was the same blanket she'd had over her earlier. But she wasn't in that room anymore—from the sounds and motion, she guessed she was in a vehicle. Daniel's truck. He was taking her someplace.

The drink he'd given her was disgusting, bitter and grainy—she could still taste the residue in her mouth. It had made her choke, but some had gone down her throat. She'd spit a lot of it up again when he moved away to get the duct tape.

An acrid odor filled the air, faint but unmistakable. *I peed my pants*. She squirmed, cringing at the clammy dampness.

Her wrists and ankles were tightly bound, but she was able to reach her hands under the blanket and loosen the tape over her eyes. Through a gap at the side of the blanket she could see daylight.

She was in a truck all right, on the floor behind a front bench seat, wedged between it and the back seat.

Where was Daniel taking her? Whatever he was

272

planning, it couldn't be good. Her throat tightened, and her eyes burned. She fought down the panic that threatened to overwhelm her.

Shifting her sight toward the driver's spot, she was relieved to see that Daniel wasn't visible. So he couldn't see her either. But he could probably hear her, so she'd have to be quiet.

She loosened the tape at her mouth as well. That helped; now she could breathe better. She left the tape partly in place so it wouldn't be obvious that it was loose, if he checked her.

Bending her knees, she tried to reach her ankle bonds, but she couldn't get her bound hands in position to touch them. She started to turn onto her side, trying not to make a sound, but she couldn't keep her movements from *skritching* against the floor. She held her breath. Daniel didn't seem to have noticed, but she'd better lie still a while before trying again.

****

Sitting in Bob's passenger seat, I gripped my hands tightly together. I realized I had wedged my right foot tight to the floor, pressing on a phantom gas pedal. I forced myself to let up the pressure.

I leaned over to check the speedometer. "Can't you go any faster?"

"No. There's too much traffic."

I fumed. Sure, there was traffic, but it was moving. Cars and trucks in the lanes ahead and beside us were travelling at a good clip. And if there was ever a time for more speed, this was it.

His phone rang, and he pressed the hands-free button to answer. It was Marie, sounding harried. "He's been seen again on the 417, just before Terry Fox

Drive. We're about ten minutes behind him."

Bob answered. "We're a little farther away than that, but we'll be there soon."

Marie said nothing for a moment. "Who's 'we'?"

I let out the breath I'd been holding. "I'm here with Bob."

"Susan? What are you doing there?" She sounded dubious. "You should leave Kevin and me to handle Kazan. This could get messy."

I didn't want to think about what she meant by "messy." And I didn't care. "If Maddy's with him, I need to be there."

She paused. "All right. I understand."

Bob broke in. "Marie, you need to get there before I do. I'm in my personal car, so it's best if I'm not the first on the scene."

"Yeah, I know. We're close. We'll have him soon."

She hung up. Bob leaned forward, attention focused on the highway, skillfully moving from lane to lane as traffic permitted.

I swallowed, trying to lubricate my dry throat. I wanted to be there now. "Don't you have a siren?"

"Not in this car. Anyway, a siren could spook him, and he's unpredictable enough as it is."

I nodded, bowing to his better tactical sense. But I was impatient, wound tight, my shoulders tensed.

****

Daniel had noticed something wrong with the truck a while back. Every so often it gave a lurch, as if the engine was skipping or hiccupping, and it was getting worse.

Now the lurching was incessant; the truck was

almost coughing. He watched the traffic in the right-hand lane, looking for a gap between cars. He was going to have to pull over—he couldn't be jack-rabbiting down the road like this.

Finally an opening appeared, and he pulled into the right-hand lane, ready to take the next exit. Both his hands were gripping the steering wheel.

He risked another quick glance over the back seat. The girl wasn't moving. He couldn't tell if she'd stopped breathing or not.

Chapter Forty-Seven

Maddy tried again to turn on her side. Slowly she shifted her body, moving as silently as she could. Reaching down, she managed to touch her ankle. *Yes!* But her fingers kept slipping on the tape, and she couldn't locate an end or a loose corner.

Her body swayed again, bumping hard against the front seat. Something was happening to the truck. It was lurching, jerking. Now it was slowing. Was he stopping?

She'd hoped to loosen her bonds before they stopped, if she had any chance to get away. But she hadn't made any progress. She wasn't ready. An icicle of fear clutched her stomach. She could hardly breathe.

It'd be obvious, the first time he looked at her, that she'd moved. She did her best to shift onto her back again and stretch out her legs. She closed her eyes and lightly pressed the tape strips back over her eyes and mouth. She pulled the blanket back into position and concentrated on not moving.

The truck stopped. She heard a scratchy sound just above her and guessed that Daniel was leaning over the back of his seat.

Lie still. She'd heard of animals playing dead. Instinct told her that was now her best option.

****

The truck still jerking and almost stalling, Daniel

pulled in behind a warehouse. He hoped he'd be out of sight here, invisible from the street.

This wasn't at all what he'd planned. He'd wanted to find a secluded, wooded area in the country to drop her in. He stared around him at the empty parking lot; at least he had the space to himself, it being Saturday, but this was still within city limits. Not a lot of options here for disposing of a body.

The far side of the paved parking area ended abruptly at a vacant lot filled with scrubby brush. Daniel eyed it speculatively. It wasn't the ideal place to leave her, but it might work. The bushes were thick enough that the deeper part of the lot was hidden. He could dump her there.

It could be days before she's found. By then you'll be long gone.

He'd need to get to a service station, get them to fix whatever was wrong with the truck, but then he'd be on his way.

But first he had to deal with her. He pulled ahead, stopping as close to the vacant lot as he could get, and turned off the motor.

He got out and opened the back door. She was lying just as he'd left her, on her back, covered with the blanket. Pulling on her ankles, he dragged her toward him so he could get hold of her. Her body was limp; it sagged until he got a grip on her, the blanket falling away as he pulled. Holding her with one arm, he propped her body against the seat so he could grab the blanket and wrap it around her again. It would help disguise her shape. She'd be a lumpy package, not—at first glance—obviously a girl.

He struggled to get a purchase under her knees and

shoulders, heaving to pick her up. Well, this would be the last time moving her.

He'd find a spot deeper in the bush and drop her there.

****

Marie called Bob's cellphone, on speaker. I could hear frustration in her voice. "Kazan has left the Queensway. We were just ahead of him, about to pull him over, but he swerved and took the turnoff at Carp Road. Now we have to drive to the next exit so we can turn around." The median on the divided highway prevented U-turns.

I knew Bob was already on high alert, but at this news his shoulders rose and his hands tightened on the steering wheel. "We'll be at Carp Road in a couple of minutes. We'll find him."

My nails bit into my palms, and I was practically vibrating with anxiety. "Faster—we can't lose him now!"

"I know. We're almost there. Watch for a dark green pickup."

A minute later we pulled into the exit, which curved off to the right and ended at a T junction. *Oh my God.* Which way did he go?

Bob didn't hesitate. He barely stopped before turning right, revving into the intersection.

****

When the truck door opened, the sudden cold air startled Maddy, but she was careful not to move as Daniel gripped her ankles and pulled her toward him.

Her heart jumped in terror, but with a huge effort she forced herself to stay limp and keep her breathing shallow. She felt herself start to slip as he pulled her out of the truck, and willed herself not to react. She hoped he wouldn't realize she was awake and alert.

His grip tightened, and he seemed to have her in balance, though he soon shifted her position again so she was slung partly over his shoulder. He was moving quickly as he carried her, his footsteps thudding dully below.

Oh my God. Where's he taking me?

His breathing was loud in her ear, and the smell of his sweat filled her nostrils.

She fought down panic and tried to think past the fog that still filled her head.

In all the movement, the tapes over her eyes and mouth had come loose again. She risked a one-eyed squint. The way he had her positioned, Daniel couldn't see her face. She opened her eye wide. Her field of vision was narrow, letting her see just a sliver of their surroundings as they moved along.

A branch slipped past her head, almost bare of leaves. A bush. Another bush. Farther back she could see an empty parking lot and a low building beyond it.

As they passed a third bush, a car pulled into the parking lot. The car doors opened, and two people jumped out. One was a small woman with dark hair. Maddy stared. *Mom?* She almost gasped, filled with relief. Mom was here.

She came.

****

"Is that Daniel's truck?" I asked as we pulled into the otherwise empty parking lot.

Our tires squealed as Bob pulled up behind the vehicle. "Yup, it's his license plate."

My eyes on the truck, I flung open my door and

leapt out. In the absence of anything resembling a weapon, I kept a firm hold on the heavy flashlight I'd found in the side pocket of the car. I could hear Bob's steps behind me as we ran.

The truck's back door was gaping wide, but the cab was empty. "They're gone," Bob said.

There were sounds in the bush ahead of us, beyond the parking lot. I heard a voice that I'd know anywhere. "Mom! Help!"

I raced toward the bush, Bob pounding behind me. Up ahead I glimpsed a figure careening through the underbrush. Daniel. He was moving awkwardly, overbalanced by the bundle he was carrying, a bundle that was now wriggling mightily.

Maddy.

I ignored the thin branches whipping against my face as I gained on Daniel. He was lurching, Maddy in a bundle across his shoulder. Suddenly he let out a yelp and stumbled, just as I reached him with a final burst of speed. I lifted the flashlight and hit him across the back of his head with all my strength, every frustration and fear I'd felt for the past days flowing into my arm.

Daniel fell to the ground, dropping Maddy.

****

Maddy hit the ground hard, air driven out of her lungs. Daniel collapsed next to her, unmoving.

Mom had done something—had she killed him?

Maddy lay there, catching her breath as her mom gathered her in her arms.

Some other people arrived. One called for an ambulance, and another put handcuffs on Daniel.

Maddy felt herself drifting away.

****

I knelt beside Maddy and wrapped my arms around her. Her eyes were squeezed shut, her breaths coming in shuddering sobs. She was partly wrapped in a dingy blue blanket, strips of duct tape hanging off the side of her face. More tape bound her wrists and her ankles.

Tears poured down my face. "Oh, sweetie. We'll get you out of here. I can't tell you how glad I am to see you."

Bob turned to me. "Well, you stopped him all right. We need an ambulance."

Chapter Forty-Eight

Two ambulances were on the way.

We'd removed all of Maddy's bindings, and I took off my coat to cover her. I shivered in the fall air, but being cold was a small exchange for the safety of my girl.

Maddy's eyes were closed. I rubbed her wrists and ankles, worried that being bound for so long might have reduced her circulation. Whatever drug Daniel had given her appeared to be overtaking her. She was short of breath and hadn't spoken more than five words.

Her hair hung in wisps and was a weird brown color. What was that about?

Marie had handcuffed Daniel, and when the ambulances arrived—pulling into the lot right after each other—the paramedics loaded him into one of them. I must have done more damage to his head than I thought; they said his condition was serious. I didn't care. If I could have hurt him more, I would have.

Other paramedics lifted Maddy onto a stretcher and headed for the second ambulance. I pulled my coat back on and followed. "I'm going with her," I told Bob

He nodded. "Of course. I'll be in touch."

In the ambulance, Maddy lay on a gurney, and I perched in a jump seat on one side. The paramedic was bent over her attentively, doing tests of some kind. "How's she doing?" I asked.

He didn't answer. His back was toward me, and he was absorbed in caring for her, adjusting equipment and the IV connection in her arm.

I asked again, my concern growing, and this time he turned to me, speaking over his shoulder. "Don't worry, we'll be at the hospital soon. The ER docs will take care of her."

That was it for conversation as we traversed the darkening highway into the city. Maddy lay still on the gurney, her eyes closed. I gripped her hand tightly as I silently willed the driver to go faster.

At the hospital, she was moved directly into an exam cubicle in the ER. I stayed in the hallway as staff converged on the cubicle. Minutes later a young doctor came out and introduced himself. "We have the paramedics' report, but what more can you tell us?"

"I don't know. She was bound in duct tape when we found her, and she seems drugged." I remembered Bob's discovery in the garbage behind Daniel's house. "We did find an empty prescription bottle for something called Zolpidem."

He raised his eyebrows. "Thanks. We'll check for that. She's dehydrated, so we're giving her fluids by IV, and we'll continue monitoring." He went back into the cubicle. I was still wound tight. What damage had she suffered at Daniel's hands?

A while later the doctor appeared again. "We're still waiting for the results of the blood tests. But I don't think there's anything too seriously wrong with her. We'll want to keep her overnight to observe her, but she can probably go home tomorrow."

"Doctor…" I wasn't sure how to put this. "Can you tell…if he…" I couldn't give voice to my deepest fears.

If Daniel had done anything more to her, I didn't think I could bear it.

He gave me a long look. "We examined her carefully, and there are no signs of injury or abuse that we can see, other than the drugging." He added, "She's sleeping now, but you can go in."

****

I went in and stood by Maddy's bed. My breath caught. She was lying still, appearing so small and vulnerable, like a little injured bird. Her chest rose and fell almost imperceptibly. She was attached to various monitoring devices, tracking her vitals. An IV tube drained into her arm.

My heart hurt for her. I pulled a chair up to her bed and settled in to keep watch. Even if she had no obvious injuries, she'd been through a horrible ordeal. How badly traumatized was she?

A couple of times I had to move out of the way when a nurse came in to check her condition or adjust something, but otherwise it was a quiet vigil. Watching the calm, organized teamwork by staff who obviously knew what they were doing, my anxiety started to subside.

In a calm moment, I texted Jenny.

—*Maddy's safe. I'm at the hospital with her.*—

Her reply came a few moments later.

—*Omg!! What great news!!*—

—*Long story. Later. But pls notify everyone?*—

—*Of course.*—

Bless her. She'd handle letting all our friends know. They would all be thrilled to hear the good news, but I didn't have the energy to handle contacting them myself.

A while later, Marie arrived and beckoned me into the hallway. She dragged a chair over next to mine and leaned in, her eyes on mine. "How are you doing?" When I shrugged, she added, "Daniel Kazan is at the Civic. I made sure he and Maddy didn't go to the same ER—I didn't want to subject you to that."

I hadn't even considered that possibility but was grateful it hadn't happened. "Thanks. How is he?" What I meant was, how much damage did I do to him?

She didn't fully answer the question. "He was in and out of consciousness. He's under guard." She patted my arm. "I'll need to interview Maddy, but that can wait till tomorrow."

****

Later Saturday night I texted Jenny again, asking her to pick up some clothes for Maddy from our house and bring them to me. When she arrived, we had a whispered conversation in the hallway outside Maddy's room. I filled her in on the day's events, but just the bare bones—she could tell I wasn't up to more. She gave me a huge hug, peeked in on Maddy, hugged me again, and went home.

I stayed at the hospital that night, dozing in a chair by Maddy's bedside. When I woke, she appeared to be in a natural sleep, not the drugged stupor she'd been in the evening before. The rattle of an attendant bringing her breakfast woke her.

She sat up, gazing around the room, and finally settled her eyes on me. "Mom? What's going on?" Her voice was a hoarse whisper.

That would be a long conversation, but not one to have now. "You're safe. You're in the hospital, but you're okay. You'll be coming home today."

She stared at me, her eyes hollow. "Where's Daniel?"

Oh God, where to start. "He's been arrested. He won't be bothering us." That was enough detail for now.

Maddy turned to her breakfast, wolfing down the two pieces of cold toast and congealed egg as if she were starving. I blinked tears away, imagining what yesterday had been like for her.

Just as Maddy finished eating, the doctor on duty came bustling in. She checked Maddy over and reviewed her chart. "Looks like you're good to go," she declared with a smile. Turning to me, she added, "She's bounced back well. We'll discharge her this morning."

Maddy did ask about her phone; I told her the police had her belongings and would be returning them.

By ten o'clock I'd signed her discharge papers and had helped her into the clothes that Jenny had dropped off. To my eyes Maddy appeared pale, but I accepted the doctor's view that she was ready to go home. A young male attendant arrived, pushing a wheelchair.

Maddy's eyes widened. "Is that for me?"

Startled, I turned to the orderly. "Does she need that?"

He shrugged. "I'm supposed to take her…"

I turned to Maddy. "Do you want a ride?"

"Sure." She plunked herself into the wheelchair and gazed around alertly as the orderly took us down to the main floor in the elevator.

"Can you stay with her while I bring the car around?" I asked. He nodded, and Maddy seemed content to wait with him.

The day was sunny. There'd been frost again

overnight, but the sun had already melted most of it and—despite the cold weather of the previous week—it was a brisk but lovely fall day. I couldn't help but take the sunshine as an omen, a sign that things were brightening for us.

In the car, Maddy said, "I didn't really need the wheelchair, but it was fun." I was glad she could enjoy something. Anything.

She was quiet on the way home, leaning against the passenger-side window. I wasn't sure if she was awake or dozing, but when we arrived and I went around to open her door, she pushed past me and stood up without my help.

"I'm okay. I can walk." She had her head down, and I couldn't see the expression on her face.

I grabbed my purse and headed up the walkway after her, reaching around her to unlock the front door. She walked into the kitchen and poured herself a glass of water, her back to me.

Putting my arm around her shoulders, I leaned over to kiss her temple. "I love you, sweetie. I'm so happy to have you home again."

She turned to me, throwing her arms around me and leaning into my shoulder. Her voice was muffled. "Thank you for coming to save me."

My eyes misted. "I'm just glad we found you." I held her tightly. I never wanted to let her go. She sobbed for a few minutes while I patted her back.

****

I needed to prepare Maddy for the police visit ahead. "You remember Constable Boucher? Marie? The one who came to see you and Emma before? She'll be coming by this morning to interview you. She'll need to ask you about everything that happened."

"Okay." We were still in the kitchen. Maddy turned toward the fridge. "I'm still hungry. Can I have something to eat?"

"Of course." I quickly put together a tomato and lettuce sandwich, while she dropped into a chair and fiddled with the salt and pepper shakers on the table. I was desperate to know what had happened—where she'd been, how Daniel got hold of her—but I didn't know where to start. All my questions were dammed up inside me. If I let them out, I feared they'd overwhelm both of us.

But if I took it one thing at a time…

I handed her a plate with her sandwich. "I was so worried! When I realized you were gone…"

Her eyes flicked to mine, then away. "I'm sorry."

I couldn't stop myself. "Why—?" I wasn't sure how to finish the sentence.

She bent her head, taking a bite of sandwich. Chewed. Swallowed. "You know why." Gazing up through her eyelashes, she added in a low voice. "We were fighting. I was sick of it."

A pang went through me. *That's what I feared.*

"Plus you said you weren't my mother."

And that. My objection burst out of me. "I didn't say that at all! I said you *are* my child. I told you the DNA test was wrong."

She took another bite of her sandwich. "That's not what Daniel said."

Ahh. "What did he say?"

I was desperate to ask how she ended up with Daniel, but I'd leave that for when Marie interviewed her.

She looked at me. "He told me the test said you aren't my mom." She blinked back tears. "And that's what you told me too."

Her words pierced my heart. "But I told you it was a mistake."

She shook her head, her eyes now on her half-eaten sandwich as she placed it back on her plate. I bit my lip in frustration. I didn't have anything further to back up my declaration. The second DNA test, the one I'd submitted samples for on Friday, might provide answers, but I didn't have the results yet.

"Listen," I said desperately, "we'll get that sorted out. But you're home now, and you *are* my daughter."

****

Maddy was relieved to be home, glad to see her mom after all the confusion. But she wasn't sure what would happen now. Her familiar frustrations threatened to surface again—had anything changed?

Her mom *had* been right about Daniel. He did turn out to be dangerous. Maddy couldn't understand why he'd suddenly gotten mean, when he'd been so nice at the beginning.

Maddy finished her milk. "Can I go to my room?"

Her mom hesitated, then nodded. "Until Marie comes to interview you."

In her room, Maddy's gaze swept over everything. She'd been away so long it was like a stranger's room. And it was so tidy! All her usual mess was gone. Her mom must have been in here, putting stuff away.

What was she doing in my room? But Maddy squelched her automatic protest. The image of Mom cleaning her room for her was actually kind of comforting.

A *prrt* at the door announced Oscar's entry. With a rush of affection, Maddy picked him up and buried her face in his warm fur. She'd missed him. She carried him to her bed and curled up, nuzzling him until he squirmed away.

She stood and crossed to her dresser, pulling out a drawer and grabbing a pair of black leggings and some underwear. She dragged several tops out of the closet and tossed them on her bed. The outfit Jenny brought to the hospital was okay, but Maddy wanted to make her own selection.

After trying out several outfits, she settled on a long green sweater over the black tights and added the silver earrings that Grandpa had given her last year for Christmas.

On impulse, she turned back to the closet and pulled out several items at random. With an inner smirk, she tossed them on the floor.

Yeah, I'm home now.

****

Watching Maddy answering Marie's questions, I ached for my daughter. She described going to Daniel's house, playing with his dog, him offering her a place to sleep, him cooking for her, playing cards. And her shock when—after treating her well, she thought—he "turned mean."

She'd trusted Daniel—God knows why, but she had—only to have her trust shattered.

It hurt to see her in pain, but I was conflicted too. I was furious at Daniel, of course, but I couldn't help feeling hurt that Maddy had run away in the first place.

Though I knew I was in large part to blame for that. I reminded myself that I was the adult here, not the victim. And my training in child development should have equipped me to do better.

I had failed to keep our relationship on an even keel. The tension between us had become so toxic that I'd driven Maddy out of the house. She was just a kid; it wasn't her fault that things had broken down.

Marie finished the interview and gave Maddy a little hug. "Thanks for that," she said. "I may have more questions for you, but that's all for now."

She put away her notebook and rose, grabbing her coat. "I'll be interviewing Daniel today," she said to me. "I'll be in touch later."

****

Daniel had been resting in his hospital bed when the policewoman appeared. Though he couldn't really call it "rest"—he had a splitting headache. The doctor who saw him this morning said they were still monitoring him for concussion. And he couldn't turn over—his arm was handcuffed to the bed rail.

Squinting, he saw it was the lady cop who'd led the search at Aunt Ruby's house. She started asking him questions, but he had a hard time following. His head was pounding.

You fool—you've landed yourself in more trouble than ever.

He'd watched enough TV shows to know he should have a lawyer if a cop was questioning him, but he didn't know how to get one, not here in the hospital.

But his first worry wasn't for himself—it was for Tucker. He felt terrible for leaving him behind. By now, Tucker must be frantic.

Lifting himself up on one elbow, he broke into whatever the cop was saying. "Where's my dog?" His voice sounded hoarse, so he repeated himself, louder this time. "Where's Tucker?"

The officer glanced at him. "Your dog is fine."

"So where is he?"

"One of our officers picked him up from your house yesterday."

"When can I get him back?"

She shook her head. "You'll be in custody. You won't be having a dog with you."

Daniel's breath caught. "So what will happen with him?"

"I don't know. He'll probably have to go to the Humane Society shelter. Maybe someone will adopt him."

Or put him to sleep, more likely. Who's going to adopt an old dog?

Daniel fell back against the pillow, pressure building up behind his eyes. He tried to shift his position to relieve the sick feeling in his stomach.

After a moment he realized the cop was talking again, saying something about him endangering the girl.

That got his attention. "Where is she now?"

The cop stared at him. "She's back with her mother, where she belongs. And she's fine—no thanks to you."

"What do you mean, her mother?"

"With Dr. Koss, of course."

Daniel snorted. "With her? You've got that wrong. That's not her mother."

"Mr. Kazan, You know Maddy's not your granddaughter."

"Yeah, I know that." That dream was gone. "But

she's not that woman's daughter, either."

The policewoman looked blank.

He half sat up. "Ask your *Dr. Koss* about the DNA test."

"What do you mean?"

"It said she wasn't the girl's mother at all."

She frowned at him. "I don't know anything about that. Maddy is back home now."

He closed his eyes. It didn't matter anymore.

Wait. Maybe...

Daniel opened his eyes again. He forced himself to keep his voice slow and calm.

"The girl and Tucker got along real well. Maybe she'd like to look after him."

The cop cocked an eye at him. "You think Maddy Koss would want to take care of your dog?"

Mustering his last reserves, Daniel nodded. "Just ask her. She likes animals. And she likes Tucker." With that he collapsed back onto the bed.

Dimly, he heard the cop talking to one of the doctors. "We'll have to interview him properly when he's in better shape, but I'll leave him for now."

Chapter Forty-Nine

It almost felt like a normal Sunday afternoon, which seemed unbelievable after what we'd been through. The house was quiet as I put on water for tea. Emma and Maddy were upstairs in Maddy's room, after a hugs-and-tears reunion in our front hall.

Emma's first comment had been "your hair!"

"I know—weird, right?" Apparently Maddy's brown hair was more comment-worthy than the rest of her ordeal. "Mom says I can change it to whatever color I want. What do you think?"

I dropped a tea bag into my mug. Oscar slept on the kitchen window seat.

The doorbell rang, interrupting the newfound silence. Peering through the window, I saw it was Marie. I opened the door and welcomed her in. "Maddy's upstairs with Emma, but I can call her down."

"No, don't call her." Marie peeled off her coat and hung it on the banister, then turned to me. "It's you I want to speak with."

Okay. "I was just making tea. Would you like some?"

She shook her head. "No, not for me, thanks."

I led her into the kitchen and unplugged the kettle, abandoning my tea-making. I didn't think I should make myself a drink if she wasn't having one.

Seated, she leaned forward. "I've just come from talking to Daniel Kazan at the hospital."

I nodded.

"I don't have a full statement from him yet—that'll have to wait until the doctors give him the all-clear—but a couple of things came up." She raised her chin. "First, about his dog."

I frowned. "His dog? Last I saw, the dog was in Daniel's backyard. Daniel had gone off and left it! Bob and I saw it there."

"Well, Bob went back last night and collected the dog. He says he can't keep it—it'll have to go to the Humane Society, unless we find someone to take it." She looked at me. "Daniel...suggested that Maddy might be interested."

I was startled. "Maddy? Daniel's dog?"

"It did seem that she liked that dog, when we talked this morning. She mentioned it a couple of times."

Maddy had always loved animals, and I could imagine her enjoying a dog. But...I shuddered at the idea of having Daniel's dog in our household. Wouldn't it always remind us of the ordeal Maddy had just gone through?

Marie shifted in her chair. "Well, think about it." She leaned back. "And there was another thing Daniel mentioned." Her eyes were on me. "Did you have a DNA test comparing yourself to Maddy?"

Oh. So that's come up finally. "Yes, we did."

"What did it say?"

I suspected she already knew the answer. "It said that I'm not Maddy's mother—but I am! It's a mistake."

Marie frowned. "What lab did you have the test at? It wasn't our police lab, was it?"

"No, it was a private lab." I suddenly hoped she'd consider a test done by a private lab less reliable.

"Why do you say it's a mistake?"

My voice rose. "I gave birth to her myself, right here at the Civic Hospital. I have all the records. My friend Jenny was in the delivery room with me. There's no question she's mine!"

Marie's expression was quizzical.

I tried to speak more calmly. "The lab is doing another test—I left some more samples yesterday. This should all be straightened out soon."

Marie got to her feet. "Well, keep me posted on that." In the hallway she added, "And let us know about the dog."

The dog. I didn't think much of the idea, but I'd sound Maddy out, see how she felt about it.

And I had to get hold of Aisha, find out if the result of the new test was available yet.

****

My head still full of Marie's questions, I picked up my ringing phone.

Nicole's voice was cheery. "We're so glad Maddy's back! How's she doing?"

I didn't want to get into the whole story, not right now. "She's fine. She was really happy to see Emma this afternoon—they're having a good visit."

"Oh, good. I hate to break it up...But Matthew's mom just arrived. Do you mind sending Emma home now?"

"Sure, I'll let her know."

"Maybe we could do something soon to welcome

Maddy home. A small gathering or a dinner, to show her that we missed her and are glad she's back?"

Oh God. Was she volunteering, or did she think I should organize it? "Let's let her settle in first, okay?"

She was silent for a moment. "Sure, I understand. The two of you need some time together."

I managed to get off the phone without committing to anything. I called upstairs to Emma, and she and Maddy came clattering down. Emma pulled on her coat and gave Maddy a hug before heading out into the chill air.

Turning from the door, Maddy's eyes fell on me, and her smile faded. A wary expression flooded her face.

Well, no time like the present to address the dog question. "Maddy, Marie had a question about Daniel's dog."

She nodded, her smile reappearing. "Tucker? Yeah, he's a good dog." Her expression brightened. "We were buddies."

Hmmm. "Well, where Daniel's going, he won't be able to have a dog. But...how would you feel about us having his dog stay here?"

Her eyes lit up. "Tucker here?" She clutched her hands to her chest. "We could have a dog? That'd be great! That's what I've been wanting!" Then her face turned sad. "Daniel will miss him, though."

I stared at her. I hadn't realized she wanted a dog so much. And I was amazed that she had it in her to feel sorry for Daniel, after the way he had attacked her.

"All right, if you're sure you want Tucker..."

She grabbed me and gave me a hug. "Thank you."

****

This time when I phoned, Aisha answered on the first ring. I threw myself on her mercy. "I need that test result as soon as possible; it's important!"

She paused, then replied, "We actually fast-tracked the analysis, and we do have the results. I believe the lab will be sending you the new report in the morning."

Oh my God. "Can't you tell me now what it says?"

After another momentary pause, she said, "I suppose I can."

I waited, holding my breath.

"I confess, I was surprised. It's a rare circumstance." I tensed, waiting for her next sentence. "You'll be glad to know that the new tests show that you are in fact Maddy's mother."

The tension melted from my shoulders. *At last.*

She proceeded to explain, confirming that the circumstances Jenny and I had encountered online likely applied in my case too.

****

I called up to Maddy. "Can you come downstairs? I have something to tell you."

After a moment, she appeared at the top of the stairs. "What?"

"Come on down. I can't holler it up to you."

She slouched down the stairs and followed me into the living room, where I took a seat on the couch. She perched on the seat of the chair opposite, pushing her hair back over her ears.

"This is great news," I started. "I just got off the phone to Aisha. She's Abel's friend who works at the DNA lab."

Maddy raised her eyebrows but didn't respond.

Watching her closely, I came right to the point.

"They retested my DNA." I took a breath. "And this test showed that you definitely are my daughter."

Maddy's eyes widened and shot toward mine. "So the other test *was* wrong?"

I shook my head. "That's what I thought, that they'd just made a mistake. But it turns out that my DNA is complicated."

Maddy frowned. "What do you mean?"

"Well. It seems I have two sets of DNA. And it turns out that some of my DNA does match yours."

She leaned back, frowning. "I don't get that. How can you have two sets of DNA? I thought people have the same DNA through their whole body."

"That's generally true, but apparently in some rare cases it's more complicated. They don't know exactly how it happens, but the most likely explanation is that when my mother got pregnant with me, there were actually two fertilized eggs. If both had developed as usual, there would have been twins."

I had Maddy's full attention.

"But what they think happened instead is that those two fertilized eggs combined, very early in development, so that together they became one baby. It's called a *chimera*——a combination of two organisms. That baby was me. So I have both sets of DNA. Some parts of my body have one set, and other parts have the other set."

Maddy looked stunned. "I've never heard of that. Twins combining to make one baby?"

"I hadn't heard of it either."

"So...you're your own twin?"

I smiled. "I guess you could think of it that way."

Maddy blinked. "And you're definitely my mom?"

I could see relief in her eyes.

"Yes. Like I said all along." I jumped up and went over to give her a hug, and she returned it with a big squeeze.

With her face crushed against my chest, she mumbled, "Your own twin. That's kind of cool, actually."

****

I let Maddy sleep in Monday morning—she needed it. I was reading in the living room when she came downstairs around ten, still in pajamas. Laying aside my magazine, I joined her in the kitchen. She had poured Cheerios into a bowl and was adding milk when I sat down across from her.

"Good morning," I started.

She looked over at me and nodded, giving me a smile. She seemed to have woken in a good mood.

"I thought you'd want to know—Bob's going to bring Tucker over today. He said around noon."

Her eyes lit up. "Great!" she said. Then she frowned. "Who's Bob?"

I realized she'd never met him, despite his frequent presence in my life recently—especially the last few days. I stumbled through an explanation, simply saying he was one of the police officers who helped find her.

Though now that Maddy was back and Daniel was in custody, presumably Bob and I would no longer have a reason to run into each other. Strange how hollow that left me feeling.

****

Before starting to make lunch, I checked on Maddy. She was in her room, sitting cross-legged on her bed, eyes focused on her phone. She flicked a look at me and smiled, then returned to the phone, tapping away.

As I headed toward the kitchen, I saw Bob climbing the porch steps. "Hi, there," I said as I opened the door. Glancing down, I saw he had a dog with him, a golden Lab. Yes, this was the one we'd seen in Daniel's backyard. Not barking today, though.

"Hi, yourself," he said. "Remember Daniel's dog? I was glad to hear that Maddy wants to give him a home, and you agreed. How's she doing, by the way?"

"She's doing all right, I think." I invited him in, along with the dog. "I worry about longer-term effects, but she seems okay for now."

Maddy came racing down the stairs. "Tucker!" The dog perked up and went to her. She dropped to her knees and gave him a big hug, and he licked her face.

Bob and I looked at each other. The two of them acted like old friends reconnecting.

"Maddy, this is Bob Russo. He's the police officer I mentioned."

She raised her head and stood, shyly smiling at him before reaching out her hand. "Thanks for helping rescue me," she said. "And thanks for bringing Tucker." She turned to me. "Can I take Tucker to meet Oscar?"

I smiled. "Sure."

The dog followed her into the kitchen, and we heard her chattering an introduction. Peeking around the doorway, I saw Tucker standing by the table, warily watching Oscar. The cat briefly lifted his head from the window seat where he was napping, then closed his eyes again.

I turned back to Bob, still standing in the front

hallway with his coat on. "I think they'll be fine. Thanks for bringing him."

"I have some dog food in the car. And I picked up a leash too." He gave me a searching glance. "And how are you doing? That scene with Daniel on Saturday was pretty wild. You really smacked him good."

I frowned. "All I could think about was saving Maddy."

"Yeah. Well, he'll be taken care of. I believe he's been discharged from hospital now, and he's in custody. He'll be facing charges."

"Thank God."

He shuffled his feet. "Well, I should go get that dog food." He headed toward the door, then stopped and turned back, giving me a searching glance. "I was wondering...would you like to go out for a drink sometime?"

I blinked, unsure how to respond.

His eyes were on me. "I just thought...it'd be nice to get together. Now that things are getting back to normal."

I forced myself to return his level gaze.

He lowered his eyes. "If you don't want to, just say so."

My face flushed. Definitely taking things off the professional level to the personal. "I'd like that," I heard myself saying. Warmth spread through me, and I couldn't help but smile.

Then I caught myself. "But not just yet. With Maddy home, I need to spend evenings with her for a while. She's been through a lot."

He was smiling too. "Sure, I understand." He raised his eyebrows. "Maybe I could come over one day and cook dinner for all three of us."

I regarded him, assessing. Wondering how far to push it. "How would you feel about cooking for a bigger group?"

"What do you mean?"

"I have a group of friends who put up posters and helped look for Maddy, people who care a lot about her. It'd be nice to get some of them together to welcome her home. Maybe on the weekend?"

"Sure, that sounds like a great idea." He grinned. "I can make my grandmother's spaghetti and meatballs."

"Ah, right—Russo. An Italian grandma's recipe. That sounds great."

"Actually she was German. But she made terrific meatballs."

Chapter Fifty

Maddy heard her mom calling from downstairs. "Do you want to go for a walk? Along the canal?"

She was going to say no—walks were boring, and she was busy watching a video on YouTube—but then she changed her mind. *Sure, why not?*

She hollered, "Okay, if I can bring Tucker." She grabbed a sweatshirt from the pile beside her bed and pulled it over her head.

Downstairs, Mom had her coat on and was digging in the hall closet. "Here," she said, holding out the toque and mitts that Maddy had last worn a week ago. Maddy smiled and held them to her chest. She'd missed them.

She slipped into her own jacket and called Tucker into the hall. She attached his leash and followed her mom out the door.

Outside, it was a cool day but not windy, and the sun was shining. Mom locked the door behind them, and they headed toward the park. The trees were bare now, and without leaves the branches formed cool patterns against the sky. The two of them cut diagonally through the park, their feet scuffing on the leaves still underfoot. They checked for traffic and waited for two cars to pass before crossing to the pedestrian pathway along the canal.

Turning south, they walked side by side, not

speaking. The paved path was just wide enough for two people. Other than one woman walking her dog, they had the path to themselves.

They weren't talking, but Maddy was comfortable in the silence. It felt great to be walking in the crisp cold air, the afternoon sun reflecting on the dark water of the canal. Walking with her mom, the two of them striding along together, felt good too. Better than she'd felt in a long time.

****

When I invited Maddy on this walk, I'd hoped for a conversation that would get us on a new track. But I didn't know how to start.

I knew I needed to loosen up with her. And I remembered the Gibran poem that Bob had recited a line from, days ago. The one that said "your children are not your children."

I thought I understood now what it meant. There's a difference between *belonging* and *owning*. I could do my best to guide her and protect her, but ultimately I couldn't live her life for her.

Her destiny had to be her own, not something shaped to meet my needs.

Walking beside my daughter, I reached deep. If I said the words out loud, maybe I could mean them. "Maddy, I want to talk about how things are going to be."

She turned to me, a wary expression on her face.

"You'll be a teenager soon, and you'll come across a lot of new situations and ideas. I'll do my best to help, but sometimes you'll have to figure things out on your own."

I took a breath. "You'll have to be patient—this is

new for me. I've never been the mother of a teenager before. I'm used to making all the decisions for our family. But now that you're growing up, we'll need to discuss things more, and you'll be deciding things more and more on your own."

There. I let out my breath. The look in Maddy's eyes was worth it. We could make this work.

Epilogue

Daniel was at the police station, waiting in an interview room for the legal aid lawyer to arrive so the cops could interview him.

When they brought him here, he'd demanded to know what they'd done about Susan, since she wasn't the girl's rightful mother. It didn't seem right that he'd be the only one in trouble.

The cop told him he was wrong: a new DNA test had proved she was Maddy's biological mother after all.

Now he was alone in the room. His head was aching, pounding.

He bent to lay his forehead on his folded arms. His mind blanked, and it seemed like tiny lights flashed behind his closed eyelids. He was swirling, swirling. Was he dreaming or remembering?

He was trudging through the snow in the back field at his farm. He was clearing brush, something he could get done before spring work started. He was carefully not looking at the road that ran past the field—past the spot where Kelly and Jacob had recently died. He didn't want to be reminded. It was still too fresh.

He was pulling low brush out of a tangled thicket when he came across it. A small bundle. Fabric—a scrap of red, another of pink. Horror gripped him as he took in the ruined face, the tiny bloodied body. It had been ripped apart. Torn at, chewed up. Some animal must have dragged her away from the crash scene that night...

He couldn't tell Patricia. It would send her over the edge. He could never tell her.

He'd dig a grave, and that would be it. His gift to Patricia, to never remember it. And his gift to himself. It was gone, never happened.

The memory, or the dream, disappeared in the fog. Gone again as if it had never existed.

A note to my readers...

Thank you for reading *Not Your Child*—I hope you enjoyed it! And I have a request: if you have a moment, please leave a review on Amazon or wherever you bought the book to tell other readers why you enjoyed it.

Nothing sells books more than good word of mouth, and I would be grateful for any words you might be willing to leave.

And if you'd like to stay in touch, please join my book club to receive monthly updates and reviews of books I've been reading: www.lisangus.com/sign-up.

—*Lis Angus*

Acknowledgments

In the four-plus years it's taken to bring this novel from conception to birth, I've been blessed with a wide range of support as I struggled my way from wannabe novelist to published writer.

First of all, there's National Novel Writing Month, which grabbed my attention in 2017. I'd always had in mind that someday I'd write a novel. "If not now, when?" I thought, and plunged into the challenge of writing 50,000 words that November.

But I wouldn't have reached that target without Jess Shulman at my side. She started as my daily writing buddy; then, as my editor, she nursed me through several subsequent drafts and revisions.

Then I had the sense to join Sisters in Crime, in particular its "Guppy" chapter, which exists to support the "Great UnPublished." Participating in its online writing classes and discussion groups helped me grow as a writer and become part of a writing community.

That community includes several writers who have become valued friends and collaborators. Eona Calli, Michelle Klump, Sharon Michalove, Zell Watson, and Joyce Woollcott all read *Not My Child*—some more than once—and offered detailed critiques and advice.

Feedback from early readers Amanda Kat Angus, Donna Dortmans, Diane Mossman, and Linda von Tettenborn challenged me to improve my plot and pacing and strengthen my characters.

The North Grenville Writers Circle and the Capital Crime Writers have also been an important part of my writing community.

Jaime Hendricks gave me valuable advice on

improving the first chapters of the novel, as well as tightening my query letter.

I'm grateful to the judges at the 2021 Daphne du Maurier contest for Excellence in Mystery/Suspense, who awarded my manuscript second place in the Mainstream Unpublished division.

I owe special thanks to three editors. I've already mentioned Jess Shulman, who guided the book through several iterations. Stephen Parolini, in his thorough review of a late draft, suggested a restructuring and some important character tweaks. And Ally Richardson, my editor at The Wild Rose Press, was the one who grabbed my manuscript from the slush pile and championed it, then helped shape its final form.

For some years I've been a regular walker. My *Ottawalker* friends—Joan Craig, Linda Cruz, Judy Field, Barbara Gallagher, Millie Mirsky, Brenda Primmer, and Kate Schissler—along with local walking companions Myrna Milligan, Nancy Muir, and Barb Potter-Angus, provided unflagging encouragement to my writing progress as we walked and talked.

My final, most important thanks go to my husband, Ian, who has been my partner in the many phases of our life together. He not only read and critiqued several versions of my manuscript but brags about me to everyone he knows. Thank you, my love.

A word about the author...

Lis Angus is a Canadian suspense writer. Early in her career, she worked with children and families in crisis; later she worked as a policy advisor, business writer, and editor while raising two daughters. She now lives south of Ottawa with her husband. You can learn more about her at her website, www.lisangus.com.